GENERAL QUARTERS

General Quarters

By

Ken Carodine

Penmorepress.com

General Quarters
By Ken Carodine
Copyright © 2025 Ken Carodine

ISBN-13: 978-1-957851-78-5(Paperback)
ISBN:-13: 978-1-957851-77-8(e-book)

BISAC Subject Headings:
FIC014000FICTION / Historical
FIC032000FICTION / War & Military
FIC031020FICTION / Thrillers / Historical

Book Cover Design : Ken Carodine
Editor : C Wozney
Emilija Rakić PR Emily's World of Design

Address all correspondence to:

Penmore Press LLC
920 N Javelina Pl
Tucson AZ 85748
Mjames@penmorepress.com

DEDICATION

To
My Children
Andrew, Kellyn & Navy Lee
Victoria

And my 1982 US Naval Academy Classmates

All Whom Remind Me Daily of the Virtues of
Honor, Courage and Commitment

GENERAL QUARTERS CHARACTERS

<u>The American Navy</u>

Captain Ben McGuire	US Naval Attaché, Taipei, Taiwan
Captain Elizabeth Nation	CO, USS PRINCETON
LCDR Paul Daniels	XO, USS PRINCETON
Lieutenant Josephina Juarez	CIC Officer, USS PRINCETON
OSC Bill Guerette	CIC LCPO, USS PRINCETON
LCDR James "Boss" Dawes	SEAL Team Leader
Chief Darrell Jackson	Navy SEAL
BM1 Carlos "DeSilva"	Navy SEAL
IT2 Paul "Guard" Boyd	Navy SEAL
HM2 Greg "Doc" Kincaid	Navy SEAL
LTJG Cody "Junior Boss" Wells	Navy SEAL
Captain Peter T. Corrigan	Prospective Naval Attaché

<u>The Cabinet</u>

Jack Langdon "Eagle"	President, United States
Victoria Aldridge	Chief of Staff, President of the United States

<u>The Government</u>

Harvey Walters	Managing Analyst, National Reconnaissance Office
Jake Harrison	CIA Station Chief, Taiwan
Michael Wong	CIA Agent, Taipei

<u>The Chinese</u>

Ho Lin Shih	President, Peoples Republic of China
Fei Chen Tzu	Chairman, Chinese Communist Party
Zieng Fong	Commissioner, Central Military Commission
Jung Li Hong	President Li's Aide
General Zhao Chin Lee	Commander, Peoples Liberation Army
Admiral Sun Xueliang	Commander, PLA Navy
Lieutenant General Weidong Muao	Commander, PLA Air Force
Rear Admiral Fong Wei	Commander, PLA Navy Air Forces
Rear Admiral Chang Hong	Commander, PLA Navy East Sea Fleet
General Yau Xingyuan	Commander PLA Navy Marine Corps
General Yang Siguang	Commander, Peoples' Strategic Missile Defense
General Cui Mai	Commander, People's Civil Defense

<u>The Taiwanese</u>

President Liu Chao-hsuan	President, Republic China (Taiwan)
Alexi Pugachev	Leader, Taiwan Drug Triad
Ciara Michaels	Contract Spy
Choi Ling	Food Worker at Taiwan Capitol
Galena Cheslav	Contract Assassin

THANKS & ACKNOWLEDGEMENTS

Captain Marc Liebman, USN (Ret.)
Commander David Fisher, USN (Ret.)
Captain Robert Donnahoo, USN (Ret.)
Captain James Hardy, USN (Ret.)
Captain Susan Hardy, USN (Ret.)
Captain Christopher Scott USN (Ret.)
Major Stephen Rapp, USMC (Ret)
Mr. & Mrs. Paul Eichelberger
Honorable Althea Coetzee
Mr. Sami Mikhail
Mrs. Margaret Whitaker
Ms. Jill Olhausen
Ms. Moira E. Burns

CHAPTER ONE
KINGSTON EXCELSIOR

Tuesday, February 23rd
Haiphong Harbor
Haiphong, Vietnam
2205 Hours

"Boss." IT2 Paul Boyd's voice had the hushed intensity that SEAL Team leader Lieutenant Commander Jim Dawes expected after countless missions together. "You have two Tangos in the pilothouse and one roving the deck on the starboard side, forward," Boyd rasped into the radio.

Dawes and SEAL Medic Greg "Doc" Kincaid concealed themselves in the starboard anchor housing of the container ship. He keyed the transmitter on his radio to transmit a "click" in acknowledgment.

Dawes smiled at his SEAL teammate's announcement of his arrival in position, conducting a good over-watch. He checked his watch. He was impressed. Now atop one of the ship's forty-foot cranes, Boyd had completed the climb in less than five minutes without detection.

"Hold fast. Tango will be over you in five, four, three, two, one," Boyd counted down slowly over the radio.

In addition to their full allotment of combat gear, Dawes and Kincaid wore relatively bulky cold-weather wet suits. And if that were not enough, each of them also carried another half of a wet suit for their "package." The packs that each of them wore, still wet and heavy from the swim, seriously impaired their mobility.

The team's collective focus now fell on their mission to retrieve "Varsity," the codename given to a defecting high-level Chinese Government official. The two special forces operatives held a deathlike stillness. Even before the smoke from their adversary's cigarette wafted over the bow to his nostrils, Dawes felt the man's warmth. He 'shallowed' his breathing so much that his breath only fogged for a split second when he exhaled.

Dawes shifted his gaze to Kincaid. His eyes transfixed with excitement; the younger SEAL also stood frozen in place. Dawes turned his mental focus toward Boyd. No need to radio him. His sniper would notify them, one way or the other, when they could move. If the sentry detected them, Boyd would silence him.

Moments ticked by at a glacial pace. "He's moving away, down the port side of the ship," Boyd reported. Dawes finally blew out his breath and some tension. He flashed Kincaid a "thumbs-up," and his teammate returned the gesture.

"Where is Junior?" Dawes asked Boyd, checking on LT Cody Wells. Already selected for promotion to commander, tonight's mission was Dawes' last mission. Wells was set to take his place.

"Junior is covering your insertion from a lifeboat on the port side," Wells replied over the net. "Let's get going," he said to Kincaid.

"Passing Tesla," Dawes said into his radio. His simple words notified those monitoring the mission from the Tactical Operations Center , or TOC, of the team's progress. USS *Pasadena*, submerged some fifteen miles away, the Los Angeles Class submarine served as the base of operations for tonight's mission.

BMC Darrell Jackson and BM1 Carlos DeSilva, also garbed in full cold-weather wetsuits, observed their teammates from a 100 yards away. They had the duty of protecting the team's means of extraction, a high-speed rigid-hull inflatable boat or RHIB. Their position kept them out of the loom of the well-lighted container ship.

Perfect meteorological conditions prevailed for tonight's mission. A moonless and overcast sky with only ten knots of wind aided their concealed intrusion. Casting the ship and surrounding area into complete darkness when the time came should prove easy.

Under the deadly cover of Boyd's and Wells' sniper rifles, Dawes and Kincaid crept onto the *Kingston Excelsior*'s main deck. Crouching with their H&K MP5 automatic weapons at the ready, they took each step with concentration.

Just like the drone photos in their mission briefing had shown, high container stacks held in place by steel cables dotted the deck as far as Boyd could see. The multi-colored metal boxes formed equally shaped canyons along both the longitudinal and athwartship axes of the vessel. While lights bathed the waters around the ship, heavy shadows covered most of the deck. He and Kincaid stole their way under the cover of the cargo, with equal portions of speed and stealth. Dawes peered toward the rear of the ship that featured a superstructure and a lighted pilothouse. Several other forward-facing portholes glowed, but darkness engulfed the rest. With the ship in port and most of the crew ashore, intelligence reports led mission planners to believe *Kingston Excelsior* sat relatively unoccupied. Regardless, they proceeded as if each space held an armed sentry. Dawes and Kincaid alternated taking the lead as they advanced, keeping their weapons always pointed ahead and upward at the portholes .

Nearing the edge of the cargo area, Dawes held up his left hand and shaped it into a fist. At the silent signal to "Halt," Kincaid knelt, holding his weapon at the ready.

An open, well-lighted area lay between them and the door to the superstructure. Taking a breath to calm himself, Dawes scanned the area like a jeweler examining a diamond for flaws. Except for the roving security patrol, all seemed quiet.

"Boss," Boyd called from his perch. "The Tango is back on the bow, smoking another cigarette. I've checked each of the portholes and you look clear to proceed."

Dawes raised his hand behind him and gave his sniper a thumbs-up. He nodded at Kincaid before stepping from the darkness toward their next objective. Kincaid stayed a step behind him, weapon at the ready.

On either side of the superstructure door, the SEALs steeled themselves. Dawes pushed up on the metal handle and quietly pulled open the access. The heavy metal door creaked as it swung.

"Passing Maserati," Dawes heard Boyd report to the TOC.

Kincaid leveled his weapon toward the interior as it opened. He nodded to signal that it was clear. Kincaid stepped in as Dawes closed the door behind them, securing it with an almost imperceptible thump.

Dawes took his place as point of the incursion. The job now was to find "Varsity" as quickly as possible and without detection. Traveling under an assumed name and forged credentials, "Varsity" berthed in a stateroom on the superstructure's third deck.

The intelligence report seemed accurate. Six cabin doors lined each side of the passageway. The stairwell leading to the upper decks stood just beyond the last set of cabins.

Dawes somehow knew things would not go according to plan. They hardly ever did.

They advanced on the first door. Dawes pulled open the door as Kincaid pointed his weapon ahead, ready to deal with whomever they encountered. The two SEALS crossed the threshold into the passageway.

IT2 Boyd pulled a candy-bar from his chest pouch. Shoulda had more for dinner. He consumed half the Payday with a single bite. He made sure to keep a watchful eye on the deck below as he enjoyed his small snack. "What's this?" Taking his final bite, engine noise from an approaching boat caught his attention.

A powerboat, at least forty feet in length, churned the water as it surged toward the ship, him, and his team. Mostly white, the blue stripes did not become visible until the craft slowed and drew near the ship. Three men occupied the craft's cockpit.

Shit! Dawes' heart almost leapt from his chest as the sound of approaching voices reached his ears. He shot an alarm-filled glance toward Kincaid. Doubling back to one of the unoccupied rooms as quickly and quietly as possible, Dawes shut the door just before the crew members entered the passageway.

"Boss. Heads up. We've got a boat coming alongside. You might want to take cover," Boyd's voice announced over Dawes' headset as he and his teammate positioned themselves. "Looks like Vietnamese Coast Guard."

"Yeah. No shit," said under his breath to Kincaid. They leveled their weapons at the door, just in case.

It sounded as if five to six men passed by the door toward the main deck. Raised voices spoke Russian in excited tones. Dawes could not hear the entire conversation but made out enough to know they were anticipating the arrival of an important person. The commotion faded as the crewmen exited the passageway.

"Boss. Two men are exiting the boat and climbing up the accommodation ladder. I count six greeters, three with rifles."

The arrival of the Vietnamese Coast Guard probably meant the compromise of the mission to take "Varsity". Dawes did the math quickly. One or two guys likely remained to guard the package. This meant the total Tango force probably numbered only eight or ten. He considered this a manageable number.

"Boss," Boyd began again. His voice had a slightly elevated tone now. "The boat's carrying a senior Coast Guard officer and an Asian civilian. I'm betting Chinese Government."

Dawes nodded. Boyd's announcement fit in with what he overheard and had surmised. "Call it in," Dawes replied just above a whisper.

"TOC, situation X-ray. I say again, X-ray," Boyd called per Dawes' order.

"Roger. TOC copies. Mission completion is an imperative."

"Roger," Boyd replied.

Boyd used the scope on his rifle to observe the eight men on the ship's main deck. He tracked them to the left as they walked toward the same door that Dawes and Kincaid used just minutes before. As they entered the skin of the ship, he shifted his scan to the forward face of the superstructure.

"Boss. They're entering the deckhouse now. Stand ready."

Boyd did not hear a response, nor did he expect one. While there was a chance that someone might overhear them, the team members on deck would only transmit a voice message if necessary.

"Few more lights on now. Stand by."

Boyd used the riflescope to examine each of the newly lighted portholes. The ship boasted six levels above the main deck. All the lights on the first and second levels remained extinguished. A few lights on the third and fourth levels now glowed brightly.

Boyd's weapons sight allowed him to see a few feet into each room. He focused on a larger porthole enough to see the chairs and sofa of an unoccupied lounge. He noted the surrounding crew quarters.

GENERAL QUARTERS

The next level up appeared to contain offices and officer berthing areas. A couple of staterooms cast their light into the darkness. Three larger and illuminated portholes on this level revealed a single occupant, an Asian man sweeping the floor. He shifted his attention to the next space.

The next room, unoccupied, contained office furniture. Boyd surmised it served as the captain's administrative area.

Boyd's eyes bulged when he focused on the final room. Two Caucasian men sat at a table across from an Asian man. Mentally comparing the man to the pictures he had seen hours earlier, he confirmed the thin balding Asian in his late fifties was "Varsity."

"Boss. Package sighted. Fourth Deck, port side, forward. Captain's Office."

With the sounds of passersby on the other side of the door gone, relative silence returned to the passageway. Only the throbbing of the ship's power plant and the warm air it shoved through the ventilation ducts above them cut into the quiet. The entourage passed their current refuge with no sign of detection, on their way to their destination, presumably to interview "Varsity".

Dawes and Kincaid acknowledged Boyd's news with only a slight nod. Dawes hoped he and his men could get in and out without detection, and without firing a shot. With yet another two guns aboard, the likelihood of that now seemed remote.

He pressed the eavesdropping device against the door. After determining all was quiet, Dawes placed his hand on the knob while his partner pulled his weapon up and aimed it at the door. They nodded at each other and pulled open the door on a three-count.

Once again, stark light blasted into their eyes, but that was all. The passageway, empty and still, made Dawes think of a ghost ship. He turned his attention to the stairwell at the end of the passageway while Kincaid covered their rear.

Dawes listened for voices as he climbed the first step. Silence. Like Kincaid, Dawes advanced with his weapon ready. The SEAL Leader stiffened his resolve to finish this Op quickly.

"Boss," Boyd called as they cleared the second level. "They've gathered in the room where "Varsity" is located."

Boyd's stomach tightened as he watched the Coast Guard officer and suspected Chinese official enter the room. Even from 150 yards away and through a riflescope, the SEAL sniper saw bulging veins in the Asian official's face and neck as he berated "Varsity".

"Varsity" sat at rigid attention as the civilian shouted at him from across the room. When he did speak, he did so with open and outstretched hands as he shook his head. The Asian civilian responded by slapping "Varsity" across his face.

"Boss. They're interrogating the 'Package.'"

"Take whatever action is necessary to protect the 'Package' We're almost there," Dawes transmitted to the entire team.

Boyd sighted in on the suspected Chinese official's head.

Cody Wells, once given the go-ahead from Boyd, made his way aft. He girded himself as he neared the equipment room positioned on the centerline. After taking a last look and listen, he shouldered his weapon and entered the space. "Boss. This is Junior. I'm in position," he reported.

Dawes and Kincaid stepped up their ascent, taking two and three stairs at a time. As they neared the fourth deck, a familiar tightness grew in Dawes' stomach. He ran through a mental checklist as he scanned the space around them. He longed to rid himself of the pack. It would make the climb much easier.

GENERAL QUARTERS

Approaching the top of the ladder, voices and heavy footsteps echoed in Dawes' ears. It was time. He signaled Kincaid by placing his hand over his eyes. The corpsman nodded, lowered his weapon and donned his night-vision goggles so they sat on top of his head versus over his eyes. Once set, Kincaid gave Dawes a thumbs-up. Dawes quickly followed his example and then quietly said, "Now, Now, Now," into his transmitter's microphone.

Wells pulled a lever in the switch room, throwing the massive ship into darkness. Wells pulled down his goggles. With Infrared-green colored hands, he reached into the switchbox and removed several fuses, placing them in the pocket of his uniform.

The pilothouse occupied the superstructure's entire top level. The ship's windows, as large as they were tall, provided Boyd a clear view of the occupants as they scurried around in the dark trying one light switch after another, to no avail. He sighted in with the night-vision-equipped scope. As long as they stayed in the bridge area, no harm would come to them. If they headed for the door, Boyd would act to protect his two SEAL teammates and "Varsity" from harm.

Dawes and Kincaid rushed up the last flight of metal steps onto the fourth deck. Two light green silhouettes in the shape of men stood by the furthest door on the port side of the athwartships Passageway. Dawes hugged the left side of the passage while Kincaid slid to the right.

Just as one of the silhouetted men turned toward them speaking Russian and leveling his pistol, Dawes and Kincaid each fired one silenced shot. The men guarding the door fell dead right where they stood.

Dawes pulled a flash-bang grenade from his belt. He used his right thumb to pull and toss away the pin. The small explosive, meant to blind and shock, remained clenched in his hand. So much for a quiet extraction. Kincaid stood to the right of the door, behind the protection of a metal bulkhead.

Dawes, his back to the wall on the opposite side of the door, turned the doorknob. As he did, someone on the other side fired several rounds. Bullets tore through the wooden door's center and into the door on the distant side of the passageway. "Damn!" Undeterred, Dawes finished opening the door, tossed in the device and pulled the door shut.

Frantic voices shouting in Russian and Chinese preceded the explosion. Crouched, Dawes again placed his hand on the doorknob and turned it. He used his shoulder to push it open the rest of the way.

When he did, someone in the center of the room, with one hand over their face and the other holding a gun, began firing. Kincaid dropped him with a single shot, the man's body falling to the deck with a thud.

The room fell silent as the two SEALS scanned the room. Five men lay dead at their feet. Dawes' nerves were on fire. He knew someone else was there, someone other than "Varsity".

Where the hell was he? Had to be behind something, hiding. Dawes surveyed the room through the green haze. A single table near the center of the room gave the only shelter. Three portholes provided air into the room. The middle porthole stood six feet above the table on the forward bulkhead. Dawes keyed his microphone.

"Come on out. Don't hurt him and we won't hurt you."

"Ha. How about you put down your weapons, and I don't kill your prize?" the voice proposed in response.

Dawes reveled at the man's command of the English language. "That's not going to happen," he finally replied. His English bore a strong Mandarin accent.

GENERAL QUARTERS

The man started laughing. "This is like one of your cowboy movies' 'Mexican standoff'. No?"

"No, this is no movie," Dawes replied. He signaled Kincaid to move around to the right of the table.

Boyd shifted his scope back down to the porthole in the room where his boss and Kincaid were facing down the Chinese official. "I don't have a shot," he announced over the radio.

Wells, still wearing his night-vision goggles, crept toward the main deck and the canyons formed by the stacks of containers. With all the lighting extinguished; the darkness provided him great cover.

"Okay," Dawes said after a long moment. "How about you let him go? And you'll get to walk out of here. You show some goodwill, and we'll do the same."

"What if I don't shoot this bastard in the head? Is that enough goodwill for you?"

A flash of light on the deck caught Boyd's attention. The Roving Guard had a flashlight and a rifle trained on Cody Wells. "Boss. I've got a situation. Stall your Tango for a second." Boyd's voice was cool and nonchalant, as if he were offering a friend a beer.

He aimed the weapon at the guard as Wells, holding his eyes, climbed to his feet. Boyd aimed toward the man's neck. A flinching movement could inadvertently cause the guard's weapon to discharge. Boyd knew his shot must not miss. He took a breath, let half of it out and squeezed the trigger. His rifle recoiled silently in the night. Far below, Wells' captor fell dead with a metallic thud.

"Okay, Junior. You're clear. Get under some cover," Boyd said into his radio to the young SEAL officer.

"Thanks. I owe you one."

"Okay, Boss. Let's get this over with." Boyd returned his attention and aim to the lounge.

Dawes took only a moment to ponder on what had just happened. He knew all he needed to know—Boyd had resolved the issue. Dawes returned his total attention to the task at hand. His mind started working. If the room was pitch-black, they still had the upper hand. But if even a small trickle of light got in, it could remove their advantage. He signaled to Kincaid to move as silently as possible.

"You know you're not going to make it out of here alive, don't you?" Dawes spoke loudly. He dragged the muzzle of his pistol across the table to cover the sound of Kincaid's advance with his own. The SEAL medic followed the non-verbal command.

"I'm not bluffing, American! I'll kill him!"

"Who fuckin' cares? I get paid for a body, alive or dead."

Dawes looked to Kincaid. Now on the far side of the table, Kincaid pointed his weapon in the direction of the voice.

"Liar. I don't believe you came all this way to have him killed. Now throw down your guns!"

Boyd shifted his aim from one porthole to the other, hoping for a target. "I need him to move right or left," he said over the radio.

Dawes, keeping "Varsity"'s well-being in mind, pressed his mind for an idea. Boyd needed a target. His eyes searched in vain in the darkness for the gunman. He finally glanced over at his partner. Kincaid, now on the far-right side of the room, stood ready with his weapon raised.

Dawes surmised the man holding "Varsity" hostage was shielding himself behind the desk. The SEAL leader aimed and fired two rounds into the bulkhead on the far side of the room. He prayed they landed above "Varsity".

"Are you mad? I said I would kill this pig," the Asian shouted as he rose slightly.

Boyd's round found the man's left shoulder. It exploded with a greenish mist. Pain and shock caused him to rise a bit more, and when he did, Kincaid took his shot. As the gunman fell dead, his pistol fired a single round. The wild shot still found a target as it impacted Dawes in the chest. The SEAL leader fell backward as his armor absorbed most but not all the impact.

On the carpeted floor Dawes writhed in pain as he watched Kincaid check the rest of the space, then the hostage, and finally him. "The Package is safe, but Boss is down," Kincaid announced over the radio.

"Thank you, thank you," "Varsity" murmured.

Kincaid only nodded.

"How bad?" Boyd asked.

"Stand by."

"TOC, passing Nissan," Kincaid reported their progress. "HVT secure but Leader is down. SITREP to follow."

Curiosity finally got the best of the guys in the pilothouse. Boyd watched as one of them walked hesitantly toward the door to the passageway. "Nope. You don't want to do that."

The sniper leveled his weapon at the pilothouse doorknob. As the merchant seaman reached for it, a 5.56x45mm round from Boyd's Mk12 rifle caused the metal object to explode into several pieces as it shattered the large window a second before. The men covered their heads as they dove for relative safety.

Boyd relaxed a bit as he studied the condition of his friend and teammate. He returned to scanning the deck and exterior portions of the vessel.

Dawes felt the medic's probing hand on his chest. Kincaid pressed in, and he wanted to scream, but didn't. Kincaid then reached under the bulletproof vest and pressed again.

"Damn it, Doc. Getting fucking shot didn't hurt that bad. Stop that shit," Dawes complained.

"He's okay. Feels like the bullet might have bruised or even cracked his sternum, but he can move," Kincaid reported.

"Well, bust a move!" Boyd ordered over the radio.

Kincaid stood and went over to "Varsity." The slightly built Asian sobbed like a baby near the nook of the table. "Get up," he ordered.

"Varsity" climbed to his feet as he wiped his eyes.

"Goggles off," Kincaid said to his boss.

Dawes used his right hand to reach for his night-vision helmet and pushed it up. He dropped his right shoulder and started peeling off the pack that had so encumbered his movements.

"Chief. You guys ready?" Dawes called over his radio. He grimaced as he spoke. Even that action caused pain.

"Affirmative. Standing by," BMC Jackson replied.

Kincaid pulled out a small flashlight and removed his pack. He placed the bag on the desk and pulled out the bottom portion of a heavy black rubber suit like the one he wore. "Put this on," he said to "Varsity" as he shoved the article at him.

Kincaid, still shining the light on Varsity, went over to help Dawes finish removing his pack, gingerly pulling his left arm through the strap. Once it was off, he helped Dawes sit up against the bulkhead.

Dawes pulled his weapon up and pointed toward the door. Doc Kincaid took the other half of the suit over to "Varsity" and helped him finish dressing.

"How we doin'?" Boyd asked. His voice had an urgent quality to it.

"Okay. Why?" Dawes asked.

No response.

Dawes was set to transmit again when his sniper came back online. "Shit."

"What?"

"The guy in the boat is coming aboard."

"Where is he?" Wells asked.

"Port side. By the accommodation ladder. He's looking up toward the pilothouse."

"I've got him," Wells replied. "Haul ass up there!"

Dawes' lower chest throbbed with each step. He found supporting himself on the handrails nearly impossible. No movement occurred without pain.

"Boss, you doin' okay?" Kincaid asked.

"Just keep going," Dawes managed to utter.

Kincaid took the point as they descended. Varsity followed next in line with Dawes bringing up the rear. Dawes and Kincaid, again wearing their night-vision equipment, guided "Varsity" with low voices and shoulder-taps, one for left, two for right.

Through the green shroud, Dawes saw Kincaid stop his progress and turn to face him. He checked his watch. Signs for the third level indicated their slow progress. Dawes agonized over his debilitated state and his drag on the mission. "Just go and come back for me," Dawes ordered.

"Bullshit," Kincaid replied. The burly Hospital Corpsman came back up two steps and lifted Dawes into a fireman's carry. He turned and headed back down the metal stairs.

"Sir. Grab hold of the Lieutenant's arm and don't let go or make us fall," he said to Varsity.

"Yes, yes."

Dawes focused his gaze on the area behind them. Each step Kincaid took jarred Dawes to the core. While painful, it hurt far less than walking on his own.

"Boyd, you still got that extra line?" he asked referring to a rope roll.

"Roger. Why?"

"We're gonna need it to get Dawes in the raft."

"Roger. No problem."

Dawes let a wave of relief wash over him. The idea of climbing down the sixty-foot side of the ship with his injury left him cold. Kincaid started down yet another flight, and the jabbing pain in Dawes' chest returned. So much for that moment of relief.

Wells crept along, his weapon up and at the ready. The memory of the guard getting the drop on him still fresh in his mind, he girded himself for the rest of the mission, his night-vision allowing him to cut through the darkness with relative ease.

By the time he got to the left side of the ship, he discovered a lone Vietnamese sailor edging his way toward the main deck door. The man extended his left hand in front of him as he walked. His other handheld pistol at the ready.

"Junior, we're almost down. Are we clear yet?" Kincaid asked over the radio.

"Stand by. He's taking care of your problem," Boyd answered for him.

Wells could not respond without giving away his position. He pressed on toward his target. He moved like a panther stalking his prey, silent and powerful. Stopping a few feet in front of the night-blinded Vietnamese Coast Guardsman, he raised his rifle butt. Wells, in one powerful jab, slammed the blunt end of his weapon into the man's skull. His quarry fell unconscious to the deck.

"You're clear." Wells grabbed the fallen Asian by his leg and dragged him away from the door.

He pulled back into one of the container canyons to observe and cover the door. Seconds later, three figures emerged from the superstructure. The last of them walked in a stoop. Dawes at least walked on his own.

"Boss, you're moving like my grandmother," Wells said as they arrived.

"I dated your grandmother," Dawes shot back. "Let's get the fuck out of here."

"Ready?" DeSilva asked Chief Jackson.

Jackson took one more look around. They now orbited almost fifty yards seaward from the container ship. He neither saw nor heard any other craft in the area. "Yeah. Go."

DeSilva pushed a lever on the rubber boat's electric outboard, and they surged forward. As Jackson pushed the handle away from him, they turned to the left, and *Kingston Excelsior*'s large black form filled their view. Jackson shifted his gaze just for a moment from the ship to his weapon to ensure it was still within reach. DeSilva sat in the forward-most part of the boat, weapon up and ready.

With the rest of his team covering him, Boyd tied off a single line of rope and dropped it to the deck below. The pitch-black sky gave way to the earliest of the sun's rays, providing further evidence of their behind-schedule status. Boyd removed his night-vision goggles and took one last look at the pilothouse and main deck. "Coming down," he said over the radio. He pushed his rifle to his side and swung himself out onto the rope. He began the descent to the main deck.

As he neared the deck, movement near the ship's deckhouse caught his attention. "Boys, we're gonna have company," he announced over the radio. "I've got five to six Tangos moving forward on the starboard side."

Boyd slowed his descent just enough to recon the situation. The men carried rifles and flashlights and advanced slowly, like a hunting party. About a hundred yards behind Dawes, Kincaid, and "Varsity", they edged toward the ship's bow and their egress area on the starboard-bow.

Once on deck, Boyd pulled the pack off his back as he brought his weapon up. He trotted as fast as he dared toward the starboard side of the bow. The Russians meant business. Locating a cleat, he attached one end of his line.

Wells and the others emerged from one of the container canyons. Boyd fashioned a bowline knot at the other end of the line as the other two SEALS, and Varsity joined him. The original plan had called for them to lower "Varsity" with it. Now, it needed to carry one more passenger.

"About time," Boyd greeted.

"Hey, blame the boss. He's movin' like an old lady at a Sunday picnic," Wells laughed.

"Yeah, yeah. We ready?" Dawes asked with difficulty.

"Yep. Boyd replied as Wells took his place at a cable roll. The younger SEAL officer directed his attention and his weapon back toward the stern of the ship, the direction of the Russians.

"Okay, sir," Boyd said to "Varsity"as he slipped the loop over his shoulders and positioned it under his arms. "Don't do anything except hold on. We'll do the rest."

He nodded as Boyd pointed toward the side of the ship.

"Over you go. There are two men in a rubber boat down there. They'll help you out of the line once you're down."

Boyd took note of the Asian's eyes. They were still wide with fear. "You gonna be all right?"

"Varsity" nodded again.

With that, their package climbed over the side, and the rope went taut. Boyd anchored himself against the side of the ship and lowered him twice as fast as usual. Time was of the essence. Boyd looked over his shoulder to find Dawes and Wells up and ready.

As the line went slack, the first bullet made its arrival known. "We've got him," Chief Jackson called over the radio.

"Corvette," Boyd reported to the TOC.

A Tango's bullet made a loud metallic pop as it ricocheted off the ship's hull. Boyd reduced his profile by hunkering down as he pulled the line back up. He checked over his shoulder again as his two teammates took aim and dropped two of their attackers.

The near silence that had surrounded the team during the mission was gone now, replaced by the sound of automatic and semi-automatic weapons fire cracking the air. Along with the noise of armed conflict, came the smoke and acrid odor of gunfire.

"Boss, you're next," Boyd said as he felt the weight of the line all but disappear. The loop's knot came over the rail a second later.

"No. You go. I'll go last."

"Sorry, Boss. It don't work that way," Wells said as he pulled the trigger on his weapon.

"You're wasting time, brother," Boyd added.

Dawes winced as he relented. He crawled over to Boyd and slipped the loop around himself. "Go," he ordered.

Boyd nodded as he anchored himself.

Dawes practically threw himself over the metal side of the ship.

Rather than lower him at the same speed as the civilian, Boyd almost doubled Dawes' rate of descent. Five seconds later, the line went slack. "I'm down. Now, get your asses down here!" Dawes ordered over the radio.

"You don't gotta tell me twice," Boyd said to Wells. Boyd threw the rest of the line over the side. He picked up his weapon and went to Wells' side.

Four men fired at them: two with automatic weapons, the other two with pistols. Boyd sighted his rifle on one of the men. A blonde man in a plaid shirt used a container for cover as he occasionally shot at them. Boyd waited until he had the man's timing. He shot, hid, shot, and hid again. The next time he came out, Boyd ended his life with a single shot to the man's head. He then turned the rifle toward the other man.

"What are you guys doing up there?" Dawes asked over the radio.

"Just taking in the view," Wells replied. "It's pretty up here."

Wells controlled his bursts perfectly. He put out just enough lead and in the right direction to keep the bad guys' heads down.

"Pull back a bit," Boyd said to him.

Wells reduced his rate of fire, and the final three Russians instantly grew bolder. When one of the men with pistols stood to rush in their direction, Wells eliminated him. The other two Russians' weapons fell silent.

"Time to go," Wells said to Boyd.

The sniper nodded as he withdrew from the line and crawled to the rope behind them. Seeing Wells go up to fire his weapon, he started down the rope to the rubber boat below.

Looking down, Boyd saw that Jackson and DeSilva weapons trained upward toward the ship's railing behind him. The line shifted, suddenly causing him to look back up toward the top. He saw Wells descending toward him. Boyd picked up his speed as the two SEALS in the boat fired toward the ship's main deck.

He reached the raft just as a Russian sailor's body fell into the water a few feet from the raft. Boyd clambered away from the end of the line as Wells arrived seconds later. As soon as he was down, Dawes hit the throttle on the outboard motor. Jackson and DeSilva continued their suppressing fire as they pulled away from the ship. The team slipped into the darkness beyond and out of sight and gun range of the container ship crew.

"Passing Porsche," Dawes reported mission success to the TOC.

CHAPTER TWO
PRINCETON

Friday, February 26th
USS Princeton *(CG-59)*
200 Nautical Miles North of Oahu, Hawaii
0300 Hours

The intercom system's buzzer volume almost rattled Captain Elizabeth Nation's teeth. Without opening her eyes, she reached for the telephone-shaped receiver with one well practiced grab. With a little luck, she could return to the dream of skiing in the Alps with her late father.

"This is the Captain," Nation answered, her voice raspy with sleep.

"Skipper, this is the TAO, Lieutenant Juarez," the young woman announced herself in a terse and exact manner. Nation tensed and her eyes went wide. Juarez paused, waiting for a coherent response from her Captain.

"Go ahead, Miss Juarez. I'm awake." Nation, aware enough to process the information, still lay in her bunk beneath warm covers.

"Ma'am, we're currently tracking a contact with an Intermediate Range Ballistic Missile profile."

Here we go.

"The contact is tracking towards our engagement envelope. Recommend we go to General Quarters," Juarez continued.

"Very well. Take the ship to General Quarters."

GENERAL QUARTERS

"General Quarters, General Quarters! All hands man your Battle-Stations!" the Boatswains Mate of the Watch shouted over the ship's general announcement system a moment later.

Still holding the intercom receiver, Nation threw off the covers and swung her 6'5" frame around, clearing her throat with one powerful cough. Even from the confines of her cabin, Nation heard rushed footfalls and elevated voices of the ship's crew wrestling from their slumber to place the improved Aegis-class cruiser in a state of maximum combat readiness. "Miss Juarez?" Captain Nation raised her voice over the ringing bells.

"Yes, ma'am?"

"Have the XO meet me in Combat," she said, referring to *Princeton*'s Executive Officer.

"He's already on his way, ma'am."

Nation descended the metal ladder between her at-sea cabin and the Combat Information Center, one deck below. Lifting her feet by bending her legs at the knee and balancing on her palms, she slid down the rails in one graceful motion. She stepped into the passageway and then into the ship's tactical operations nerve center.

"Captain's in Combat," one of the enlisted watch-standers announced her arrival.

Nation instantly detected more noise in the space than usual. She frowned at the prospect of trying to fight her ship with so much background clutter.

The space, crowded with equipment and personnel, grew instantly quieter as the tall, former Olympic skier strode to her station.

"Good morning, Ma'am."

"Good morning, Miss Juarez. What have we got?" Nation's vision adjusted quickly to the subdued lighting. Blue-hued fluorescent bulbs bathed the space in pale light from overhead, allowing computer monitors and sensor screens to appear with greater clarity in the arcade-like room.

LT Juanita Juarez, clad in the Navy Working Uniform and a *Princeton* cap, remained seated at her Battle Management Console station.

Juarez served as Nation's combat systems and tactics expert. Four years of at-sea experience in destroyers and cruisers, as well as graduating from the Navy's TAO School, thoroughly qualified her in the use of the ship's combat suite.

The short, curvy young Latina turned in her seat to face *Princeton*'s Commanding Officer. "Ma'am, National Reconnaissance Office assets have detected the launch of an intermediate-range ballistic missile. It's north of our current position and tracking westerly. It'll enter our engagement envelope in two minutes."

Nation nodded as she took her place at Lieutenant Juarez' right. She studied the displayed computer-processed sensor information. The ballistic missile's red icon featured a long vector extending from it towards the left edge of the monitor screen indicating its supersonic speed.

Juarez positioned the trackball on her console to select the missile's icon. The target's vital contact information appeared to its right in a dark box with white lettering. Speed, altitude, and its computer-generated identification number displayed in a small window to the contact icon's right.

Now at just under 60,000 feet, the missile had reached apogee and was headed earthward. "Mach Five or better," Nation read aloud.

"Yes, ma'am."

"Executive Officer's in Combat," the same voice announced over the growing spectator chatter.

Lieutenant Commander Paul Daniels' tall and muscular frame came into view. "Have we got a targeting solution yet?" the African-American officer asked as he took a seat next to her.

"Yes, sir," Senior Chief Guerette shouted from his station a few feet to their rear above the once again growing din. Senior Chief Operations Specialist Bill Guerette served as the ship's second most senior enlisted person. The non-commissioned officer ran the Combat Information Center as well as operated the Air Warfare console.

Captain Nation liked her Executive Officer. She thought him a brilliant administrator, great ship-handler, and an even better tactician. She humorously considered his Naval Academy pedigree his only real shortcoming. Like her, however, he numbered among the few officers in the Navy who gained their first commands as lieutenants. Witty and personable, the crew loved him. In her twenty-four years in the Navy, fortune allowed her to work for more than a few future Admirals. Paul Daniels displayed all the same characteristics as those men and women daily.

Nation and Daniels turned in their seats to look down the left most of three rows of sensor operators. Air Alley, or the row of sensor operators who handled the Air Warfare picture, buzzed with spectators and activity. Several personnel, officers and enlisted alike, crowded around Senior Chief Guerette's station. The contingent of embarked civilian contractors joined the throng as well.

"This is not a peep show, people," Daniels scolded.

The resulting hush reminded Nation of a classroom of students on the receiving end of admonishment by a teacher for talking. The room grew instantly quieter. That's more like it.

The intercom beside Nation's chair rang, and she reached for it without taking her eyes from the large screen displays. "Captain," she answered.

"Ma'am. Zebra is set. All stations report manned and ready," LT Jefferson, the Officer of the Deck, reported from the Bridge.

She checked her watch. Less than three minutes had passed since calling away General Quarters. "Nice work, Mr. Jefferson. That's our best time yet."

"Yes, Ma'am."

She put the receiver back in its holder and turned to LT Juarez.

"Ma'am, the forward magazine is ready. We've got target acquisition," Juarez reported.

"Okay, XO. Call it in."

Nation knew the reason for the crowd. The first two tests had resulted in failures. Bad weather caused the last cancellation. Everyone, herself especially, yearned to get this system fully qualified for deployment. Tonight meant another year of research work or getting her warship back to its real job.

"Yes, ma'am." Daniels keyed the microphone on his headset to contact the Pacific Fleet Operations Command Center. "BAD KARMA, this is SLEDGEHAMMER," he called. "VAMPIRE, VAMPIRE, VAMPIRE. Tango Track 821051 designated as IRBM. SLEDGEHAMMER engaging. Over."

"SLEDGEHAMMER, this is BAD KARMA. Roger. Out."

"TAO, you have weapons release authority for one SM-4 missile," Nation said to Juarez. "Make it count."

"Air Weapons, TAO. One SM-4 Missile. Weapons Free," Juarez spoke into her mic to the Weapons Control Station.

Captain Nation watched Senior Chief Guerette nod as he responded to Lieutenant Juarez. He reached for the firing key and turned it with one confident motion.

A second later, the ship's frame groaned and vibrated as if it had a bad case of indigestion. A closed-circuit camera provided a clear picture of the forward vertical launch missile magazine on *Princeton*'s bow. The camera transmitted the image of the Navy's newest missile on a nearby television screen. The noise and vibration faded as the missile made a fiery ascent into the night sky.

"Bird's away," Senior Chief Guerette announced.

A few crew members started applauding, until their contemporaries hushed them. An enforced silence returned to the space as Nation watched the air plot on the large display screen in front of her. A second or two later, the screen updated and displayed *Princeton*'s missile in a blue semi-circle icon. A long vector reached out towards the ballistic missile's icon.

"I think we've got it this time," Daniels said. "That's gonna leave a mark," he joked.

"Hope you're right," Nation replied, not taking her eyes from the screen.

Moments passed. Nation sat perched as if on the edge of a tall cliff, ready to jump off for the downhill run of her life. The red and blue icons moved towards each other with increasing speed until they merged. When *Princeton*'s SPY-1 radar and AEGIS weapons systems updated the screen again, neither contact appeared.

"Target destroyed," the enlisted radar operator announced from Air Alley.

Nation didn't stop the applause. Handshakes and backslaps abounded in the dimly lit space. She exchanged smiles and handshakes with Daniels and Juarez.

Daniels, still grinning, pulled out a cigar and put it in his mouth, offering another to Nation. She smiled as she accepted her Executive Officer's gift. Juarez shot Daniels and her Commanding Officer disapproving glances.

"SLEDGEHAMMER, this is BAD KARMA-Actual. Target destroyed. Bravo Zulu," the Pacific Fleet Command Center congratulated them over the radio.

"BAD KARMA, this is SLEDGEHAMMER-Actual. Roger, out," Nation replied with a smile.

"Nice work, Lieutenant," Daniels said to Juarez.

"Thanks, XO."

Nation turned to her XO after placing the radio transceiver back into its holder. "Stand down from General Quarters, XO. Set the normal underway watch and let's turn for home."

"Aye. Aye, ma'am."

***

Guiyang, China
11:15 PM

The knot in his stomach grew with every passing minute. He listened intently as the CNN International News anchor carried on a conversation with one of his colleagues. The hour's lead story concerned a break-in at a Lyon, France, bio-medical research laboratory and an ensuing search.

"Jack, have the police made any statements about what the thieves were after?" the anchor asked.

The scene behind the field correspondent spoke volumes. Several blue and white police cars, their strobe lights still flashing, sat parked in front of yellow crime-scene tape. Two or three men in dark blue Gendarme police uniforms kept crowds of curious on-lookers from crossing into the crime scene.

"No. They're remaining quite mum on the subject," the reporter answered with a distinctly English accent. "What is at the top of their comments are the four Asian men killed as they attempted to evade arrest."

He slammed his fist against the table. An ashtray and teacup resting adjacent to him nearly flew off the edge from the force. "Damn!" What the hell went wrong?

"A fifth man remains at large. According to police, this man shot three officers with an automatic weapon before he escaped on a stolen motorcycle."

"Have the police mentioned how the other suspects were killed?" the anchor quizzed.

"Yes, Tom. The police say that the men were all stopped at the rear gate to the facility. When police demanded their surrender, the fifth man shot his comrades before turning the gun on the police."

"He shot his accomplices?" Tom asked, incredulously.

"That's correct. He then turned the gun on the police, killing three and seriously wounding a fourth. That officer, with less than a month on the job, is fighting for his life in a local hospital."

He sat on the edge of his couch. The large-screen television illuminated the entire room, casting dark and bizarre shadows all around him. Smoke from a smoldering cigarette diffused the remaining light as it clouded above the couch.

"How long has this fifth man been on the run?"

"The robbery took place almost two hours ago. The police have checkpoints all around the city and are confident they will find him."

"Thanks, Jack. We know you'll keep on top of this. We'll check back with you later during the broadcast."

The field reporter nodded as the cameras returned focus to the news anchor. He moved the program along with news from the Middle East and the escalating violence between Israel and Iran.

Just as he raised the remote to turn the television to another news channel, the telephone rang. "Yes?" he answered. He did not pause to examine the Caller-ID before answering. He made no effort to hide the edge in his voice.

"Sir?" a familiar voice on the other line greeted him.

"Lu? Where the hell are you? The police are searching for you everywhere! How did this get so fucked up?"

"Not to worry, sir. I am safely away and making my return."

He detected a loud droning noise in Lu's background.

"Where are you?"

"I am on an airplane. I obtained it earlier today."

"And our men?"

"They are dead. I could not chance our mission failing, or one of them falling into the hands of the police."

He let the information sink in without commenting. Lu was right, of course. The most important task was completing their mission and returning with the item. "Do you have it?"

"Yes, sir. I do."

He sighed. "I hope it is worth it."

"As do I. I will see you in a few days."

***

Londoner's Night Club
Taipei, Taiwan
11:45 PM

Alexi Pugachev dined alone at his favorite table in his best nightclub. The sound system blasted a techno-dance tune to the packed dance floor below. Multi-hued spotlights and several glittered disco balls threw intermittently synchronized colored beams of light through a thick cigarette-smoke haze. Pugachev liked the sound of human voices and music. A good crowd meant more money.

Stephan and Petrov, two of Pugachev's lieutenants, stood guard on his left and right. Their coats bulged from their concealed automatic pistols. Pugachev sipped from a beer bottle before taking another bite from his plate of sashimi. His table, on one of three balconies overlooking the dance floor, gave him a bird's eye view of the goings-on below. He scanned the crowd and forced himself to ignore the knot of anxiety in his stomach so he could take another bite of dinner.

"Good crowd tonight, huh, Boss?" Petrov asked above the noise of the crowd.

Pugachev looked up to make sure his bodyguards remained focused on their surroundings. They were. "Yeah." He returned to his meal while casually running his hand across the 9mm pistol on his lap.

Pugachev took mental note of his holdings. Working for the Chinese, so far, proved very profitable. Finding a way to hide it all proved more and more difficult every month.

Keeping the police away from his "other" businesses while remaining on call for his Chinese clients served as a daily challenge. Pugachev's empire included drugs, gambling, and prostitution. He managed to provide access to these "services" through several strategically located bars in Taipei's Combat Zone.

He took a sip from his half-empty beer bottle as another of his lieutenants approached. Sean Schugard, their lone American, earned his way by running Alexi's operation. The former football and rugby player looked more like one of Pugachev's enforcers, but his business acumen and intelligence distinguished him as his best operator.

"We've got more trouble," Schugard announced.

Pugachev looked up at the tall, dark-haired man and scowled.

"Hey, don't be pissed at me. I just deliver the bad news; I don't make it."

"What now?"

"Well, we got a shipment in, but it wasn't what we were waiting for."

"Speak plainly, damn you!" Pugachev shook his finger.

"Boss...well. You need to come to see this," Schugard gestured with both his hand and his head for Pugachev to follow.

Pugachev threw down his chopsticks and stood to follow his operations manager. Stephan and Petrov fell in a step ahead and behind Pugachev. The four men shoved their way through the crowded lower floor toward the rear of the building.

The noise from the sound system and the partiers in the disco faded as they left the bar. After passing through the kitchen and the dozen workers preparing food, they entered the warehouse.

Several hundred meters wide and about ten meters high, the space hosted an array of crates of varying sizes and two marine shipping containers. The object of Pugachev's curiosity sat in the middle of the most open part of the concrete flooring. A single large crate sat apart from the rest with two of his men standing a respectful distance from it.

As he neared the container, the smell of rotting human flesh reached his nostrils. At three meters, the odor overpowered him. He reached into his pocket for a handkerchief to cover his nose and mouth. Pugachev frowned at the stench as he exchanged glances with Schugard.

The crate's cover, although it showed damage from the crowbar that lay on the floor, still obstructed his view. "Open it!" he ordered.

Coughing and gagging, Stephan and Petrov picked the lid up on either side to slide it away. When they did, the decaying corpses of three men came into view. Gunshot wounds riddled the bodies. Their chests and stomachs lay open, exposing their intestines and the insects that now fed on them.

Pugachev gestured to put the lid back in place when he felt his dinner trying to come back up. "Get rid of it," he said to his men.

They nodded their understanding as he turned to walk away. He needed some fresh air. He felt Schugard and his two bodyguards close behind him.

As Pugachev reached the door, his mobile telephone rang. The Caller-ID confirmed he didn't know the caller.

"Yes."

"Did you receive my package?"

Pugachev knew the male voice instantly. "You? Did you do this?"

"Of course."

Pugachev's men stood around him with expressions of shock, surprise, and curiosity on their faces. Schugard strained so hard to hear the conversation that he nearly pressed his cheek against Pugachev's.

"But why? I did as you asked," Pugachev pulled away from Schugard when he heard the pleading in his voice.

"Yes, you most certainly did. Then you tried to follow my people after our last meeting. I warned you."

Pugachev wanted to kill the bastard on the other end of the line. However, he did not know where or even who he was. Since their first conversation some three months earlier, the caller brought a considerable sum of money and trouble. Pugachev now considered himself nothing more than an errand boy. With each passing day, this deal seemed less and less like a good one.

"Alexi, you are a man who requires..." the voice paused "motivation." The voice laughed.

Pugachev's hand shook with rage as he listened to him. He exchanged glances with Schugard. His operations manager gestured with his hands, asking the identity of the caller. Pugachev turned his back to him.

"What do you want?"

"I'll be in touch. Unless you want to end up like your associates, you will start following my instructions," the voice said before the line went dead.

CHAPTER THREE
STRAINED RELATIONS

(Six Months Later)
Monday, August 11th
Residence of the Naval Attaché
United States Diplomatic Residential Compound
Taipei, Taiwan
0515 Hours

"This is CNN News' continuing coverage of the 'Crisis in Asia,'" The news anchor announced with such gravity that it made Ben's stomach churn. Their now-famous "Breaking News" marquee covered the bottom portion of the screen. "Just moments ago, the American and Chinese Ambassadors to the United Nations openly traded barbs, one accusing the other of trying to start a world war."

Ben McGuire studied his wife's luggage for a long contemplative moment. Four bags in all, two large, two small, silently spotlighted her impending departure for home. The last three and a half months had flown.. Until just recently, he regarded their temporary overseas assignment as a fun-filled adventure. He pulled his gaze away from the depressing sight to the television as the prevailing news story demanded his full attention.

The broadcast displayed two well-dressed men, one Asian and one Caucasian, in a split-screen format. The Chinese ambassador shouted something in Mandarin while pointing his finger at the American. Almost at the same time, the American ambassador stood and shouted, "Stop dishonoring this body with your lies. Stop pretending to be in search of peace when you obviously have other intentions."

"Geez," Ben said as his legs tried to give out beneath him. He plopped himself down onto the sofa.

"What?" Claire asked as she entered the room, still putting on earrings.

"The UN ambassadors look like they're ready to throw down." Ben tried his best levity to lighten the situation.

Claire finished fiddling with her jewelry and seated herself on the arm of the sofa.

Secretary-General Ortiz, a lanky Argentinean, kept shouting "Order! Order!" as the exchange continued unabated.

The Chinese ambassador picked up a group of papers and launched them into the air toward the American delegation. The other delegates seated near him drew back in wide-eyed nervousness. The Chinese ambassador, followed by the rest of his contingent, stood, turned, and stormed out of the General Assembly. The camera followed them for as long as they remained visible.

The news anchor's image returned to the screen. "Of course, this whole mess all started almost six months ago when US Intelligence published photographs of Chinese trains delivering goods to North Korea. Things escalated when intelligence officials released documents describing the shipping contents of those trains as miniaturized electronics technology. United Nations nuclear energy experts further testified that the equipment had no other purpose other than to shrink the size of nuclear weapons for placement in North Korea's No Dong missiles."

Sensing the need to reassure Claire, Ben pulled his attention from the television to his wife's lovely face. Claire instinctively reached for his hand as she continued watching the screen.

"Today's flare-up started when the US Ambassador again pressed the Chinese for an answer to President Langdon's invitation to a summit with the President of Taiwan and himself, now just a few days away. Rather than answer, the verbal fireworks began. And honestly, that's the only kind of fireworks we hope to see."

As the broadcast continued, Ben's mind turned to the sequence of events that landed him in the middle of a global hotspot. At the time he took the assignment, it felt like a perfect alignment of the planets. Now, it felt like something else entirely.

Claire's company, always amenable to one of their favorite executives, agreed to place her in their Asian Foods Division for a quarter. War could engulf the entire region within the next few days, or hours. Now on vacation and expecting the arrival of their two teenagers, the couple changed their plans. Ben canceled the family vacation and moved up her departure.

"When are you coming home?" she asked.

"Not sure. My relief isn't ready yet," Ben replied, referring to his successor.

"I want you out of here. This place is gonna blow up any second now."

Ben shrugged. "Sorry, you're CINC Home, not CINC PAC," he half-joked, using the Navy's jargon for Commander-In-Chief, Pacific Forces. His wife's face bore the tension she processed. She was worried, and truthfully, so was he.

Claire didn't laugh as she shifted herself from the sofa-arm to his lap. "Seriously."

Ben shrugged. "Corrigan and I are turning over as fast as we can," he lied. Navy Captain P.T. Corrigan's progress so far remained muted. He barely made a dent in his required reading material. Further, he comprehended only a passing familiarity with the area geography and force structure. Ben believed that

GENERAL QUARTERS

Corrigan's four years as a Pentagon staff-weenie took its toll. He returned his attention to the television broadcast.

"Our sources at the Pentagon report the Chinese Military has continued its build-up along their eastern coasts, supposedly to repel a US-led invasion. Their Navy is on high alert, prompting the US, Japan, and Taiwan to respond in kind," the anchor continued reporting as Ben and Claire kissed in the dimly lit room.

Ben McGuire, too young to remember the Cuban Missile Crisis of 1962, only knew of the event through reading. As a fan of history, he appreciated the story well enough. In addition to consuming several books on the subject, Ben read every classified report available on the subject. He knew that due to 1960's era lack of openness and rudimentary media technology, most people did not understand how close the world came to nuclear war. Now, thanks to leakers in the involved governments, the 24-hour news cycle and the Internet, nearly everyone understood the gravity of this crisis.

***

Intelligence Operations Center
United States Embassy
Taipei, Taiwan
6:15 AM

"Okay, just tell me this. Why so much interest in McGuire?" Wong asked.

Jake Harrison, carrying a full coffee cup, took a seat in one of his assistant's guest chairs. Yawning, he covered his mouth with his empty hand.

"I don't get it. McGuire's hardly a big fish. I mean, the guy is a total suit," Wong laughed as he spoke.

Jake closed the file and looked up at his apprentice. "A suit, huh?"

"Yeah. That guy is all 'gung-ho, ooh-rah.' Typical military type."

Jake smiled as he placed the classified document back on his desk. As the rhetoric between the US and China had increased, so had the amount of high-level Chinese government chatter about the US Naval Attaché. Captain Ben McGuire's name now appeared daily in their communications intercepts.

Wong represented the new breed of CIA operatives: non-white, advance-degreed, second-generation American, and extremely patriotic. The 29-year-old grew up in a Mandarin-speaking household in the Bay Area before going to Stanford and then on to graduate school at Yale. As Jake's second in command in Taipei, Wong balanced between the office and fieldwork. He also served as their unofficial liaison with the Taiwanese Intelligence Agency. As the Embassy's Intelligence Chief, Harrison considered himself lucky to have Wong on his staff.

"What?" Wong asked. "What do you know?"

Harrison took a sip from his cup. "What is the first thing they teach you about our work?"

"That nothing is as it appears," Wong replied.

"Correct. So, just to make you feel better, I thought the same thing for a while. But here's what you need to know: Mr. McGuire comes highly recommended. I did some digging around..."

"And?"

"We had a classified project going on over here a few years back that was compromised. McGuire was out here on Reserve Duty at the time. He got pulled into it and pretty much saved the day."

"Define 'saved the day'," Wong pressed.

"He and some SEALS took on a company-sized unit of Chinese Marines before they blew up an island."

"Wait a minute. I remember this. Senkaku Islands, right?" Wong asked.

"Yes."

"I thought a dormant volcano exploded."

Jake hushed his voice. "That's the cover story. The real story is pretty interesting. There's an on-going joint project with the Japanese to perfect the process of generating energy from a nuclear fusion reaction."

"Fusion. Is that even possible?"

"Yeah, it is, but still extremely experimental."

Wong nodded.

"It would seem that the Chinese found out about it and tried to take it. McGuire uncovered a spy and kept the whole thing in our hands by blowing up the reactor."

"McGuire?" Wong frowned in confusion as he asked the question.

"Yeah. Like I said, he's not a suit."

***

Beijing, China
8:45 AM

"I have been watching the events at the United Nations with great interest," Central Military Commissioner Zieng Fong mused. The President of China sat across from him at a large and ornate mahogany table. President Ho Lin Shih studied Fong's face for a long moment before shifting his gaze to Communist Party President Fei Chen Tzu.

Light rays cut beams of different shades of gray in the thick cigarette smoke. The high ceilings, marble floors, and relatively dim lighting gave the room a cavernous feel. As they spoke, their voices echoed in the vast space.

"Yes, interesting isn't it," President Ho asked as he sipped piping hot tea from a white cup. China's real head of state scanned the two men for their facial expressions and body language. They presented what his American schoolmates used to call a "tough room."

Under the People's Republic of China's (PRC) Constitution, the Communist Party of China, or CCP, governs China. While the CCP dominates policymaking and execution through its government members, the National People's Congress ranks as the highest legislative body. The cabinet, or State Council, headed by the President, actually run the country.

At any given time, one of the three gathered individuals serves as the "Pinyin," or Paramount Leader, literally "the highest leader of the country." This person may hold or have held the office of Chairman of the Communist Party of China, President of the People's Republic of China, or Chairman of the Central Military Commission. At present, Ho Lin Shih, as President, had a very tenuous hold on the role of Paramount Leader.

"What?" Fei asked. He folded his stubby arms across an ample chest as he momentarily put down his fourth cigarette in thirty minutes. Blowing out a heavy cloud of smoke , he shook his head in disagreement.

"American politics." Ho gently placed his cup back in its place on a flower-ringed saucer. He forced a pleasant smile at the fat man monitoring him on behalf of the Communist Party.

"Interesting is hardly the word I would choose." Fei's tone and manner were matter of fact. He wore a "bad taste in his mouth' expression. "The Americans are a rabble — a dangerous mob with too many guns and too little patience. They want what they want, and they want it all now."

"Perhaps what is most interesting is how they are reacting to the mess you created, Comrade Zieng."

Zieng's eyes grew wide and then thinned, as he did not attempt to hide his anger. "The time to act was now," he barked back.

"Perhaps, but the decision to do so was mine," Ho shot back. "I am the Pinyin. Not you."

"Yours?" asked Fei. He laughed as he took a drag from an American cigarette. "I'd have to disagree with both of your statements."

Ho took a breath to regroup. He agreed with Fei. He shared the job of setting policy with the Party and the People's Congress. "At a minimum, we should have all discussed it."

Neither of the men responded.

"Now, the Americans are pitting world opinion against us, and our ambassador's behavior in the U.N. was most unseemly."

"What do we care about world opinion?" Fei snapped as he crossed his arms.

"You studied too long in America, Comrade Ho. You have an acceptance for them that many of us find...troubling."

Fei uncrossed his arms and took another long drag from his cigarette. He shot Ho a stern glance before turning to Zieng with a smile. "Besides, some of us discussed the North Korean issue before acting."

Ho knew that Fei mentally commended himself for getting in a daily jab at him and his policies. Still, in his first year as President, Ho Lin Shih knew he should move slowly. Ho harbored grand plans for China, perhaps his version of Perestroika. He also knew that to affect those plans, he must remain in office.

He turned his gaze toward Zieng. The Central Military Committee Leader tried to avoid eye contact for a moment. When their eyes finally met, Zieng lowered his head without verbally commenting on Fei's opinion.

The Chinese President smiled at Fei's dig as well as Zieng's lack of support. Ho knew Fei hated all things Western, including his education. When the Party decided to nominate him, Fei voiced the strongest and most vocal opposition.

The Old Guard explained to him they thought him too young and liberal. Ho chaffed at the deal that brought him to office. It came with a rider: Fei's close geographic and political proximity.

Ho understood Zieng's position. Siding with him placed Zieng at odds with Fei. The Party Chairman would interpret it as weakness. Removing Ho from office required an act by the Party and National Congress, a difficult task. Removing Zieng from his duties as the Central Military Commissioner required far less effort and besides, Ho needed Zieng, for now.

"The American President has strongly expressed his beliefs. He plans to make formal recognition of Taiwan the centerpiece of his foreign policy," Zieng commented.

"And the only reason for that is our decision to assist the North Koreans with nuclear missile technology. I fully expect the UN to vote for sanctions. Comrades, you have set our economic progress back ten years." Ho grunted as he sat forward in his chair.

"And that would be a mistake on their part," Fei joked.

"Comrade, do you plan to fight the entire world?" Ho asked.

"No, but I think that we should have a strategy in place to ensure the renegade province understands their future lies with no one else but Mother China." Fei shifted his large body to sit up in his chair.

"I think we make sure they know we are ready for war," Zieng added.

"Yes. In no uncertain terms," Fei agreed.

"And jeopardize all that we have gained?" Ho pressed.

"What have we gained?" Fei laughed.

"Our economic plan is in its fifteenth successful year. Each day more and more Western companies are doing business here. We have had the fastest-growing economy in the world, even faster than the Americans. If we go to war, we will fall behind and possibly never regain our place."

"At what cost? If we compromise on this, we will have a difficult time maintaining our National stature."

"Compromise is the currency of diplomacy," Ho said.

"It is also the language of cowardice," Fei interjected.

Ho looked at Fei with pursed lips.

"I can think of nothing that is worth surrendering our claim to Taiwan," Zieng stated.

"Then I suggest you should open your mind, if not conceptually, then economically."

Fei frowned.

"You have a plan?" Zieng asked.

Ho smiled. "More tea, Comrades?"

Fei did not accept the offer of tea.

"So what if the Americans are crazy to climb into bed with Taiwan? Let them have their diplomacy," Ho suggested.

"What you offer is insanity."

"Hear me," Ho pressed. "We retrieve the technology from the Koreans, let this diffuse, and, in time, we go back and get Taiwan. Must we act now?"

Fei shot Zieng a glance before he spoke. He crushed the life out of his cigarette. "So, you're saying we will act?"

"Yes, but not now. It would cost too many live..."

"And too much money," Zieng ended the sentence for him.

"Besides," President Ho added. "There is a much bigger prize to be had just now."

"And what is that?" Fei shot back with a snort.

"The Spratley Islands."

Zieng's eyebrows went up at the remark.

"I see I have your interest, Comrade."

The Philippines, Japan, France, Portugal, Spain, the United Kingdom, Republic of Vietnam, People's Republic of China, and the Republic of China all claimed, at one time or another, the Spratley Islands. Both China and the US had maintained observation stations there.

Rich in oil reserves, Ho believed it the solution to China's long-term energy consumption issues for a generation or more.

"Our island-building initiative will only allow us to project power in the region. Owning it all without a fight at this point is an impossibility. But if we make a deal…"

Ho examined the faces of the other men as he laid out his strategy. They relaxed their postures just a bit. Ho pressed.

"We will back off if the US will not only relinquish its claims but also push to solidify our claim on the world stage."

The fat man reclined in his chair and stroked his chin as he seemed to think the proposal over. He finally turned to Ho and nodded. "That is acceptable."

"Meanwhile, we will continue the build-up, to keep the Americans on edge?" Zieng asked.

"Yes, for a while. When we finally negotiate, we will make them think it is on their terms."

Zieng also nodded his concurrence.

Ho, careful not to let it show, relaxed for the first time in three months. He remained in some semblance of control, for now. Getting rid of both Zieng and Fei Tzu figured next in his grand strategy. They and their thinking conflicted with his plans. His comrades were dangerous, and he was sure they harbored the same thoughts about him.

***

People's Liberation Army Navy (PLA-N) Headquarters
0930 Hours

Vice-Admiral Sun Xueliang's conference room occupied the top floor of a 1920's era building that served as the People's Navy Headquarters. The room normally commanded a third-floor view of China's capital city. Today, however, electronic curtains cast the room in relative darkness and complete security from electronic eavesdropping.

GENERAL QUARTERS

The PLA-N Commander's staff consisted of China's three operational fleet commanders and the head of their Marine Corps. North Sea Fleet Commander, Rear Admiral Chek Khan Li; East Sea Fleet Commander Rear Admiral Chang Hong; and South Sea Fleet Commander Rear Admiral Zheng Xu, Naval Air Forces Commander Rear Admiral Fong Wei, and Marine Corps Commandant General Yau Xingyuan sat in the last day of their two-day quarterly meeting. All five men listened intently as the East Sea Fleet Commander made his case.

"The two Wuhan-class cruise missile submarines must be kept on active duty. They represent a critical component of our offensive striking capability," Rear Admiral Chang Hong pleaded.

Sun, seated at the head of the table, frowned. Even as he listened, he struggled to find logic in Chang's argument. He glanced at the pile of documents and folders strewn on the table in front of him. Sun reached across several to pull a red-colored folder from near the bottom of the stack.

"The shipyard has yet to repair them adequately. They are in the poorest of material condition," Sun said. He leafed through several pages until he found the line he needed. "Here. It is in your report from a year ago that 'these ships are in such disrepair that the Commander feels it is unsafe to operate them.' When we take into consideration how much the current mobilization is costing, we must be ready to make cuts."

Seated across the table diagonally from him, Chang shifted in his seat. The heavy-set two-star flag officer winced at his commander's barb. He looked at each of the other officers seated beside him for support, but they barely acknowledged him.

Sun, the first aviator to command the People's Navy, felt somewhat uneasy in the presence of his fleet commanders. The Central Military Committee chose the country's senior officers, himself included. Just as he, these other men rose through the ranks until their promotions to Senior Captain. Political allies backed these other officers' promotion to flag rank and appointment to their current postings just as they did for him. Any loyalty they might someday feel for him must come from the relationships he forged. As Sun debated with his subordinate, he looked around the room at the other four men for reassurance. Only Rear Admiral Fong and General Yau nodded in concurrence.

Sun continued, "We have no idea how long this mobilization will continue. Nearly all our ships are either at sea or in port on boilers. General Yau has two divisions of Marines sitting aboard amphibious assault ships in Shanghai and another assisting with security here in the city. Are we really positioned to keep these aging platforms operational?"

"Sir, that report also continues with my recommendation to overhaul and improve them," Chang pressed. "The C-803 Sea Eagle missile is…"

"A key weapon for us," Sun finished the sentence for Chang. Designed to counter the American Aegis cruisers and destroyers, the newest version of the C-802 Sea Eagle featured upgraded software and a new booster. The newer missile flew lower and cleaner than its predecessor. Unfortunately, the Chinese Navy could only deploy it on their patrol boats. "The new 803's will soon be fully deployed, but we cannot configure the Wuhan-class to launch them."

"Admiral…"

"Enough." Sun ensured his voice had the right amount of finality to it.

The room grew quiet. Sun hoped the three fleet commanders found the silence uncomfortable. "Enough debate. I will take your concerns under consideration, Admiral."

Chang nodded.

Ten clocks on the far wall represented the key time zones of interest. Sun examined the one for Beijing Local Time. "We've been together for several hours. Perhaps it is time for a small recess," Sun suggested as he stood.

The other officers came to their feet. They bowed from the shoulders in semi-unison. Sun acknowledged them with the same gesture before turning for the door to his adjoining office.

"Admiral?" Chang called as he caught up to his commander.

"Yes, Admiral?" Sun replied without slowing his pace.

"Sir, no disrespect was intended-"

"And none was taken," Sun replied.

The PLA-N Commander brought his gaze to meet Chang's. "I value the perspectives and information that come from an open discourse. I think that it is one of the few characteristics of our American friends worthy of emulation." Sun smiled at the East Sea Fleet Commander.

***

Daily Situation Briefing
US Embassy
Taipei, Taiwan
10:15 AM

Six months earlier, when Ben arrived in Taipei, no formal US government offices existed in Taiwan. Until then, a private organization called the American Institute managed the relationship between the US and the small island nation.

The Langdon Administration changed all that. Upon discovering that China provided nuclear weapons technology to North Korea, President Jack Langdon wasted no time in implementing his new policy toward Taiwan. Insiders called it "CGFY," a kind abbreviation for "China Go Fuck Yourself."

A few short months before, Navy SEALS looking to assist a defection, ended up whacking a hornet's nest. The defector, aka "Varsity", brought news of a dangerous alliance that generated new turbulence in an already tense part of the world. In just a few short weeks, the building complex that once served as the United States' unofficial legation now hosted the official U.S Embassy to Taiwan.

"We estimate the Chinese have amassed at least two divisions of Army and Marine regulars in the vicinity of Shanghai at the Ningbo Naval Base," US Army Colonel David Painter explained to a captivated audience. Painter, a dark-haired, short man, spoke in an almost casual tone as he gave his briefing.

"These guys are looking for a fight," Jake Harrison murmured to Ben as they examined the graphics.

Ben nodded as he took a sip of water from an open bottle. The situation seemed to worsen each day. More troops, more ships, more tension, it just keeps gettin' better.

"I'll let Captain McGuire go into the details, but they have also assembled a fairly large number of ships in the area. Drone reconnaissance shows several amphibious landing ships and escorts are also present," Colonel Painter continued as he brought up an enlarged photo of the area.

A Google Earth-based presentation occupied the ten-foot screen behind the Army officer who served as the US Military Attaché. Red icons shaped like men and ships highlighted the major base and port locations in the eastern part of the People's Republic of China.

"Do you think this is a show or the real thing?" Ambassador Wooten asked.

Twelve men and women sat around a large wooden table. Ambassador Thomas Wooten III sat at the head of the gathering. Wooten, a stout African-American man in his late fifties, possessed a deep and resonant voice that reminded Ben of the Baptist ministers he knew as a child. Fluent in six languages, including Mandarin, Wooten came over to State from one of several large manufacturing firms now doing business in China.

The ambassador's deputy, on the other hand, reminded Ben of a wormy hipster. Most of the time, James Dudley wore his stringy black hair too long, even for a civilian. He was constantly pushing it back in place. Ben realized that Dudley always seemed to inspire his antipathy faster than anyone he had ever known.

"No way to tell, sir," Ben answered from his chair. Ben switched on his laser-pointer and aimed the beam of light at one of the dark patches dotting the picture. "That's smoke from ships' boilers. That means these ships are running their engineering plants—expensive unless you're planning to go somewhere."

Jake Harrison and Ben's relief, Navy Captain Peter T. Corrigan sat adjacent to Ben. Harrison's nameplate read, "Counselor to the Ambassador," code-speak for Central Intelligence Agency Station Chief.

At six feet, Harrison's muscular frame weighed in at almost 190 pounds. With short reddish-brown hair and green eyes, Harrison usually wore a stern contemplative expression. Rumors about his background included everything from his being a paid assassin, to working with the Kurds in Afghanistan and Iraq. Ben never inquired, but he suspected that was one of the reasons Harrison never let anything interfere with their Thursday afternoon tee-time. The veteran intelligence operative had a rugged complexion and a deep scar across the right side of his face. Harrison always looked like ready for anything.

Corrigan, the former commanding officer of an Ohio-class submarine, wrung his hands as Ben stood to make his presentation. Corrigan, like Ben, had a slender build. Bald, with blue eyes, the career submariner looked more like a college professor than anything else.

Corrigan thought himself ready to take over for Ben right now--if not sooner. Ben knew this because his colleague had mentioned it to countless others since his arrival just days before.

"Captain McGuire?" Chief of Staff Dudley called. Ben's brief was next on the agenda.

Ben McGuire nodded for the projectionist to change the presentation as he took his place at the lectern. He looked up to find Ambassador Wooten ready to take notes. Dudley, sporting his normal bad comb-over, played with his hair. McGuire successfully fought back the urge to laugh.

Ben's first slide displayed a 300 nautical-mile area map of the northern half of the island nation. Two groups of ship-shaped icons figured prominently, one group to the east and the other located in the Taiwan Straits north of the island's furthest point.

Ben used a laser pointer to highlight the eastern group. "This is the *Ronald Reagan* Carrier Strike Group. They are maintaining a range of 100 nautical miles from the eastern coast. If we need them, they can close the distance fairly rapidly. We are under their air cover even now. Aircraft from the strike group are working with the Taiwanese Air Force flying combat air patrols."

Ben looked over his shoulder to see Wooten nodding his understanding. He shifted the pointer to the naval units in the waters north of the Taiwan Straits. "This is *Princeton* Surface Strike Group. It consists of three ships, one Aegis Cruiser, the *Princeton* and two AEGIS Destroyers, the *John Paul Jones* and the *William P. Lawrence*. They are acting as both a deterrent and ballistic missile shield for the island."

"Mister Ambassador, sir," interrupted Dudley. "I cannot repeat my objection to their presence more strenuously than I already have. The Chinese will undoubtedly look upon those ships as a provocation,"

Here we go again. Ben winced in anticipation of yet another long debate.

"And how do we know one of your trigger-happy sailors won't accidentally fire off a missile and start World War III?" Dudley persisted.

Are you really that fucking ignorant or stupid? "Because, sir, the systems don't work like that-" Ben commented successfully suppressing his inner-most feelings and thoughts.

The Ambassador's administrative assistant, Gayle, entered the room quietly. The short, petite woman with red-tinted hair made a beeline for the Ambassador, handed him a white slip of paper, and departed as quickly and as quietly as she entered.

"Oh, really?" Dudley interrupted. "I seem to remember one of your Aegis ships accidentally shot down an Iranian airliner not too long ago."

Ben grimaced at his memory of the USS VINCENNES' 1988 engagement in the Persian Gulf resulting in over 200 civilian deaths. The Iranians contend to this day that the shoot-down was deliberate while the Navy still believes Iran conjured up the incident, an intentional act to embarrass the US.

As Dudley relayed his revisionist view of naval history, Ben watched the Ambassador's face. His eyebrows went up. When he saw Ben watching him, he put down the note and returned his attention to the discussion.

"Mr. Dudley, that was over thirty years ago, and this is hardly the forum for that discussion. May I continue?"

Dudley did everything he could to turn his back toward McGuire as he leveled his gaze at Ambassador Wooten. "Sir, again, I..."

"I understand your point, James. But I have some news that requires we leave those ships right where they are," Wooten announced with gravity.

The occupants in the room brought their collective attention and gaze to the Ambassador.

"Gayle just handed me a note," Wooten said as he held it up. "It would appear the Chinese have blinked."

Ben frowned. What did that mean?

"Chinese President Ho will be joining President Langdon and President Hui for the Summit," he said. "Here in Taipei."

Civilians in the room erupted in applause and cheers at hearing the news. The military personnel exchanged wide smiles but held their verbal exultations in check.

A wave of relief washed over Ben with such impact that his knees weakened just slightly. He took in a deep breath as he let the good news finish the job of settling his nerves. *I might just live through this mess after all.*

"We'll ask the Navy to leave the ships there for now," Wooten said. "The Presidential Security Detail wants them there, so we'll keep them there." He shifted his gaze back to McGuire. "We're far from out of the woods on this one yet. Proceed, Captain," he ordered.

"Yes, sir," Ben replied as he brought up his next slide, yet another high-resolution drone photo of the Ningbo naval facility. "The Reds have amassed an amphibious strike group that appears ready to sail within a few hours' notice. As the Colonel pointed out, there are several amphibious operations ships, two of their newest Wuhan destroyers, and about six missile patrol boats."

"Capabilities?" Wooten asked.

"Well, there's good news and bad news," Ben replied as he put down his laser pointer.

Dudley, though he didn't speak, wore a "Do tell" expression.

"The Chinese are relatively new to the Amphibious Warfare game. They can't project that much troop strength at one time."

"So, you're saying that we don't have anything to worry about?" one of the other civilians at the table asked.

"No, I didn't say that." Ben changed his presentation back to his original slide before he strode to the presentation screen.

"Their whole strategy is to land platoon-sized units, run home, load new troops, and deploy them." Ben used his finger and pointed to the relatively short distance from Taiwan to Ningbo. "And to keep doing that until they get enough people onshore. The good news is that they would have to have air superiority. We own the skies."

"So, you consider the troop concentration to be a minimal threat?" Ambassador Wooten asked.

"Yes, sir. That's the good news. We own the air, and consequently, anything that floats. If they try this, we will clean their clocks."

"What's the bad news?"

"The bad news is that I'm sure they're planning to airdrop troops, too."

Ben shot his Air Force colleague a glance to see the man shaking his head in violent disagreement.

"We've got total air supremacy here, Ben," Colonel Scott Johansen retorted.

"Listen, all they have to do is place one platoon-sized unit on the ground. They'll link up with the terrorist cells that are already here, and Taipei will make Baghdad look like a Sunday walk in the park."

"Aren't you getting a little ahead of yourself, Captain?" Dudley asked with condescension.

"No, sir. I don't think so."

"Why do you believe the Chinese have cells in Taiwan?"

"Because it would be foolish not to," Jake Harrison interjected. "And Captain McGuire is no fool."

Ben shot his colleague and golfing partner a half-smile.

"Any other comments?" Dudley asked in an obvious attempt to move the meeting along to another, and perhaps less controversial subject.

"No, that's all I have."

The meeting continued as the other department heads stood and made their presentations. Ben took his seat and girded himself to stay focused for the next hour.

Ben would make a point of thanking Harrison for his support. Over the last four months or so, they had become fast friends. As near as Ben could tell, he was the only person at the embassy that enjoyed that status, including most of Harrison's staff.

***

Chi-Li, Taiwan
6:15 PM

Even before Choi Ling brought his vehicle to a stop, the usual gaggle of neighborhood children mobbed his car.

"Hi, Mr. Choi!" they greeted. "Did you bring us candy? Are you going to play soccer with us?"

Choi, touched by their exuberance and affection for him, did not restrain his feelings. He smiled widely as he gently pushed open the car door. He made sure to grab the bag of lollipops on the passenger-side floorboard.

The children, eight in all, ranged in age from five to nine. Choi, as a matter of habit and choice, sought out his favorite, little Ming. The six-year-old girl, as beautiful as she was shy, stood quietly at the rear of the clamoring rascals. His smile grew as she met his gaze.

Two years before, at a neighborhood party, Lu Ming found her way into a jellybean jar. Choi, while making his exit, heard a woman's scream. The shriek held so much anguish and despair that Choi stopped in his tracks. He did not remember running to the scene nor finding Ming's parents frantically shaking their child's body as it turned bluer by the moment.

Choi noticed several of the small candies on the floor near her feet before he shoved the father aside. Once at Ming's side, he pulled the young child into his arms, placed her facedown on his left hand, and swatted her on her back between the shoulder blades with his right. The first two swats proved unproductive and roused the anger of Ming's frightened and frustrated parents. The father tried to pull the child away from him.

Younger and stronger, Choi shoved the man away and gave the child two more well-placed, yet firm swats to the back. The force ejected a slimy red jellybean from her mouth as Ming began coughing her way back to consciousness. Choi turned her over as she regained her breath and her color.

Their protesting and pleading voices brought Choi back to the present. He knelt, reached into the bag, and pulled out a cherry lollipop. "Now, now, Ming," he said as the child began to tear off the plastic wrapper. "You must not ruin your appetite for dinner. Ask your parents if you can have that before you open it."

She smiled, hugged his neck, and ran toward her house. Choi looked up to see Ming's mother waving from her brownstone steps. He returned the gesture as the other children jumped and begged for treats as well.

"Okay, okay. Here you go," he said as he reached in and pulled out handfuls of candy.

***

Yamenkou, China
(35 Kilometers West of Beijing)
9:15 PM

The old farmhouse, seized long before by the Government, guarded an open and green pasture. As it usually sat empty, the structure made the perfect meeting place.

Chinese Communist Party Chairman Fei Chen Tzu's security detail kept watch outside while he paced the straw-covered dirt floor. He made a point of flicking his ashes onto the occasional scalps of soil that poked through the yellow flax. When the hot ash sometimes turned the dry covering to flame, Fei stamped it out with his foot.

"Sir," one of his aides called to him from behind.

Fei turned to see General Zhao Chin Lee's short, muscular frame coming through the door. Zhao always reminded Fei of a Shar Pei, the famous breed of Chinese dog that once guarded and protected the emperors.

Zhao, dressed in a dark suit, wore a stern expression. The two men approached each other with confident strides. Zhao, despite his civilian attire, marched. Once within a half-meter of each other, both bowed their heads in greeting. "General," Fei began. "Thank you for coming on such short notice."

"Minister, I live only to serve China."

Fei smiled at the General's words for a short moment then let the expression evaporate from his face. "We are facing dire times, General. I hope that you are prepared to stand by your words."

"Minister Fei, you know that I am."

"You may be branded as a traitor," Fei warned as he gestured with his arm for the career soldier to walk at his side.

"There are those in power who have behaved with much more contempt for Mother China than I will."

"I quite agree."

Fei and Zhao strolled a few steps in silence.

"President Ho has accepted the invitation to the Peace Summit with the Americans," Fei said plainly. "This is playing out just as we expected."

"Does the President think we are still 'rattling our sabers' with the mobilization?" Zhao asked.

"Yes. Ho is planning to use the relaxation of our military posture as one of two bargaining chips when he negotiates away Taiwan."

"His treachery has no limits. I assure you, he will pay for this, not Mother China."

Fei stopped their stroll and turned to face his fellow conspirator. "General, when last we spoke, you were having some issues with Admiral Sun. Has he agreed to join us yet?"

Zhao frowned at the question before he crossed his arms. "Truthfully, Admiral Sun and I have yet to speak on this matter. He has proven to be," he paused, "elusive."

"We must have the People's Navy in this endeavor…"

"I know, Comrade Chairman. I have made other arrangements," Zhao interrupted. "Just in case."

"What arrangements?"

Zhao took a breath. "Chairman, I have the situation under control. Be assured. We will have the support of the People's Navy. I promise you." Zhao brought his gaze to meet Tzu's.

Zhao nodded. "Then, Comrade, we are committed," Zhao replied as he stopped walking. The face of the Commander of the People's Army's came into full view, as he drew even closer to Fei. "When we leave here today, things will be set in motion that we cannot stop," he said just above a whisper.

"I understand."

Zhao grabbed Fei's forearm. Though he was not using much force, Fei felt his strength. He knew that Zhao could break his arm, or his neck, with ease.

"But know this," Zhao continued. "We will be watching to know if you act for China, or yourself."

Fei's eyes met Zhao's intense stare for a long and silent moment.

"I understand that, too," Fei finally replied. "I have China's best interests in mind."

Zhao released his hold on Fei's forearm. He pulled away and took a step back. The General bowed his head, and as Fei moved to return the gesture, Zhao turned to walk out of the barn.

Fei followed Zhao with his gaze until the sound of a closing barn door told him the General was gone.

"So, it begins…" Fei's mind turned to the next task in placing his country back on its proper footing.

***

Near Taipei Taoyuan Airport
Taipei, Taiwan
9:20 PM

The limousine's tinted windows intentionally made it difficult for the occasional passer-by to see the goings-on inside. However, the passengers and their driver commanded a clear view of the streets around them.

"How long will you stay in our city this time…ah… What do I call you since you won't tell me your name?" Alexi Pugachev asked. His voice always reminded Song of a hissing snake.

"Why do you constantly try to engage me in these pointless conversations?" Song Fann replied. "You will never know my name or when I'm coming or going, Alexi. We are not friends. You have a service, and I have a need."

Alexi readjusted his position in the automobile's plush leather seat. He crossed his arms as he blew smoke from his cigarette without bothering to remove it from his mouth. "And if I choose to stop supplying that service?"

"Then you will disappear just like your predecessor. My superiors pay you for the inconvenience of my unannounced arrivals and departures. We also pay you for the quality of your services. But don't for one moment think that we can't find another supplier."

Like him, Pugachev still wore a military haircut. Bulky and rugged looking, the former Soviet army officer looked anything but defeated. Part of Song's reasons for keeping his comings and goings secret was to keep Pugachev from killing him, or his superiors.

GENERAL QUARTERS

Alexi took another deep drag from his cigarette. This time he pulled it from his lips and crushed out its life in a nearby ashtray. He blew out the smoke and inhaled a deep breath of smoke-filled air. "You are my favorite customer. Why would you even consider another vendor?"

Song nodded. He did not like associating himself with criminals, especially Russians, but moving secretly in Taipei without them was virtually impossible. And as much as he hated to admit it, Alexi Pugachev was the best, so far. Perhaps it had been his former life in Soviet Intelligence that had prepared him for his current life. Whatever it was, Alexi commanded quite the array of services: drugs, human trafficking, prostitution, smuggling, security, and today, arranging a viewing.

"What is so interesting about this building?" Alexi asked as he tossed Song a pink folder.

Song did not answer, but instead, he slowly opened the package to examine its contents.

Alexi took a small bottle of Chivas from a lighted bar and poured himself a glass. "I would offer, but of course we know you don't drink," the Russian said in a mocking tone. "Everything has been arranged. The landlord is expecting new tenants who are referrals from me."

"Good."

CHAPTER FOUR
TAIPEI

Tuesday, August 12th
People's Liberation Army Navy (PLA-N) Headquarters
1301 Hours

The intercom on Admiral Sun's desk buzzed and pulled his attention, if only for a moment, from a souring relationship with his paperwork. "Yes?" he said into the device after pressing the 'Answer' button. "Admiral, General Zhao is calling for you," his administrative assistant announced.

Sun stroked his chin, took in a deep breath to calm himself and sat in silent reflection for a long moment.

"Admiral? Are you there?"

Sun contemplated the conversation with his superior. Too many irregular happenings in the last few weeks coursed through his mind, too many that did not follow any logical paths. Good tactics demanded a better grasp of the situation before engaging in a conversation, any conversation. Zhao Chin Lee had proved himself a dangerous man over the last few years. Engaging him without adequate preparation did not make good sense.

"Yes. I'm here. Tell the General I am indisposed."

"Indisposed?"

"Yes." That should be plausible enough. "Take a message."

"Yes, Admiral."

Sun turned off the intercom.

GENERAL QUARTERS

Taoyuan District
Taipei, Taiwan
1:15 PM

Song Fann looked on from the driver's seat of the van as his partner, Guo Tao, paid for their apartment. He divided his attention between Guo and the street. The apartment building, with steel bars on the dirty windows, looked as old as their information indicated. On the street, commercial vehicles of one sort or another comprised most of the traffic. Few, if any, pedestrians made their way.

Guo completed the transaction, bowing graciously in unison with their landlord before turning toward the van. Song continued studying his surroundings. The sound of an airliner taking off from nearby Taoyuan International Airport pulled his attention skyward. He looked up, momentarily seeing the eppenage of a jumbo jetliner as it quickly appeared and disappeared between the tall buildings.

"We are set," Guo announced as he climbed into the van. "We're on the sixth floor."

"Perfect," Song replied as he glanced over his shoulder at the three large, black cases behind them. Strapped to the van's floorboards, they would remain there until nightfall. Once darkness fell, they planned to move them into their new and temporary home.

"Let's find a place to park. We'll stay with the van until it's time to move in."

Song's first operation since the mission in France, his superiors subsequently sidelined him. Not at all happy with losing so many personnel, Song's fears for the worst faded when the call came for this effort. Though happy to be back at work again, he did not like or want this mission.

Guo nodded his understanding, placed the vehicle in gear, and slowly pulled into traffic.

***

Office of the President
Beijing, China
1:30 PM

Ho's aide, a young man in his twenties, entered the President's office and made his way to the desk. "New messages, Comrade President," Jung Li said as he placed a red folder on the edge of Ho's already cluttered desk.

"Well, Jung Li," Ho said as he crushed out his cigarette. "I think I may need to have you start answering some of these for me. Are you ready to be president?" he joked.

"It would be my supreme honor to someday serve the people as President," Jung Li said with a wide smile.

Already opening the folder, Ho looked up and stared at his aide across the top of his glasses. He smirked for a moment at the confidence in Jung Li's voice. He shifted his focus to the first dispatch.

After a short while, President Ho looked up from his papers to find his aide studying him as if he were an amoeba on a microscope slide. Jung Li tried to turn his gaze away in time but to no avail. "What's on your mind?" Ho asked as he removed his reading glasses.

"Nothing, Comrade President. I was, ah," Jung tried to lie. The young man's face turned red as he lowered his eyes.

"Sit down, Jung Li," Ho invited.

He stood at attention, throwing his shoulders back as if he were a military officer. "You are terribly busy, President. I honestly did not mean to...-"

"Sit down, Jung Li," Ho said again, but this time with a more direct tone.

GENERAL QUARTERS

The aide eased his thin young frame into one of the visitor's chairs on the far side of the desk, his eyes again directed toward the floor.

"When I appointed you to my staff, I did so because you are inquisitive and bold. You have a habit of speaking your mind even when it would be best for you to do otherwise." Ho smiled. "I like that. It reminds me of people I once knew long ago. Why do you shy away now?"

Ho flashed back to his days as a student at Boston College. He wondered what became of the American friends who once welcomed him as one of their own, taught him to dance and sing their music, and introduced him to things like cotton candy, chocolate fudge, and milkshakes.

Jung folded his arms and then unfolded them. He shifted in his seat; first leaning to his left, then to the right before finally leaning forward with his hands folded on his lap. "Respectfully, President..."

"Yes, Jung?"

"I do not understand why we are giving in to the Americans and the Nationalists. Do we fear them? Is their army so much greater than the People's Army? I do not understand." His eyes were back up now, wide and inquisitive.

"So, your friends are saying your Pinyin is a coward, eh?"

Jung lowered his face again.

"Ah, so it is true?" Ho laughed at Jung's reaction.

Jung Li brought his eyes up to meet Ho's. He frowned as he pursed his lips. "Why do you laugh at me, Comrade President?"

"I am not laughing at you, Jung. I am laughing at all the blind and ignorant ridiculing you must receive for working for me."

Ho stared across the desk at Jung. He reminded Ho more of a child than a young man. Handsome, virtuous, and smart, Ho found himself envying his aide's youth. The changes he will see in his lifetime!

"I am sorry, Comrade President. I am confused."

Ho reclined in his chair as he took a long reflective scan of his expansive office. A marble bust of Chairman Mao caught his eye for a moment. Then, he moved his attention to the map of the world that took up most of the far wall. When Washington, DC came into focus, he eventually turned back to Jung's prying and still inquisitive scrutiny. "How many bicycles did you pass on your way to work this morning?"

Jung's eyes widened at the question. He then shook his head. "I do not know."

"Five? Fifteen? A hundred?"

He rubbed his chin as he scrunched his face in thought. "I would have to say hundreds."

"Have you ever been to the American capital, Washington?"

"No, President Ho. I have not."

Ho thought he detected some level of pride in Jung's answer. He dismissed it and pressed forward with his point. "I have. The only people on bicycles in Washington are the ones on holiday."

"How do they travel, then?"

"By automobile."

"Then their capital must be very small," he retorted.

"No, Jung. It is very large."

He watched as amazement washed over Jung's face.

"I dream of a China where all of our people have a choice between bicycles and automobiles," Ho added with gravity. "I dream of a China that is better than the one I was given."

"But the Nationalists, and especially the Americans, are greedy and wasteful," Jung replied.

"True. They garner wealth for themselves. But we will acquire it for the people."

Jung rubbed his chin in contemplation again. "This will require great change. I do not know if everyone is ready for that. I do not know if I am ready for that kind of change." His tone was firm now, almost cautionary.

"Whether we care to admit it or not, the world is changing around us. If we wait too long, I fear it will be too late."

Jung shook his head. "I think many of the people will be afraid."

Ho smiled as he remembered something he once read. "To see what is right and not to do it is for want of courage," he said softly.

"Confucius?"

"Very good, Jung Li. I am impressed. The youth of today do not read the teachings as we once did. I hope you see that I am not looking to change everything."

Jung nodded.

"I will take you with me to Taipei. You will meet the Nationalists and the Americans. And you will see they are nothing for Mother China to fear."

***

The Badaling Section of the Great Wall
Northwest of Beijing, China
2:00 PM

In Chinese culture, the color red holds great significance and allure. The proverb of Guo Nian, the story that tells the origin of the lunar year, features a beast with an enormous mouth capable of swallowing people whole.

The beast, a dragon named Nian, terrified people until an old man tamed and rode it into the sunset. Before the man departed, he directed the people to hang red paper decorations on their windows and doors at each year's end because that color frightened the dragon and would serve to keep it from returning. Hence, the tradition of "Guo Nian" began.

Guo, which means "to pass" or "to observe," and Nian, which means "year," once meant "survive the beast" but now connotes "celebration of the New Year."

Chairman Fei slid his hands inside the pockets of his business jacket as a stiff breeze from the north carried away most of the day's warmth. Multitudes of tourists walked the five-meter-wide parapets and stood inside ancient battlements despite the cooler, windy weather.

Fei stood near a watchtower as he waited. Staring at the skyline to the north, he noticed a thin layer of clouds covering the uneven mountain landscape.

Secret societies in China predated the Qing Dynasty, ebbing and flowing in popularity in direct proportion to the level of chaos in the land. The anti-Manchu White Lotus Society revolted against the Qing in 1796. In 1853 the Small Sword Society led an uprising around Shanghai, and the White Lotus brotherhoods formed the nucleus of anti-foreign forces during the Boxer Rebellion that ended in 1901.

The Hung figure prominently as one of the oldest and most famous of these societies. Hung translates into English as "Red" or "Brave." The Hung draw their fame from their southern China roots in the provinces of Fujien and Guangdong, and their descendants who took their legend and protocols to North America and beyond.

The Hung Yāoguài, or "Red Dragons," came into existence a few days after the death of Chairman Mao Zedong in 1976. As Chairman Mao's health declined, a group of followers known as the "Gang of Four," including his wife, attempted to hijack and subvert the government. The Government, under the influence of the Hung, acted quickly by arresting the members, bringing them before the Politburo in the Great Hall, charging them with crimes such as high treason, and hauling them off to prison. While all four died in captivity, the Gang of Four incident reinforced the need for a quiet group consisting of the Party faithful, to ensure China's government always acted on the peoples' behalf and did not again run the risk of becoming a cult of personality.

Hung Yaoguai holds as its greatest accomplishment the removal of the Gang of Four and the placement of two of her favorite sons, Deng Xiaoping and Zhou Enlai, as President and Paramount Leader. Hung membership stretches throughout the government, from the Office of the President to Party leadership, from the Foreign Service to the Military. As lifelong Hung members, Fei Tzu, Zhao Chin Lee, and Zieng Fong all took the oath of service to China long before their appointments to official leadership occurred.

"What it must have been like standing guard all those centuries ago," a voice said just above a whisper from behind him.

Fei smiled. "Greetings, Comrade. Not too unlike how we stand watch today," Fei said without turning around.

"Why do you bring me out on such a blustery day?" the Leader of the Hung Yaoguai asked.

"I, we," Fei corrected himself, "have a problem."

Being sure not to face the man standing behind him, Fei leaned against the two-thousand-year-old structure. Over the years, Fei and this Patriot of China met in this fashion several times. Protocol and custom demanded that Fei not see his face.

"I'm listening."

"The President has abused the People's trust. He plans to conspire with the Imperialists to make us weak."

"That is a serious charge...and a strange one. Was it not you that helped arrange events to assure his ascension into office?"

"Yes, I did. We hoped that his experience as an officer in the People's Army would influence his decision-making."

"And now you want him...purged." The Hung Yaoguai leader's voice held a direct and inquisitive tone.

"It must be public and untraceable to us."

"Of course."

"And it must appear to be the work of the Nationalists or the Americans."

The Hung Yaoguai leader was silent for a moment. "Why?"

"The time has come to resolve the Taiwan issue once and for all. The President's demise will assist in accelerating the inevitable conclusion."

"What you suggest could be viewed as treason."

"Not to act would be worse than treason."

"And how do you propose to replace him?"

"Our constitution will act to place the President or one of our Party comrades as Paramount Leader. But you know all this. Why do you ask?"

No one answered.

Fei slowly turned around only to find a group of camera-laden students snapping photos of each other. He returned his focus to the northern frontier. Protocol demanded he remain there for another half hour.

***

Office of the Commander
People's Liberation Army Headquarters
Beijing, China
2:30 PM

Seated behind his desk, General Zhao scanned his expansive office. Just five years before, he commanded the 1st Information Warfare Brigade as a one-star general officer. That role gave him access to electronic resources and the ability to gather information on anyone in China.

Now in command of the entire People's Army, he also occupied a seat on the prestigious Central Military Committee. Knowledge truly gave him power.

GENERAL QUARTERS

As the most senior officer in his country's armed forces, he commanded respect, influence, and deference from the other service chiefs,—but not their forces. While he did not command the Air and Naval forces directly, he directed the policies that influenced their decisions and actions. Under the rule of his country's constitution, no one person ever wielded such power. Only those in the United States or Great Britain governed with such foolishness.

Zhao Chin Lee, clad in his green dress uniform, checked a file labeled "Air Force" as he took an occasional sip from the hot teacup on his desk. He leafed through each page with an even pace. "Pan, you do good work," he said to himself of his protégée.

A knock came at his door, and Zhao checked his watch. Right on time. "Enter," he ordered.

His executive assistant, a young male lieutenant, opened the door and marched two paces into the office. "Sir. Lieutenant General Weidong Yi Muao has arrived and is waiting to see you."

"Very well. Bring him in."

"Yes, General." The young officer executed an about-face pivot and marched out, stopping only to close the door behind him.

Zhao used the time to finish browsing through the file. Towards the end, he rearranged several pages and photos, placing one at the very beginning of the dossier.

He stood, walked over to a nearby closet, and opened the door. Zhao checked his appearance in a mirror on the door's far side. An expected knock at his office door ended his self-inspection.

"Enter," he replied as he closed his closet.

Zhao took seven normal-sized and rehearsed steps to meet General Weidong at the exact center of his office.

Weidong, taller and thinner than Zhao, owned a pale and acne-scarred face. Zhao had long ago judged him unsuitable as an Army officer. However, if one could find some way to serve Mother China, then one should, even if it is in a lesser service.

"General. Good to see you again," Zhao said.

Weidong, his hat tucked securely under his left arm, came to a halt, stood at attention and saluted. "It is good to see you as well, sir."

Zhao returned the salute, and the two men shook hands.

"Please, have a seat." Zhao used his right hand to gesture toward a small sofa.

As Weidong moved toward the lounger, Zhao returned to his desk and picked up the folder

Zhao took a seat in one of two chairs across from Weidong's seat. He plopped the file on the table and watched Weidong's attention focus on the package. "May I offer you some tea?"

His attention fixated on the file, Weidong said, "No, General."

"And how is your son? I hear he is quite the pilot."

Weidong finally looked up with pride in his eyes. "He is fine, General. Exceedingly kind of you to ask."

Zhao raised his hand from his lap just an inch or so and gave a slight waving gesture. "Not at all."

The two men sat in complete silence for a long moment. Zhao locked his eyes on Weidong's as he waited for him to look away. *How strong is he? How long will he challenge me?*

After fifteen seconds or so, the Air Force officer finally gave up the contest and seemed to focus on something behind Zhao.

Ahh, finally. "Tell me, General. How ready are your forces?"

Weidong's gaze came back to Zhao's in an instant. "We are fully combat-ready."

"Fully?"

"Yes, General."

"To go to war against anyone in the world?"

"Against anyone the People direct us toward."

"The Russians?"

"Yes, General.

"The Japanese?"

"Anyone, General. Even the Americans," Weidong answered with a slight edge.

Zhao nodded. "What about disloyal Chinese?" he asked after a pause.

Weidong frowned. "I don't think I understand, sir."

Zhao gestured toward the file. "Pick it up."

Weidong jumped at the chance. He almost tore open the envelope.

Zhao reclined in his chair as the Air Force officer opened the red folder to expose the first artifact.

Weidong's eyes bulged in shock as he examined the first photograph.

"That, General, is a picture of you having sex with an American female intelligence agent last month. Your official schedule had you hunting in Mongolia. I suppose the real question is just what were you hunting?"

Weidong looked up from the picture, but only for a second.

"The next few artifacts document your complicity in an ongoing scheme to improve your wealth through the illegal sale of military equipment," Zhao added.

Weidong's normally pale face and extremities were now flushed. His hands handled the folder's contents with increasingly poor dexterity, shaking like leaves in a heavy breeze.

Zhao leaned forward in his chair. "General."

Weidong did not respond. Rather, he kept reading the text and examining the other pictures, all of them, one sexual embrace or another.

"General, I need your attention. That file is yours. You may take it home and read it on your own time."

Weidong slowly returned his gaze to Zhao's. "What do you want?"

"Now, that's the spirit. I knew we could work something out."

"I'm listening."

"Though I cannot give you any details just now, you need to stand with the Central Military Committee and me when the time comes."

Weidong shifted in his posture. "A coup?"

"No. Not a coup. A realignment of leadership."

"Hmm, I see. Why should I help you break our laws?"

"Because, General, just based on what is in that file, I could shoot you tomorrow."

"But you may shoot me anyway."

Zhao smiled. "Yes, but wouldn't you rather be shot the day after tomorrow, or next week, rather than today?"

Weidong fell back on the couch.

Zhao reclined as well but in a much more relaxed manner.

"Have you contacted the Naval Commander, as well?"

The question brought Zhao's concerns about Admiral Sun to mind. Entrapping a dishonest man is always easy. Co-Opting Admiral Sun, thus far, proved challenging. Sun avoided direct contact with him. Normally, tolerating such insubordination fell outside of Zhao's patience. He longed for the return of normalcy.

"General, I would suggest that you concern yourself with your own well-being for now."

"Yes, sir."

Zhao stood.

Weidong clambered to his feet in response.

"General Weidong, you are a coward and a traitor! You have this one chance at redemption. Do not fail me. To do so would be for you to fail China twice. She may give you a second chance, but I will not."

Weidong, his eyes wide open and mouth hanging slack-jawed, nodded.

"Get out."

He took a step toward the door, but then stopped to pick up his hat. He looked up at Zhao when he reached for the file.

Zhao nodded his approval and Weidong jerked it up, papers and pictures sticking unevenly out of the sides. The Air Force general officer did not bother with the normal military courtesies as he nearly ran for the door.

And now, we deal with my insubordinate Navy friend.

***

Guiyang, China
3:30 PM

Set against the mountainous terrain to the north, the pharmaceutical plant more resembled a prison than a manufacturing center. The building's gray color, high fences, armed guards, and barbed wire presented the image of a fortress.

Inside, all employees wore badges. More guards, stationed at key choke points, ensured that certain portions of the complex remained isolated only for those with the proper credentials. Fluorescent lights cast the facility in stark white lighting. The administrative offices, laboratories, and conference rooms all featured the same bright illumination.

The Hung Yāoguài Leader walked into the lab, and two of his technicians stopped their work. The younger of them, Shen, walked over to him. Each step seemed charged with energy. He wrung his hands with nervousness as he spoke. "Good morning, sir."

"You have something? What progress have you made?" The Hung Yāoguài Leader did not try to hide his impatience. They were running out of time.

73

So far, his scientists' failure to develop a new and undetectable method of assassination drew the Hung Leader's daily angst and ire. The weapon, whatever form it took, must deploy with ease and leave no evidence, but leave all blame on the Nationalists or Americans. While he realized accomplishing that task presented difficulties, he knew the task fell well within the abilities of his people. He compensated them well enough to afford their own homes, a couple of automobiles, a private school for their children, and most importantly, the ability to work in China's most advanced laboratory without Government oversight and monitoring.

"I think we have done it," Shen replied.

The Leader felt his stomach churn. Just two days ago, one of his scientist's concocted an elaborate device that when charged with a small electrical battery produced a powerful explosion. Everything seemed fine until the Leader posed the question, "How will we explain the presence of a battery to the President's bodyguards and security team?" The Leader wanted to throw him out of the company but instead yielded to his patience. Rather, he dressed him down in front of his peers for his lack of imagination.

"How so?" The razor-sharp edge in his voice even surprised himself.

"You may remember that we acquired some nanotechnology assets a short time ago," he explained.

The Leader remembered the France operation very well. He should in that he sanctioned it against his better judgment. "Yes. I remember. Damned waste of resources," he said as he thought of the men who were lost.

"We have engineered a nanite."

"A what?"

"A nanite."

"What is a nanite?"

Shen walked over to a nearby computer and double-clicked on a file. An image that resembled a hexagonal-shaped spider appeared on the screen. It rotated offering a 360-degree view. The Hung Yāoguài Leader frowned at the screen.

"A nanite is a computer-engineered micro-mechanism that, when programmed, can carry out many functions. Only it is very small."

"How small?"

"About a billionth of a meter. Think in terms of a bacteria-sized robot."

He looked up at Shen with dismay. The young scientist had his interest. "Proceed."

Shen nodded. "As I was saying, our original goal was to produce a nanite that would attack cancer cells and destroy them, thereby removing the need for chemotherapy."

"Yes, I remember this now. I saw a report a few months ago saying that we had run into problems targeting the right cells. The drug was attacking healthy cells as well as sick ones."

"Yes, sir. That was no 'drug.' It was nanites. The research division used the word 'drug' to keep their activities well-hidden."

The Leader nodded his understanding.

"While they are still having difficulties, one of their experiments yielded some interesting results."

The Hung Leader reflected on the best benefit of his role. The job gave him access to some of the greatest minds in his country. Most of China's best and brightest worked and invented in this facility. In the last five years, they earned over a hundred new patents.

"Yes," Shen replied with excitement mounting in his voice. "They tried everything to come up with some way of identifying the cancerous cells from the uninfected cells, gene analysis, microscopic, chemical testing…"

He felt his head starting to spin. "Shen," he said in frustration.

The young scientist's eyes went wide with anguish. "Sir?"

He also mused on the top drawback of working with such gifted men and women—their inability to get to the point without first demonstrating their intelligence. He fought the urge to let his eyes roll back in his head. "The point?"

He took a breath to regroup himself. "One of the methods they attempted to identify the bad cells from the healthy cells was by comparative magnetic field analysis."

Despite his best effort, he did not understand a word of what he had just heard. His frustration mounting, the Leader rubbed his eyes.

"Sir. Don't you get it?"

"No, I'm afraid I don't."

Shen walked over to a whiteboard and picked up a marker. He drew an oval shape. "This is a cell," he explained. "It, just like everything else, has a magnetic signature."

Still not completely following his line of thought, he understood at least that much. "Yes. Continue."

"The human body uses electricity to function. Everything has an electrical charge and magnetic signature but at a sub-microscopic level."

The Leader nodded.

"When we tried to use the nanites to detect the differences between the electromagnetic signatures of the healthy and cancerous cells, something bad happened. They disrupted the electrical function of the body."

The Leader's eyes opened wide.

"In effect, they caused the body to short-circuit. The test subject almost died from the procedure."

Shen fully engaged the Leader's interest now. He stood and crossed his arms as he, almost leaning forward, yearned to hear more.

"So, we took their work and improvised."

"Improvised?"

"We posed the question: What would happen if we programmed the nanites to attach themselves to the spinal cord and disrupt the electrical current there?"

"And?"

Shen walked back over to his computer and pulled up the interface to the system's digital media player. He expanded the window to encompass the full screen and pressed the "PLAY" icon.

The screen flickered on to show a man in gray prison clothing laying on a gurney. The prisoner, a middle-aged Asian, wore a ragged full-length beard. His eyes and mouth went wide with fear as he strained against the bonds holding his head, arms, and legs in place.

Another man, this one wearing a white lab coat, came into the frame. The Leader, while he did not recognize the technician, recognized the crest above his left breast pocket, identifying him as a member of his research team. He placed a cup at the subject's mouth and poured in a clear fluid. The prisoner coughed as he gagged on some of the fluid.

"The subject has just received a solution of water with about a thousand nanites in it."

"A thousand?"

"Yes. We could have used more but wanted to understand how long the minimum yield would take to do the job."

The subject finished the drink and relaxed just a bit when the technician walked away and out of the frame. The camera zoomed in on the man until he took up most of the screen.

Several moments passed without incident. As the Leader sighed in boredom, the man began convulsing. His body twisted and contorted with so much violence that his leg came out of the restraint. Once free, it flapped around like the tail on a kite in a brisk spring breeze.

"The nanites have attached themselves to his upper spinal cord and are now intermittently blocking and amplifying electrical impulses sent from the brain. Death will occur in three, two, one, now," he said.

All motion on the screen ceased as the man's loose leg fell without restriction to the side of the table like a wet noodle. Thick, red-colored goo seeped from his eyes, nose, and mouth.

"His body beat itself to death in just under thirty seconds."

The Leader, unmoved by the horrific sight, drew nearer to the screen to take in more detail. His mind turned. "What about an autopsy?"

"Unless a medical examiner knows exactly what to look for, the death will be a mystery."

"But won't the nanites be detected?"

"They will dissolve into the remaining bodily fluids because they are primarily made of carbon. I believe they will be virtually undetectable."

"Is there another way of getting them into the subject other than in a drink?"

"Yes. They can be ingested with food or water or be injected."

"How long before they dissolve?"

"We've kept them suspended in blood for up to two hours. After that, their ability to do the job becomes impaired. One additional benefit is that in time we can code the nanites to attack only a specific DNA pattern."

"Making it a weapon designed for only one target?"

"Yes, in time."

"What does that mean?"

"We have succeeded in partial DNA targeting. We know we can target at a course level, say all Caucasians vs. all Asians. We have some work to do concerning targeting DNA to a specific person."

"How much time do you need?"

"I am not sure, sir."

The Leader unfolded his arms and turned away from the screen. He looked at his scientist and bowed slightly. "Congratulations, Shen. We go with what you have. You are a true patriot."

Shen returned the gesture with a wide smile. "Thank you, sir."

"You have done well."

The smile suddenly left Shen's face. "Sir?"

"Yes. Is something wrong?"

"No. I was just wondering. How will you deliver the nanites to the target?"

He smiled at the question. "Our reach is wide and deep, Shen. Our reach is wide and deep."

***

USS Princeton *(CG-59)*
Patrolling the Northern Taiwan Straits
1655 Hours

Lieutenant Commander Paul Daniels loved his life and the irony that steered it. Finishing as the Anchor Man, dead last, in his Naval Academy class ten years before, he defied the odds. Not only did he graduate first in his Surface Warfare Officer's School class, but he also finished first at Department Head School garnering him this amazing role.

While his contemporaries went on to serve as Engineering, Combat Systems, and Operations Officers aboard cruisers, destroyers, and frigates, the Navy selected him for command. Daniels served as the commanding officer of the Cyclone-class Special Operations Patrol Craft USS TYPHOON (PC-5) for two and a half years. Those three accomplishments along with eight years of top marks on his annual performance reviews culminated in his appointment to one of the Navy's most powerful warships as her Executive Officer. Everything in his life, except one area, was perfect.

Making his way to the wardroom for dinner, Daniels grinned to himself in pride as he glanced at a large painting of the ship's crest. His boatswain's mates, at the Captain's urging, adorned the bulkhead adjacent to the wardroom door with the five-foot-tall multi-hued graphic.

Princeton's crest was replete with symbolism. Four components of the image spoke the loudest: A trident, lighting bolts, five stars, and the background. The upward thrust of the trident symbolizes the ship's vertical launching system. The three tines represent its multi-mission war fighting capabilities: anti-air, antisubmarine, and surface/strike warfare. Lightning bolts interlaced with the trident signified the ship's quick striking ability. Five stars honor the five previous US Navy ships that bore the name Princeton. Finally, the background's quasi octagonal shape represents the ship's SPY-1 radar arrays, the core of the revolutionary AEGIS missile system. George Washington's profile rested on an azure scroll inscribed with the words, "Honor and Glory" in gold.

The sixth ship of the fleet christened as *Princeton*, CG-59's name commemorated battles of the American Revolution won by George Washington in and around Princeton, New Jersey. The 13th Aegis Cruiser *Princeton* embodied grace, technology, and deadly striking power. The 567-foot ship used four gas-turbine engines to push it along at speeds over 33 knots. But in the style of Cleopatra, Mata Hari, and other femme fatales, *Princeton*'s sleek modern styling belied her deadly potential.

Built around the Aegis Weapons System, *Princeton*'s technology suite allowed her to continuously scan a 360-degree area and simultaneously track and engage multiple air and surface targets. Also equipped with a vertical missile launching system, her two magazines carried up to 122 Standard-3 surface-to-air, Tomahawk cruise, or Anti-Submarine Rockets, or any combination thereof. Eight Harpoon anti-ship cruise missile launchers adorned her stern. Just as deadly under her skirts, *Princeton*'s hull-mounted and variable-depth sonars gave her the capability of targeting and engaging multiple sub-surface contacts with six wire-guided torpedoes.

Paul anxiously awaited his opportunity to command one of these fast, sleek, and deadly ships. His *Princeton* sailed with a proud and professional crew who repeatedly earned the coveted Battle "E" for Combat Readiness.

"In a good mood, XO?" CAPT Nation asked as he sauntered into the wardroom.

"Yes, ma'am. The best."

"May I join you?" Daniels requested permission to sit at her table in the traditional manner.

She gestured toward the open place on her right.

Daniels liked his captain. She liked her crew, and it showed. Rather than taking her meals in her cabin, CAPT Nation preferred to dine with her officers, and occasionally with the enlisted personnel.

Daniels' arrival left only one open place setting at the wardroom table. Roughly half of *Princeton*'s twenty-four officers sat quietly, listening to their Commanding Officer. The rest were elsewhere on the ship, either going on or coming off watch.

"I'm glad you're here, XO. Maybe you can help me educate Mr. Pickins here."

"Oh?"

A tall, heavy-framed mess attendant brought Daniels his table setting. He thanked the man with a nod of his head.

"He seems to think we put too much emphasis on tradition."

Daniels caught himself frowning at the red-haired, round-faced Junior-Grade Lieutenant seated across the table from him as if he were a nut case.

"All I was saying, Ma'am, is that I think we would be much more efficient if we spent that time on other pursuits," he explained.

Pickins, nicknamed "Slim" among the other junior officers, graduated from Yale with a degree in business. Unable to find a job, he sought and received a commission. Only there for a three-year tour, everyone knew Slim longed for corporate-America and an office on Wall Street.

"I mean, take morning quarters for instance. We make everyone come to their workspace, whether or not they have work, to stand around for fifteen or twenty minutes while we take muster. I think we ought to look at how much time we could get out of the workday if we dropped a few of the things we do out of pure tradition."

Daniels shook his head at Slim's ideas, naiveté, and nerve. Daniels served himself by stabbing a juicy-looking chicken breast from the platter in front of him.

Three loud raps on the wardroom door temporarily saved him. A second later, a short, dark-complexioned African American enlisted man entered the space. His traditional blue cracker-jack uniform was inspection ready as he marched four steps to Nation and halted.

"Ma'am," he started with a salute. "The Officer of the Deck sends his respects and reports the approaching hour of 12 o'clock. All chronometers have been wound and compared, and he respectfully requests to strike Eight Bells on time."

The second-class boatswain's mate presented his captain the Fuel, Water, and Navigation Reports after lowering his salute.

"Mr. Pickins. I suppose you'd get rid of this little activity, too?"

"Well, ma'am. We really don't wind and compare chronometers anymore."

Nation shook her head and turned to the enlisted man. "Petty Officer Templeton, nice job. You may tell the OOD to strike Eight Bells on time."

He saluted. "Aye. Aye, Ma'am." Templeton pivoted around and marched back out of the room.

"Tradition, Mr. Pickins, is one of the things that separate us from the animals," Nation began. "It is certainly the thing that makes us a real service instead of something like the Air Force."

"Well, that and the fact we've got a clue," Daniels quipped with a grin.

The officers sitting on the periphery of the conversation laughed aloud. Nation grinned. "Would we be more efficient without it? Maybe. But we would lose the culture of our organization. Our culture is what allows us to use words like honor, courage, and commitment with meaning."

"Hear, hear," Daniels said as he took a bite of his meal.

"I'm hoping you will learn that before you head off to Wall Street. If you do, maybe you can keep your company from becoming another Wells Fargo or Boeing," she added.

As quiet returned to the table, Lieutenant Juarez entered the wardroom. Daniels looked up just in time for his eyes to meet hers. He returned to his meal a second later.

"Request permission to join you, ma'am?" she said to the Captain.

"Please," Nation replied, gesturing toward the open seat at the end of the table.

"Any thoughts on tradition vs. efficiency in the Navy?" Captain Nation asked.

One of the other lieutenants gave her a "cut" gesture.

The beautiful young Latina officer smiled. "No, ma'am. I don't think so."

"Good. Have a seat."

Juarez nodded at her skipper and took her place.

"Smart girl, huh, XO?"

Daniels, his mouth full of food, nodded. He looked up from his plate to see Nation eyeing him like a radarscope. When Daniels finally winced at her scrutiny, Nation broke off her gaze and returned to her plate.

Daniels eventually did the same.

***

Office of the Communist Party Chairman
Beijing, China
6:20 PM

After dialing a memorized number, Fei Tzu placed the telephone receiver against his beefy face and listened to the system ring the telephone at the remote location. It felt like an eternity between each tone and even longer before a familiar voice answered.

He heard a Russian-accented woman's voice say, "Good day, sir."

"Hello," Fei replied.

"I take it that you are calling to check our status one last time," the woman on the other end asked. Fei judged her Chinese language skills barely passable due to a heavy Slavic accent.

"I just want to ensure we are getting what we paid for," Fei replied.

"We are professionals. To do less than that would be dishonorable. And besides, you have made it more than worth our effort."

"And if you fail us, we will hunt you down like the Russian dog you are."

"Now, now, sir. There is no need to insult each other."

Silence.

"Have you made a decision on that other issue?" the Russian asked.

As much as Fei disliked Russians in general, he admired this one's directness. Her priority was making money. "Yes."

"Shall we take care of it, too, for a relatively small premium?"

Intelligence Minister Fong Du So's frail image took over Fei's mind. The former Intelligence Minister served as Fei's life-long mentor until his death a few years before. Fei planned to avenge his master's demise, and he considered a few hundred thousand American dollars a small price. "For the price we discussed?"

"Yes," the Russian replied.

"Good."

"We will not fail, and we will expect payment in full."

"Very well, then. Goodbye," Fei said as he hung up the phone.

American hubris knew no bounds. First, they insult China by recognizing the runaway province, and if that were not enough, they place the instrument of his mentor's demise as an official in their embassy. Someone in America sent them a message. Fei intended to ensure China responded in kind.

***

People's Liberation Army-Navy (PLA-N) Headquarters
Beijing, China
18:25 Hours

Vice-Admiral Sun bit his lip as he examined a classified message from General Zhao. The People's Army Commander authorized the movement of additional personnel and hardware toward Beijing and the coast without any rationale for the activity. Despite his best effort to the contrary, Sun's suspiciousons grew.

Special Forces units from several regions all converged on Ningbo. Sun did the math. By the time they gathered, Sun estimated their total number approximated a division or more, adding to the two divisions of regulars already present. Further, some of the regular units moved out of their assigned areas to the larger cities. Zhao's orders also directed two tank battalions and three military police companies to Beijing.

Zhao's request for Sun to step up his submarine patrols in the Taiwan Strait felt more like a directive. Additionally, Zhao wanted the subs to deploy with full torpedo and cruise missile loadouts. Why did he need that much firepower for a ruse? This is strange.

Sun reread the message several times. With each review, he hoped he had misread the words or misunderstood their intent. As he finished examining the terse request for the fourth time, Sun quizzed the general in absentia. What are you doing?

The second portion of the message dealt with the status of the Navy's troop transports: What was their readiness state? How long would it take to place all their boilers on-line for at-sea operations? Sun frowned at these unanswered questions, too.

He eventually put down the printed message and pushed it to the side. He planned to continue dragging his heels, not acting until more information became available, or until the situation exhausted all other options. He reclined in his chair for a while before turning to his desk and the framed picture of his last aircraft, a Xian JH-7 fighter-bomber. Even with the prestige and grandeur of his role, Sun missed going to sea as an aviator.

He returned his full attention to the present and reaching across his desk for a thick, multi-sectioned folder. Each morning his aide compiled the fleet's readiness reports into a single collection for him. Sectioned by fleet and division, he turned the folder on its side and leafed through the pages until he found the East Sea Fleet's section.

GENERAL QUARTERS

Admiral Chang's two Wuhan-class cruise missile submarines' readiness status showed the troublesome ships now fully operational. The report also showed them at sea and headed for the Taiwan Straits.

He sat up in his chair. How could these two ships go from barely functional to this level in just a day? Though only five years old, engineering issues plagued them since their commissioning. Everything from diesel engine breakdowns to ballast system failures occurred. Sun suspected the shipyard used faulty engineering practices during manufacture and produced something that the Americans called "lemons." These two ships would better serve China as museum pieces. "Stupid son of a bitch!"

He picked up his desk phone and dialed his aide.

"Yes, Admiral?" the young woman answered.

"Get Admiral Chang on the line," Sun barked.

"Yes, sir."

Sun slowly replaced the phone; his eyes still fixed on the readiness report. He imagined the conversation between Chang and his submarine squadron commander. Sun did not doubt that he ordered those men to do whatever it took to sail, safe or not. He shook his head in disbelief of Chang's bad judgment.

The intercom buzzed and Sun reached for the phone expecting to hear the East Fleet Commander's voice. "Admiral Sun," he answered.

"Sir, General Yau is here to see you, and he says it is urgent," his aide announced with gravity.

Sun pulled his eyes away from the report to the phone as if the Marine Commander were visible on it. He frowned, "Send him in."

"Yes, sir."

"Any luck finding Admiral Chang?"

"Sir, the Admiral is on the waterfront, and they are sending for him," she replied.

At the sound of a knock, Sun looked up to find General Yau Xingyuan entering. His muscular frame came through the door and marched across the room to the front of his desk and saluted. "Thank you for seeing me, Admiral."

Sun nodded and noticed the Marine officer's taut and ashen face. Yau lowered his salute and stood at attention between two guest chairs.

"What's happened?" Sun asked.

Yau shifted his eyes from right to left as if he were looking for something. "Is it safe to speak here, sir?"

Sun shrugged. "I hope so."

"Sir, I have it on good authority that a coup is in the planning."

Sun's eyes nearly popped from their sockets. He shifted his attention from Yau's face to Zhao's message. A chill ran through him. Damn. He looked back up at the Marine who now looked as afraid as Sun felt. Now things make sense. "Sit down. Tell me what you know."

CHAPTER FIVE
TENSIONS

Wednesday, August 13th
Taipei, Taiwan
5:15 AM

Guo Tao studied engineering at the University of Science and Technology of China in Hefei. Before his recruitment into the People's Army and the Hung Yaoguai, Guo planned to become a builder of roads and highways. After leaving the university, his work took him in a far different direction.

While Guo's graduate school plans once consisted of advanced engineering courses, the last five years included bomb-making, flight training, and marksmanship. As more time passed, he grew further and further from his boyhood dreams. This mission, ironically, called on one of his most basic engineering skills. Guo carried a familiar tool in a one-meter-long black plastic case.

Armed with a standard-issue Tokarev 213 7.62mm pistol, Song Fann watched the darkened stairwell behind them as they crept along. The top floor of their seven-story apartment complex featured twenty apartments along a long and dimly lit corridor. As the pair stole past the closed doors, Guo pointed at the doors that showed light under their thresholds. Guo and Song took great care to pass these doors without making any noise.

The door to the roof stairwell loomed ahead. Guo smiled at the quality of the information their intelligence operatives provided. He dug into his pocket for a key as he reached the access. Song faced back down the corridor as Guo inserted the key and turned it. The lock disengaged with a small "pop" and he turned the knob. The door opened away from him, exposing a small metal stairway. Song followed him through the door and gently closed behind them.

As unspectacular as the ramshackle building itself, the view from the top proved equally uninspiring. Most of the city's newer buildings surrounded them, blocking any eye-worthy vistas. Except for one small gap, Guo saw only the windows and sides of taller and more modern office buildings. Illumination from the surrounding buildings bathed them in dim fluorescent light. The one exception to the otherwise obstructed view provided the reason for their presence.

"Get set up," Song ordered as he walked the perimeter of the rooftop. Small gravel pebbles crunched beneath his feet. "We can't stay here too long."

Guo nodded, knelt, and placed the case on the building's roof. He opened it to expose a Total Station, telescoping tripod, and personal digital assistant.

The Total Station, an optical instrument normally used in modern surveying, combines an electronic theodolite and an electronic distance-measuring device.

Total Station instruments measure angles utilizing electro-optical scanning of extremely precise digital barcodes etched on rotating glass cylinders or discs within the instrument. A modulated microwave or infrared carrier signal, generated by a small solid-state emitter within the instrument's optical path, measures distance by bouncing off the measured object.

An integrated computer interprets the speed-of-light lag between the outbound and returning signal into a distance measurement. Afterward, the operator downloads the data from the theodolite to a computer, and application software generates a map of the surveyed area.

Guo quickly got to the job of setting up the unit. Once he erected the tripod and mounted the theodolite, Guo connected the unit to his PDA. He took a small can of spray paint and made a red "X" on the building's roof directly beneath the unit. Next, he turned the viewer toward the gap in the concrete canyons and sighted in on his objective.

Guo's unit also featured a GPS component, eliminating the need for an assistant staff member to hold a reflector prism over the point to be measured. The operator holds the reflector and controls the machine from the observed point.

As he peered through the lens, the VIP Terminal at Taoyuan International Airport came into focus. He activated the Total Station, and the PDA displayed its reading, 5.58 kilometers. When he looked up from the unit, he found Song's confident smile. "It is fine. We have a solution."

***

5:35 AM

Jake Harrison woke from a dreamful sleep to find Ciara's arm draped across his chest. He glanced down the length of the bed to find her nude and spectacular form "spooned" against him as she slumbered. The sound of her breathing filled his ears.

Oh, man. What are you doing? However, as quickly as that thought crossed his mind, Jake confessed to himself that he more than looked forward to seeing her.

Jake's relationship with Ciara Edwards began as a business arrangement: she needed a legal job, and he needed a spy without a discoverable background. Beautiful and fluent in Mandarin and Russian, Ciara Edwards only lacked training. Jake started cultivating her skills almost from their first

91

meeting. Sleeping with one of his employees broke all the rules. Worse, he was falling for her.

"What are you thinking about?" she asked with a dreamy voice.

Jake, surprised to hear her speak, thought quickly. "Work," he lied.

She shifted, and her head came to rest on the nape of his neck. Her perfume, something floral and delicate wafted into his nostrils. She snuggled closer, and primal urges stirred. "You might as well admit it," she moaned.

"What's that?"

"You're crazy about me."

She shifted again, and this time he felt her weight on top of him.

Jake opened his eyes to find her beautiful face millimeters from his. Pre-dawn rays of light illuminated the otherwise darkened room. He barely made out her green eyes as she smiled.

"I think I heard two words that I agree with," he grunted.

"Oh yeah? What?"

"You're crazy."

She elbowed him in the stomach and Jake flinched.

"Ouch."

"So, what am I? Just another lay?" she joked.

"Yeah. I treat all my contractors like this. As a matter of fact, I've got another business meeting on the other side of town in an hour."

"Well," she said as she kissed his mouth. "You might wanna call and tell 'em you're gonna be late."

Jake fell under the spell of her sensuous and powerful caress yet again.

***

GENERAL QUARTERS

6:30 AM

With the sun barely in the early morning sky, Jake finished dressing without the aid of the bedside lamp. The shower in Ciara's new apartment worked to bring him back to his senses, at least partially. He felt the pull of her sensuality again as soon as he walked out of the bathroom and spied her beauty. He felt the constant weight of her stare as he dressed.

Ciara Edwards' curly red mane fell just below her shoulders. Thick and curly locks of long red hair contrasted against her milky white skin. She was simply radiant. She pulled it back to reveal a widow's peak, reminding him of the quintessential vixen. Despite his best efforts, his eyes kept finding her breasts.

"You're rushing," she finally said.

Glancing at his watch as he shoved his left foot into a shoe, "I'm running late."

"You sure that's all there is to it?"

Jake sighed as he went over to the bed and sat next to her.

His mind flashed back to their meeting in a dark bar some nine months earlier. Destitute, a desperate Ciara Edwards considered starting a life of prostitution, and Jake Harrison almost became her first customer.

"Yeah, I'm sure." He looked into her eyes as he took her hand in his. Jake leaned forward to kiss her mouth. She came up to meet him and placed her arms around his neck.

"What time are you going in today?" he asked, gently pulling away.

"Not 'til this afternoon."

Jake nodded his understanding. "Watch your ass for the next few days."

Weeks before, an NSA intercept had tipped Jake off to a combined Chinese-Russian Mafia alliance in Taiwan. As near as they could tell, several two-person teams planned to attack US interests in Taiwan. Those assaults ranged from cyber hacks of US-owned banks and companies to blowing up a merchant ship in Taipei Harbor. Subsequent Intel indicated they also planned to assassinate a US dignitary thereby sending a message to the US government to stay out of Taiwan affairs.

Ciara intentionally worked at the bar owned by the Taipei Mafia kingpin. If all went well today, the combined American-Taiwanese task force would arrest Alexi Pugachev and his cohorts on espionage charges.

Ciara sat up, exposing even more of her stunning figure. She eventually pulled her long legs around and climbed out of bed. "Something I should know?"

"No. Just be careful. Okay?"

"Okay," she replied from across the small room. "We need to have that conversation, you know?"

Jake, heading for the door, stopped in his tracks. "I know."

"When will this be over, Jake? I mean. I just want to know when I can go home, that's all."

He remembered conducting her background investigation before bringing her on as one of his contract spies: "Ciara Jane Edwards. Thirty years old. Unmarried. College dropout. No real skills. Parents still living in Texas." Back in the States, authorities listed her as missing and presumed dead. She was anxious to return home, but he still needed her.

"Soon. Okay?" Jake asked as he tried to keep an edge from his voice.

She nodded.

"See you later?" he asked.

"That depends on you, doesn't it?" she asked.

Touché. He gave half a nod as he opened the door. Jake took one last look at his lover as he closed the door behind him and stepped into the apartment hallway. He looked up to see one of Ciara's neighbors also leaving his residence.

He and the Asian man nodded in greeting as Jake hurried past him.

GENERAL QUARTERS

***

PRC National Military Command Center
Beijing, China
0820 Hours

The conference room, located deep within the immense complex, featured no windows. Dimmed incandescent lighting cast bluish hue on the assembled group. Each of the officers, all men between the ages of 50 and 65, puffed American cigarettes and blew out the smoke in irregular order as they huddled around a large wooden table. A heavy cloud of smoke hung over the area like fog, as a mostly one-way conversation continued.

The assembly consisted of Air Force Commander General Weidong, Strategic Missile Defense Commander General Yang, and Civil Defense Commander General Cui, as well as two of Zhao's Army deputies. Admiral Sun was conspicuously absent. Even as Zhao briefed the plan, he girded himself for questions about Sun and the Navy's role in the operation.

Zhao sat at the head of the table, littered with butt-filled ashtrays and half-empty water glasses. Several folders containing maps, timetables, and photographs moved around the table as the others examined them. He kept close tabs on the contents to ensure their continued secrecy.

"Our ability to complete this operation depends on each of us keeping to schedule and working as if we know nothing of the other," Zhao explained.

"Then perhaps, General, you can tell us something of the plan," General Cui, the Civil Defense Commander asked. Zhao did not personally know Cui. This man had been Yang's recruit. Cui, tall and gaunt, had once been one of China's Olympic marathon athletes.

Zhao nodded as he stood and reached across the table for one of the folders. He pulled out a picture of President Ho Lin Shih and his aides arranged in an organizational chart format.

"As you know, the President has made plans to join the summit with the presidents of the United States and Taiwan. This creates an opportunity for us as his decision to attend has only occurred in the last few days. Hastily prepared, security for him will be at an all-time low."

Zhao looked intently, in turn, at each of the men as he spoke. He had their complete attention.

"The President of the United States and the President of Taiwan will host a formal dinner with our President as the guest of honor. At that dinner, we will make our intentions known."

"How?"

"The President of China will not survive the event. Of course, we will blame the Taiwanese and Americans for his death. We will act to defend ourselves from attack by enacting martial law and regaining control of the renegade province."

"The Americans will be vehement in their denial," one of Zhao's deputies said.

"But his blood will be on their hands," Weidong added with a smile.

"We will launch our fleet to take Taipei, act to consolidate our territory and make claim to the runaway province," Zhao added as he spoke of Taiwan. "By the time calm returns, we will be reunited."

"What about the American President? He will no doubt be ready to send in forces."

Zhao smiled. "We will take steps to persuade him otherwise."

"What steps?" Yang asked.

Zhao looked across the smoky room at him. "General, with respect, I must decline to answer your question at this time. But it will become clear soon enough."

Yang bowed his head, signaling his concurrence.

"This is a bold plan, General. It only takes one thing to go wrong for it to fail," General Cui added.

"And your point?"

"What is our contingency?"

Zhao frowned. "There is no contingency. We succeed, or we die."

He scanned the room, focusing on each of the men. They all, in turn, nodded in agreement.

"You shall all be honored as heroes of our nation," Zhao said with a wide smile.

"No, General," Yang said as he stood. "You will be remembered as the hero of China for bringing Taiwan back into our control."

Zhao's chest swelled with confidence. Nothing would stand in their way. By the end of the month, a new president would lead a greater and victorious China. "Any questions?" Zhao asked. He examined his watch. This briefing, already over two hours in length, needed to end soon. Having others miss them served no purpose.

"General Zhao, sir," Air Force Commander General Weidong began.

Zhao felt his stomach go taut at hearing the traitor's voice. After this is over, Zhao vowed to execute him personally. But for now, "Yes, General?"

"Where is Admiral Sun?"

"I should think that you have your hands full in dealing with the Air Force. What is your concern with the Navy, General?" Zhao shot back.

The room at once grew uncomfortably quiet and tense. He quickly glanced at the faces of the other men. They lowered their eyes out of respect, or fear, of him.

Zhao did not like his answer any more than the others in the room. The truth proved even harder for him to process. Surely, Sun's spies knew something was afoot.

Zhao's experience told him that Sun's silence and absence sowed seeds of dissension. Sun even went so far as to skip the Annual People's Army Leadership Conference. Zhao stared at them with unblinking eyes. "Admiral Sun is focusing on the issues of getting our ships and submarines in place, just in case the Americans and the Japanese try to take advantage before we can obtain complete control. I only tell you this so that you will remember that each of us will sometimes conduct actions without the knowledge of the others. Do not ask impertinent questions again."

This answer silenced them. Several of them nodded in understanding as their eyes came up to meet his. Zhao's confidence in his ability to control the situation returned in full.

"Even so, General. I am anxious about starting this operation at this time. I..."

"You don't have a choice," General Yang cut him off.

General Yang, the Strategic Missile Commander, standing a few centimeters over one and a half meters, possessed a small stature. He wore round glasses that made him look more like a cartoon character than a three-star Army officer. However, Yang, in contrast to Weidong, stood apart as an honorable man and a hard-core true believer. If he ever found out Weidong's secret, keeping the Air Force Commander from harm would prove problematic. Yang's reputation for using clandestine means of disposing of his enemies rivaled only Zhao's.

"None of us do," Zhao added. He checked his watch. "In just a few hours, events will take place to move our plan into action. Once actions are set in motion, they will be impossible to stop," Zhao added. "I will call you each with a simple message when we are two hours from D-Hour. The message will be simple, 'A Greater China.'"

Only one issue plagued him. Sun: Where was he and what was doing?

GENERAL QUARTERS

***

Office of the Naval Attaché
US Embassy
Taipei, Taiwan
8:35 AM

As offices go, Ben's didn't offer much curb-appeal. His, like most in the building that once served as the unofficial consulate, was carved from almost nothing. At 30' x 20', his corporate office in the States dwarfed this small space. A large mahogany desk with an attached computer station and credenza took up most of the room. Three large safes didn't leave much room for the two guest chairs. A large screen television sat across from him, displaying a muted US network news channels. He routinely switched back and forth between CNN, Fox and MSNBC.

The image of a poster Ben once saw in a novelty store never strayed far from his mind. The placard displayed a bathroom stall with a white porcelain toilet and a traditional black seat. Next to it, a full toilet roll stood ready for a user's employ. The most arresting feature was the words written at the top of the graphic, "No job is over until the paperwork is done." This job certainly had its share.

Only on 50 of the typical 200 daily emails, Ben scanned his computer screen, sipping coffee from his favorite Naval Academy mug. Back home, the Naval Reserve Command Selection Board was convening. He hoped for a second command assignment. Ben reasoned the knowledge of heading home to a great reserve job might ease some of the anxiety associated with sitting in the middle of the world's hotspot.

He submitted the paperwork supporting his assignment request weeks earlier. The drill of reading countless emails took his mind off the waiting and worrying over the Board's decision. A knock at the door pulled his attention back to present and CAPT Corrigan's smiling face.

"Hey, Benny. You got a sec?" he asked as he invited himself into the office.

Benjamin McGuire hated "Benny." "What's up?"

"I was wondering how comfortable you'd be with me doing the briefings from now on." Corrigan seated himself in the guest chair to Ben's left.

Ben caught himself frowning at the question as he reclined in his chair. This oughta be good. "Hmm. I'm not sure I'm comfortable with that."

"Well, I just don't want a repeat of yesterday," Corrigan replied.

"Excuse me?" While Ben successfully fought back to urge to speak his first thoughts, his back went up.

"Well, pissing off the Ambassador and his staff isn't really making us look too good."

Ben took in a deep breath and let it out slowly. The divorce from his first wife taught him a very valuable lesson: Choose your words carefully. Once they're out there, you can't recall them.

"As a matter of fact," Corrigan continued. "I was thinking we could conduct our relief sometime this week. I know Claire must be anxious about you being over here and you've got that business of yours to get back to. So, whaddya think?"

Ben cleared his throat as he sat up in his chair. "I appreciate your candor, Pete."

He smiled and nodded.

"So, let's be clear. You haven't done any of the required reading that I gave you when you checked in-"

"Oh, come on," he interrupted. "You can't tell me that stuff is really that important."

"Yeah, Pete. It is. Not only that, it's not required by me, it's required by SecNav." Ben refered to the Secretary of the Navy.

Corrigan crossed his arms.

"I know you don't think highly of Reserve Officers, Pete. You've made your feelings known to too many people here. And I know you don't think very highly of this particular Reserve Officer, but here's the bitch of it: You're ready when I say you're ready."

Ben only shifted his eyes from Corrigan's leer long enough to reach into his desk and pull out a blue folder. "And in case you think one of my short-comings is an inability to read and comprehend orders, let me read yours to you." Ben located the appropriate paragraph and read the pertinent portion aloud. "You will relieve the current Naval Attaché' at his discretion." Ben put the orders back in the folder and set it on his desk. "At my discretion. And not pissing off the Ambassador or his staff isn't part of the job description. Giving honest assessments is."

Corrigan stood to leave.

"One more thing?" Ben called after him.

"Yeah?" The officer turned slowly to face Ben.

"If you ever mention my wife with regard to this job-" Ben stopped himself. "Scratch that. If you ever mention my wife again, it'll take something short of an executive order to remove my foot from your fuckin' ass! You read me?!"

Corrigan didn't answer at first. He simply stared back with a blank expression.

"DO YOU READ ME, CAPTAIN?" Ben asked again, this time with considerably greater emphasis and volume.

"Yeah. I read you. Sorry about that. That was way out of line," Corrigan replied.

Ben took another breath and nodded.

"I'll go get started on that reading," Corrigan offered.

Ben nodded as he put his head back down to finish reading his message traffic. He did not watch Corrigan leave. Rather, he listened to his footsteps fade from the office.

When he was sure Corrigan was gone, Ben took another breath to calm himself further. Shit, he really winds my watch. He again reached for his coffee cup. When he did, Ben looked up to find Jake Harrison standing in the doorway. He whistled a little tune as he turned to watch Corrigan walk away from the office.

The tune sounded familiar, but Ben couldn't quite place it.

"What is that song?"

Harrison smiled wryly. "If I Only Had a Brain."

"You look busy," Jake greeted.

"You don't," Ben jabbed back with a grin.

Harrison flashed a rapid smile at the joke.

"What's up?"

Harrison strolled over to one of two guest chairs and eased himself into the one on Ben's right. "I need a favor. Actually, I need a couple of favors."

Ben dragged his attention from the computer monitor to his friend's haggard and battle-scarred face. Harrison always wore a serious "I've got it under control" expression.

"If I can," Ben replied. He found himself modulating his answers whenever he spoke to Harrison in the work environment. One never knew what the spymaster was up to and Ben didn't want to inadvertently sign up for something out of his lane or comfort zone.

"Are you still going over to the Taiwanese Naval Headquarters to talk to them about the Aegis destroyer agreement today?"

Ben reclined in his chair and folded his arms. "Are you still hacking into everyone's calendars?"

"Not everyone's. Just yours," he shot back.

Ben didn't know if he joked or not. After a long moment of waiting for even the slightest of lilts, Ben concluded that Harrison was serious.

"Yeah?" he finally answered. "Its getting me out of standing at attention for two hours."

The meeting with the Taiwanese bumped up against the arrival of President Langdon. Most of the entire embassy staff was required to attend. Missing Dudley in action-a lucky break Ben decided.

"I need you to take their temperature for me."

"Take their temperature?" Ben asked. "What does that mean?"

"See how they're feeling. You know, are they warming up to us?"

Ben frowned at the request. On the surface, it seemed innocent enough, but things were usually never what they seemed when it came to Jake. Everything from his golf game to his social life seemed steeped in mystery and intrigue. For instance, before playing their first game, Harrison passed himself off as a hacker. Since that time, Ben watched in awe as he finished several rounds below 80, two of them with a hole-in-one.

On the social front, Jake never brought the same woman to any gathering. On at least four occasions, his dates used the same assumed name of "Julie." Meeting the first Chinese woman named Julie was "unusual." Ben judged the fourth successive person with the same name an "unlikely" circumstance. After a third encounter, Ben figured Jake would do everything he could to keep a tight envelope around his personal affairs.

On the Taiwanese Navy request, this felt like Jake was up to his tricks again, but this time with good reason. Since the formalization of relations, the Taiwanese people and their government seemed conflicted about their newfound friend. And that conflict surfaced at all levels, from the average person in the street hailing the move, to the news media painting it as "opportunistic American diplomacy." As with all things, Ben figured the truth lay somewhere in the middle. When visiting members of the Taiwanese government, one never knew what kind of reception to expect.

"So, if I go over there and get kicked out on my ass, will that give you enough information?" Ben asked with a smirk.

"Yeah, that'll pretty much tell me everything thing I need to know."

Ben sighed. "That's it? No stealing classified documents or photographing Taiwanese sailors in drag?"

"No," Jake said as he stood. "At least not this time." He winked as he turned to leave.

"You mentioned two favors?" Ben called after him.

"Oh, yeah. Can you stop by Beng's? I dropped a club off to have it re-gripped."

Mr. Beng ran one of the best and most reasonably priced pro shops in town. A little out of the way, it was downtown near one of the indoor driving ranges.

"Sure. No problem. Even though you'll probably use it to kick the shit out of me again."

Jake nodded. "Yeah, you're probably right about that."

Ben feigned a smile. "You're such an ass."

Jake turned to walk out again. "To know me is to love me."

Ben couldn't be sure, but he thought he saw his friend grimace as he left the room.

CHAPTER SIX
THE BAIT

Wednesday, August 13th
Intelligence Operations Center
US Embassy
Taipei, Taiwan
10:15 AM

With an approving eye, Jake scanned the Taipei Intelligence Station through a large plate-glass window separating the workroom from his conference center. Compared to the Intelligence Operations Center in Kabul, Taipei felt extravagant. Analysts labored at computer workstations while others either spoke on the phone or flipped through documents. Well lit, loud, and spacious, the room featured scores of televisions, hanging from black mounts. Most of the screens displayed Asian stations, but three of the monitors showed images from the PRC's State news channel.

Forty men and women from the CIA, FBI, along with a few other cats and dogs like Secret Service and Customs, crowded the conference room. Jake alternated his attention between the goings-on in the analysis center to Michael Wong's briefing.

"This is their target," Wong said as he used a remote to bring up two pictures of Captain Benjamin McGuire on the main presentation screen. The image on the right featured McGuire in a Navy Service Dress Blue uniform. The second featured him in a dark gray suit, the normal attire for Embassy officials.

"While he is the bait, this man must be protected at all costs," Wong continued.

Wong brought up a schematic of downtown Taipei next. A red circle and several blue squares indicated key locations. "Point Alpha is Beng's Pro Shop. We've broken enough of their code to know that they have an interest in McGuire and the shop," he said of the red circle.

"Does he know he's the bait?" one of the FBI agents asked.

Wong's face grew taut at the question.

"No," Jake answered for him.

Almost on cue, all the eyes in the room moved from Wong to Harrison. "We want him acting naturally, as if nothing is wrong. If they go for it, we want them to go for it all the way."

"We will deploy to the locations marked with squares. Your team assignments are in your handout. The object here is to maintain total surveillance on the area as McGuire moves in," Wong added.

"Do we at least know who we're looking for?" another agent asked.

Wong changed the display again. This time photographs of six individuals appeared, all in their late twenties or early thirties. Four of the six were Caucasian, three men and one woman. Two Asian men appeared in the other photos.

Wong used a laser pointer to highlight the non-Asians. "These people have been positively identified as Russian mobsters. They started entering the country a few weeks ago; the last of them, this woman, arrived a day ago."

Jake changed the display to a close-up photo of the attractive blonde woman featured in the first picture. In this image, she wore a conservative dark blue pants-suit. "Her name is Galena Cheslav."

"Who is she?" someone asked.

A second later, the Russian woman's picture displayed on two other monitors. The screen on the left showed a mug shot front and profile. The other displayed a full-length photograph. A tag on the left bottom indicated British Intelligence provided the images.

"Galena Cheslav. Credited with two assassinations in Lebanon, and three more in Bosnia, the Congo, and the Philippines. Ex-KGB. She went freelance about five years ago. She's awfully expensive."

"So the Russian Mob is working with the Chinese?" someone else from the audience asked.

"We've long believed the regime on the mainland has been working with the local Russian mafia," Jake said. "If this hit attempt is made, we will not only have cracked the PRC's code but will make a big dent in their Taiwan operations by taking down part of the organized crime problem here."

"Do we know where the Russians are?"

"Yeah, we've had them under constant surveillance since their arrival," Wong answered. "We believe they will lead us to any cells operating here."

"What about the Asians?" another audience member asked.

Wong sighed. "They are Chinese Military Intelligence; Captains Song Fann and Guo Tao. We think they're Special Operations officers. They've been in the country for about two weeks, but that's all we know. They've gone under. We can't find them."

Jake stood and walked to the front of the room to join Wong. "Listen, we have almost every conceivable angle on this thing covered. We've done some really good work over the last couple of months. The only thing we need to fuck this up is for us to get McGuire killed. And I really don't want to have to get a new golf partner. Okay?" Jake locked eyes with the other leaders before he checked his watch.

"Let's get going. Ben should be half done with his meeting."

KEN CARODINE

***

Fleet Headquarters
Republic of China Navy
Taipei, Taiwan
1215 Hours

Ben McGuire sat as the lone US Navy officer in the expansive conference room. Two ROC Officers and members of their staffs outnumbered him 15 to 1. A US State Department representative and translator served as the seventeenth member of the gathering. McGuire only hoped that the bookish young woman was relaying his words accurately.

"And with the agreement, we propose Taiwan would gain a significant tactical advantage over the PLA-N," Ben said, referring to the People's Liberation Army's Navy component. He reclined in his chair as a translator communicated for him in Mandarin. Ben studied the faces of the officers clustered around him. They were no friendlier now than they had been two months ago.

"But why give us these ships without the necessary training and logistics support?" Admiral Lu shot back angrily and in near-perfect English. "It's like giving a caveman an airplane and expecting him to fly it. These are sophisticated systems that will require months for us to reach proficiency!"

No matter where an American went on the island nation, it was anyone's guess as to how they might be received. One faction, those vehemently opposed to anything related to the People's Republic of China, embraced the closer relationship with the United States. Those on the opposite end of the spectrum believed the US was once again meddling in the affairs of an independent nation, and further, they were placing them in grave danger. War rhetoric from the PRC filled the newspaper headlines and newscasts daily.

GENERAL QUARTERS

The other Flag Officer, Admiral Taung, only leered at him. As his armpits grew uncomfortably moist, Ben pictured an iceberg to calm himself. *This sucks.*

He estimated the military sat somewhere in the middle of the opinion polls. The Taiwanese armed forces, since the US discovered the PRC openly supporting North Korea's nuclear weapons program, received top-of-the-line hardware and technology in droves for the first time in many years. It did not escape Ben's today's negotiation around the discount sale of ten Aegis Destroyers only came about because the US needed Taiwan to act as a foil against the PRC.

"Sir. I understand your concerns, and I will take them back to my superiors," Ben relented. He knew giving the Taiwanese the Aegis system met one goal, scaring the hell out of their brothers on the other side of the straits. However, properly training officers and crews in the efficient tactical management of the ships took months, possibly years.

Ben checked his watch. He still had an hour left. His stomach flip-flopped as Lu started ranting again. Ben's mind turned to Jake Harrison's request to "take the Taiwanese's temperature." *Okay, that's done.*

***

PLA-N Headquarters
Beijing, China
1315 Hours

The guards at the gate to the People's Navy Headquarters first gazed at each other and then at Zhao with wide-eyed surprise when the General of China's army stepped out of his car. Of course, headquarters sentries routinely greeted general officers. However, such visits usually came after planning and advanced scheduling.

Zhao stood in the Admiral's reception area adjacent to his office suite. The space featured historical artifacts, including wooden helms from sailing ships and glass-enclosed ship models and swords. Zhao seated himself prominently in the center of the largest sofa. He took note of the occasional staff officer or sailor noticing him.

"General Zhao, sir," a very youthful Senior Captain addressed him. The officer, dressed in their formal blue uniform, came to attention a half meter away and smartly saluted. Zhao remarked how much like a boy this man of at least forty years looked.

Zhao rose with majestic calm and came to attention as well. He returned the officer's salute in a similar, but slightly more relaxed manner. After all, he was the Commander of the People's Army.

"Sir, Admiral Sun apologizes for inconveniencing you. He has cleared his calendar and respectfully seeks the honor of your company."

Well done, Sun. You have trained your officers well. Zhao nodded and bowed his head slightly.

"If you would accompany me, sir, it would be my great honor to escort the Commander of the People's Army to the Commander of the People's Navy."

"Yes, Captain. Please." Zhao extended his hand for the officer to lead. "And the honor is mine."

The Captain turned on his heels and marched off toward the door to Sun's office. Zhao maintained two paces behind him. As Zhao passed the desks of several of the other members of Sun's staff, these officers and enlisted personnel rose to their feet and saluted. Zhao returned their greeting with a simple nod of his head.

The Senior Captain pressed on toward an ornate wooden door. He stopped at the doorway, stepped to the side, and conducted an about-face maneuver to face Zhao. "Sir, Vice-Admiral Sun," he said with a salute.

Zhao returned the officer's salute and continued through the doorway to find Sun, standing at attention beside a set of guest chairs.

"Good day, Generalissimo," Sun said as he saluted the Commander of the People's Army.

"Thank you for seeing me," Zhao said as he closed the distance between them to within a meter or so.

"Please forgive me for not clearing my schedule sooner-"

"No need to apologize, Admiral," Zhao said as he raised his hand. "You had no way of knowing that I would be so rude as to arrive unannounced."

"Thank you, General. You are most gracious." Sun smiled, but only for a moment. "General, please be seated."

Zhao nodded as he accepted Sun's invitation. He placed his gold-brimmed hat on the coffee table and took a seat in one of Sun's guest chairs. Sun seated himself across from him on a small light-blue sofa. Zhao crossed his legs casually as his eyes met Sun's.

"Cigarette?" Zhao offered as he dug into his jacket for and retrieved a silver metal cigarette case.

"No. Thank you."

"Admiral, again, I apologize for this unconventional meeting," Zhao began. He lit the cigarette and took a drag as he spoke. "But we have an unusual situation, and I fear that your assistance may be required to resolve it."

Sun, already sitting almost at attention, in his chair, became that much more so. "Go on, General."

"May we speak in confidence?" Zhao asked in a more hushed voice.

Sun frowned for a moment in thought before answering. "General, I must answer your question with a question."

An exceedingly careful man. Honest and careful. This will be difficult. "Yes. Of course."

"Is this situation something that we should report to the President or the Central Military Commission?"

Why you impertinent son-of-a-bitch. You're asking me is this legal? Who the hell are you to question my honor? Zhao took a breath and kept his anger in check. He took a long drag from his cigarette. That helped. "I believe that course of action is up to me, Admiral. And frankly, I'm surprised that you would ask such a question."

"No disrespect was intended, General. I simply want to ensure that I represent myself and my intentions clearly."

"Duly noted, Admiral. Any more questions?" Zhao felt his edginess creeping into his voice. I hate dancing with this ass.

"No, General." Sun's tone was, again, apologetic.

"I fear we have a traitor among us."

Sun frowned so greatly at hearing the news that his whole face seemed to take on the appearance of a prune or raisin. "Who?"

"I cannot be sure. But I suspect someone in the President's office, perhaps even the President himself."

Sun took a deep breath. "That is an extremely dangerous charge, General. How have you come to this conclusion?"

"Taiwan, Admiral," Zhao said plainly. "Taiwan."

Sun frowned again. "I'm afraid that I do not understand."

"I believe that the President or someone in his organization has fallen under Western influence. I have it on good authority that the People's Republic of China will endorse the Americans' recognition of Taiwan as a sovereign nation."

"That is troubling," Sun agreed.

"I hoped you would think so."

"So, tell me, General..." Sun brought his hands up and rubbed his face. "How can we be of assistance?"

"I'm not sure yet, Admiral. For now, keep your ears open. Report to me anything that you hear, even that which you might dismiss as irrelevant."

Sun nodded. "We can do this."

"And…"

"Yes, General?"

"Be ready. If we fail to unearth this traitor, it may be necessary to commit forces to either get the Americans' attention or to retake Taiwan finally."

Admiral Sun's eyes grew wide at the request.

At least I have my answer. Sun must go.

***

Captain's Cabin
USS Princeton *(CG-59)*
Northern Taiwan Straits
1400 Hours

Paul Daniels stood ready to knock on his commanding officer's stateroom door when it suddenly opened. Daniels' gaze immediately found that of the ship's second most senior enlisted man, Senior Chief Operations Specialist Bill Guerette. Guerette ran the ship's Combat Information Center, as well as provided a conduit to understanding the crew's morale and well-being. The two men routinely worked together.

"Afternoon, Senior Chief," Daniels said with a smile.

The burley and haggard-faced man cleared his throat. "Good afternoon, XO." Guerette looked away as he spoke.

Frowning, Daniels asked, "Is everything okay?"

"Come on in, XO," Captain Nation ordered from the depths of her office and living quarters.

"Yeah. Yes, sir. Excuse me, sir," Guerette, still looking away, said as he brushed by Daniels.

Weird, Daniels said to himself as he closed the door and completed his arrival. "Evening, Skipper," he said.

"XO," she replied. "Do you have the CASREP?" She gestured toward the folder in Daniels's left hand. A Casualty Report transmitted mission-impacting equipment failures to the chain of command.

"Yes, ma'am." He pulled a document from his notepad and placed it in her hands.

"Who wrote the narrative?" Captain Nation asked.

"I had the MPA do it. I figured he needed the practice. Not a bad job, huh?"

Nation proofread the Number 2 Evaporator Casualty Report. The device turned seawater into fresh potable water for cooking, drinking, and showering. With it down, the crew needed to manage their fresh-water usage carefully.

"And we're sure we can repair this underway?" she asked.

"Yes, Ma'am. CHENG swears up and down all he needs is a new separator," Paul Daniels relayed the ship's Chief Engineer's assessment.

"Hmm."

"You sound doubtful, Ma'am."

"Well, I do think he's got a 'Mister Scott' Complex going on," she smiled. "But if he can get this done without us having to pull into port or live on water rations for the rest of the cruise, I'll consider calling him the 'Miracle Worker.'"

Daniels smiled at her joke as she handed him the redlined paper.

"Anything else?" he asked.

"No, ma'am. That's it for tonight." Daniels slid the paper into his notepad and was turning away when she spoke.

"Paul?"

"Yes, ma'am?"

"Have a seat. We need to chat."

He nodded. "Yes, ma'am."

The stateroom was spacious, featuring enough room for a bunk, desk, toilet with shower, and a table with guest chairs. Paul openly coveted a Captain's assignment to an Aegis Cruiser. Quarters such as these served as only one of reasons for his ambitions.

He took a seat at the table, opened his pad to take notes, and their eyes met. "What's up, Skipper?"

"I want to talk to you about LT Juarez."

"Is there a problem with her?"

"I want to talk to you about your romantic relationship with LT Juarez."

Daniels felt the life go out of him. He tried a couple of times to maintain eye contact with Nation but could not. He eventually let his gaze fall away.

"So, you don't deny it."

"I may be guilty of bad judgment, Captain. But I'm not a liar. You have to believe that nothing has happened on this ship between the Lieutenant and me." His confidence was back now. He brought his eyes back up to hers.

"I know that, and I appreciate it. But that's not good enough. You should have told me about Hawaii."

"Yes, ma'am like I said... Bad judgment."

"So how did this start?"

Paul Daniels usually spent each day trying to keep thoughts of his life with Juanita Juarez in Hawaii out of his mind. Now his Captain had ordered him to relive those days again. "It started when I was an instructor at the Fleet Training Center."

"Was she a student?"

"No, ma'am. She was the Combat Information Center Officer on a destroyer. We met at a wedding. She was a friend of the groom. I knew the bride." What he did not tell Nation was that from the moment they met, their relationship had been electric.

His captain nodded. "How long did you see each other?"

"For almost a year," he replied as he successfully pushed back the urge to smile at the memory. Every day in Paradise had been just that. "On the day I received my orders to *Princeton*, I bought a ring."

Nation's eyes widened as she sat back in her chair. "So this was serious?"

"Yes, ma'am. But ironically, she also received her orders to this ship on the same day."

Nation shook her head at the irony.

"She was so excited and happy, just like me. She drove over to tell me the news. When I heard where she was going, I almost fell over."

"So did she accept the ring?"

Daniels felt embarrassed at the question. "I never gave it to her. It's in my stateroom safe. I told her where I was going and decided to hold on to it until a more appropriate time. Ma'am, when we found out we were coming here, we put things on hold."

"Well, your chiefs and other senior enlisted personnel think you two are still an item. And whether it's true or not, something you or she or the both of you are doing is propelling that belief."

Daniels sighed and shook his head in disbelief. He closed his notebook. "What do you want me to do?"

"My first concern is for this ship. We have a leadership problem. And I need you to help me solve it," she said plainly.

"I understand." Daniels stood.

She nodded.

"You'll have my request for a transfer in writing in the morning."

She nodded again. "I'm sorry it had to end like this, Paul."

"Yes, ma'am. Me, too. But..."

Her eyebrow went up.

GENERAL QUARTERS

"I should have decided this a year ago. Now, I've screwed up two careers instead of just one."

***

Downtown Taipei, Taiwan
2:05 PM

"Mr. McGuire, welcome," Beng said with a lilt as he greeted one of his more regular customers.

Beng's Pro Shop held iconic status in downtown Taipei. With an indoor driving range on its second floor, club fitting, and instruction, Beng's provided a full-service offering to golfers. Only a few kilometers from his residence, Ben McGuire spent countless hours there since his arrival in Taiwan.

"Hello, Beng," Ben greeted.

"I see you did not come to practice today. How can we help you? New clubs, perhaps?"

Ben smiled as he recognized the owner's now-famous entrepreneurial style. "No, not this time. I came by to pick up a club for Jake Harrison. He's having it regripped."

"Ah, yes. He mentioned that you would be by. This way," Beng said as turned toward the club-making area.

Beng's retail area reminded Ben of the sports superstores back in the states. As far as the eye could see, golf equipment and apparel filled the aisles, giving testimony to the popularity of golf in Taiwan.

"Did I tell you that I have the new TaylorMade irons?" Beng asked as he continued toward the inner reaches of the store.

His words had the same effect on Ben as offering liquor to an alcoholic. Ben's head and eyes riveted so quickly that he gave up any opportunity of presenting a poker face.

"Ah, so you would like to see them?"

Ben grinned in anxious embarrassment.

CHAPTER SEVEN
MURPHY'S LAW

Thursday, August 14th
Taoyuan Airport
Taipei, Taiwan
2:00 PM

Ambassador Wooten and Taiwanese President Liu Chao-hsuan stood at the end of a long red carpet with most of the Embassy Staff and a small army of international news media. As the door to Air Force One opened, a military band sounded the first strains of "Hail to the Chief". President Marshall Langdon proceeded down the aircraft gantry to meet the President of Taiwan and his State Department delegation.

***

PLA-N Headquarters
Beijing, China
1415 Hours

As soon as Zhao left Sun's building, Sun started making telephone calls. He first called Marine General Yau. He requested his friend's presence as soon as possible.

He next called his fleet commanders, North Sea Commander Admiral Chek and South Sea Commander Admiral Zheng. Anxiety filled Zheng's voice as he reported the status of his destroyer and frigates. Nearly all the ships reported 100% operational readiness with only three at sea. The Northern Fleet

Commander, Admiral Chek, responded in almost the same manner as Zheng.

"Admiral, I will issue written orders very shortly. But I want you to order those ships that are at sea into port."

"Sir? I don't understand."

"You heard me, Admiral," Sun ensured he used the proper measure of intensity and sternness. "I also want you to place the destroyer and frigate crews on leave for the next seventy-two hours."

A long silence ensued. "All of them, sir?"

"Yes, Admiral, all. All destroyer and frigate crews. Immediately."

"Admiral, this is highly irregular. May I know the reason for this action?"

Of course it is irregular. What can I say? "Admiral, all I can tell you is that I just had a visit from General Zhao. There is a traitor among us, and I am doing what I can to place as many loyal Chinese military personnel in-country as I can. Our motherland is counting on us. Can I count on you?"

"Yes, Admiral." Chek's response was instant and, once more, respectful.

A familiar knock at the door was followed by Marine General Yau opening it and leaning in for permission to completely enter. Sun waved his permission as he finished his call with Chek.

"Thank you, Admiral. I will be in touch as soon as possible." Sun put down the telephone receiver and looked up to see his comrade's watchful stare.

Sun stood. "I am in trouble, my friend. And I'm afraid because you have been a good friend and ally, you are too."

"Hmm. I assumed as much."

"I estimate that General Zhao will issue an arrest order for me in less than a day. You probably will have a few hours more."

Yau seated himself in one of the guest chairs. "What should we do?"

"You could probably get out of the country... if that is your wish. I am in a position to assist you, if necessary."

"And go where?" Yau shot back. "This is my home, and it is under attack. Would not running away be the act of a coward?"

Sun smiled at him. "That's what I thought you'd say."

"So, what do we do?"

Sun seated himself. "Bear with me, General," he replied as he dialed Admiral Chang's number. Chang, the East Sea Fleet Commander, since being called to account for placing two of his problem-ridden submarines back into active service, went quiet. Sun knew Chang did not like him. The animus began when the Central Military Committee promoted Sun over him to command the People's Navy. The recent clash served to estrange the two men. Sun suspected Chang's participation in this coup attempt.

"Yes, Admiral?" Chang said as he answered the phone with a burdened tone. Sun tried to dismiss his subordinate's terse manner.

"Admiral, I have ordered the destroyers and frigates in the Fleet to return to port and place their crews on leave."

"What? What has happened?"

"I anticipate trouble here at home, and I want as many loyal military personnel on the ground as possible," Sun quibbled.

"If you expect trouble, then these ships belong at sea to keep our enemies from taking advantage of the situation," Chang shot back.

"Admiral, I think the Strategic Missile Command will more than ensure our security from external threats," Sun jabbed back. "Please stand by to receive these ships in Ningbo," he added.

"Admiral Sun, I must protest this action-," he began.

"Admiral Chang," Sun cut him off. "This is not a request. If you cannot comply with this order, surrender your command to your deputy and report to your quarters."

A tense silence fell over the line for the third time in as many telephone calls. Sun exchanged a weighty glance with Yau.

"I understand, Admiral," Chang finally said.

"Very well, Admiral. I will be in touch," Sun said as he removed the phone from his ear and slammed it into place.

"Admiral," Yau began as if he were stalking a wild animal.

Sun did not respond verbally. Rather he looked up and raised an eyebrow.

"I don't understand. What will we accomplish by keeping the destroyers in port?"

"Honestly, Yau. I do not know. All I know is that once this is all over, we need to have a fleet. Can you think of a place where it will be safer? Besides, Zhao wants them at sea."

Yau nodded at his commander's assessment.

"Now, I want you to order your Marines out of their garrisons and into the cities. If rioting breaks out, they need to be available to keep order. If we need to retake the capital, we will not be able to do it if your forces are under arrest."

Yau nodded again as he stood and walked over to Sun's desk. He picked up the phone and began dialing.

***

Downtown Taipei, Taiwan
2:50 PM

Jake walked into the mobile command post. "How long has he been in there?" Jake asked about Ben.

"About five minutes," Michael Wong replied. Wong, dressed in black urban cammies, wore a holstered pistol on his belt.

Technology, as a rule, did not easily impress Jake Harrison. He generally took considerable pride in his audio cassette player, typewriter, and book collection. The idea of CD's, DVD's, iPods, and most things digital, except for his mobile telephone, left him cold.

His agency underwent many changes in his twenty-four-year career, but none more troubling and destructive than its departure from relying on field operatives to high-tech means. However, the National tragedy of September 11th and its aftermath vindicated men and women like him who knew no technology could ever replace well-practiced tradecraft.

Still, he found himself marveling at their mobile command post on every visit. Almost 30 feet in length, the converted RV featured drone and PCS communications systems, computer workstations, a small conference room, whiteboards, and a small-arms weapons locker.

Five workstations arranged in tandem took up most of the right side of the vehicle. Eight flat-screen monitors, positioned above their heads, displayed the GPS locations of Ben McGuire, and the four Chinese and Russian spies under surveillance.

"How are we getting this info?" one of the Secret Service representatives asked.

"We placed beacons on their vehicles. We're piggy-backing the cell towers and processing the signals here," Edna Hennessey, the senior technical analyst, answered.

"And just in case this shit fails, we have people tailing them," Jake added.

"My shit don't stink. You oughta know that by now, Jake," Hennessey shot back. A thick Southern accent fit her short, stout frame perfectly. In her mid-fifties, silver-grey strands ran evenly through a thick head of dark brown hair.

"We'll talk when this is all over," Jake replied without taking his eyes from the screen.

GENERAL QUARTERS

Hennessey flashed Jake the finger, which he pretended not to see.

Wong smiled at Harrison's distrust of their systems while Harrison continued to scan the different screens. A pulsating green dot indicated Ben McGuire's parked vehicle in front of Beng's Pro Shop. The other contacts showed up as red dots moving across their respective electronic landscapes. Jake's eyes narrowed when one of the dots drove into the same two-square-mile grid as McGuire's location. The others were moving away from the city center.

"Here we go," Wong murmured.

Harrison only nodded before he grabbed a nearby radio microphone and pressed the transmit button. "Okay everybody, the shooter is in the area. Her picture is in your info packs."

"Gotta go," Wong said as he charged out of the trailer.

"Good luck," Jake shouted after him as each of his three teams acknowledged receipt of his transmission. Wong departed to take on-scene command of the strike team.

Jake took a seat at the conference table in the rear of the vehicle. A monitor near him flickered to life to display the GPS information for McGuire and Galena Cheslav. Harrison reclined on the small sofa and folded his arms as the suspect assassin's vehicle closed on their location.

"How's this gonna go down?" the Secret Service guy asked from the doorway.

Without taking his gaze from the display, Harrison said, "We'll let her get into position, just in case we can nab any accomplices. But I want her down before she can even aim."

Harrison returned his full attention to the blinking GPS display.

Ben McGuire, blue suit jacket removed, necktie loosened, and with rolled shirtsleeves took a full swing with the demo TaylorMade 3-Iron. The crack of the club-blade hitting the ball pierced the air a second before the sound of the ball hitting the back of the simulator reached his ears. The computer took over the rest of the ball's flight. The machine even simulated the required time-delay for the ball to hit the ground. A graphic appeared seconds later indicating Ben's stroke had sent the golf ball almost 200 yards in a nearly straight-line trajectory.

"That's pretty good," Beng said even before Ben could mentally applaud his performance. "You've been practicing."

"Shit, Beng. Claire's gonna kill me," McGuire laughed.

"Shall I include a complimentary box of Pro V's?"

"A box? Hell, for the price of these suckers you ought to throw in a whole carton," Ben shot back half-seriously.

"Done," Beng replied.

McGuire's jaw dropped. "Are you kidding?"

Beng shook his head. "You and Mr. Harrison are good customers."

Ben shrugged. "Thanks, Beng. I appreciate that. Wrap me up a set," he laughed.

Special Agents Roxanne Xiu and Brett LeMaster trailed behind their target by half a block or so. Xiu drove the vehicle while LeMaster held the tracking unit's display. A GPS-enabled transmitter attached to Galena Cheslav's vehicle emitted a signal that showed up as a pulsating yellow light on the hand-held display unit.

Xiu wove the vehicle in and out of traffic to both blend in and keep within electronic tracking range of their target's auto. A device attached to the top of Galena Cheslav's rear axle transmitted a low-powered signal to avoid detection. They lagged behind no more than half a mile or so to keep their receiver/transponder in contact.

Her fourth year as a member of the Operations Directorate, Xiu hailed from Taiwan. She expertly placed several vehicles between herself and their target on an intermittent basis. Their green Ford Taurus' dirty and battered exterior faded into the city traffic around them. LeMaster, just out of the academy, came to the team by way of the Defense Language School.

"How are we doing?" she asked LeMaster in Mandarin.

"Everything is working properly," he responded in the same language.

LeMaster frowned when Xiu rolled her eyes.

"What?" he asked.

"You're too formal. Until you start sounding more natural, you're not gonna be of much use to me," she replied.

LeMaster nodded. He liked his senior partner, most of the time. Her candor often took the air out of the room. He appreciated her forthrightness. He made a mental note to have her teach him more conversational Mandarin when time permitted.

He looked up to visually compare his actual location to the display on the Receiver/Transponder. The device placed them in the middle of Taipei's famous Combat Zone, a five-square-mile area filled with bars, clubs, and low-rent apartments and hotels. The unit had two basic functions.

Screeching brakes and deceleration threw LeMaster's body forward and the transponder out of his hands. He looked over to see Xiu swirling the steering wheel to the left. The automobile's rear-end swung around to the right as the vehicle came to an abrupt stop. They ended up at a 90% angle to the back end of a large truck.

"Shit, that was close!" This time he spoke in English.

"Get that tracker off the floor before we lose her," Xiu ordered as she pulled back into traffic with screeching tires.

Jake Harrison covered the ten feet between his small office and the main portion of the mobile command post in two angry steps. "What the hell do you mean you lost her?" he shouted at no one in particular.

Edna looked up from her station. She wore a helpless expression as if she were a child and someone had taken her toys. "Xiu and LeMaster almost had a wreck. She slipped out of range before they could get back on the road."

"Shit!"

"Here's where they last had her," Edna added as he pulled a map up on his screen and pointed to a downtown Taipei intersection. "There's a cell tower in the area, but we're not getting a signal," she complained.

Jake scanned the area. At his last known location, Cheslav was only a mile from the golf store. Bile rose in Jake's throat. *This is starting to go bad. Fucking Murphy's Law.*

"Get Xiu on the line. You tell her to fucking get her shit together and find Cheslav!" he ordered Edna as he headed for the door.

"Yes, sir. Where are you going?" Edna asked.

"To try and save this. Just call me when you get something." "My shit don't stink," he added mockingly, as he bounded out of the van.

Edna Hennessey picked up a ringing phone. The display showed Roxanne Xiu's name and number. "What've you got?"

"Nothing. Where's Jake?"

"On his way to your area. Look, I'll get back to you in a sec," Edna said as she ended the connection. She turned to the technician next to her. "Henry, I've got an idea. It's kinda wild, but it might work."

"I'm open. Shoot," he replied.

"Do we still have a bird covering the area?" she asked, referring to a UAV.

"Yeah, we ordered one when all the chatter started. A second one came online when POTUS decided to pay us a visit."

"Well, we know where Cheslav was ten minutes ago..."

"Got it," Henry replied as he picked up on her idea.

"Michael, you heard?" Jake asked Wong over the radio.

"Yeah. We're standing by. We can be anywhere in a three-block radius in less than a couple of minutes."

"Okay. Standby."

He keyed the microphone a couple of times before making another call. "Edna, what have you got?"

"Wait one, Jake," she came back immediately.

"We don't have 'one,'" he replied.

She didn't answer.

Back in the mobile command post, Edna and Henry worked with such intensity that their hands blurred against their keyboards. Edna conjured up a simple plan: Isolate the portion of the digital drone data that contained the suspect vehicle and then track it to its final location.

"Got the car," Henry announced in a terse but excited manner.

He froze the action and moved his pointer to select the target image. Once he clicked the mouse button, a circle formed around the vehicle. He set the software to run slow forward in automatic mode. As the picture started moving again, the cursor stayed locked on the vehicle.

"Edna?" Jake called over the radio.

She ignored him as the picture progressed.

Soon everyone left in the trailer gathered around Henry's screen to watch the vehicle's recorded image progress through the street. A full two minutes later, it came to a stop in front of an office building.

Edna picked up the radio microphone. "Taipei Energy Corporation," she declared. "She got out of the vehicle four minutes ago carrying a brief black case."

"Roger. All stations converge on Taipei Energy," Jake ordered. "I'm going after McGuire."

Michael Wong approached the front of the Taipei Energy Corporation Headquarters from the north. As he brought his sedan to a screeching halt in front of the modern high-rise structure, the box van carrying his assault team came up behind him. Three Taipei Police Department cars came to an abrupt stop from the south as he exited his car. Police department vehicles also deployed on each of the other sides of the building to prevent the would-be assassin from completing her mission and escaping.

Wong sprang out of his vehicle as ten other men and women emerged from the large black van a few feet away. He stormed up the steps, taking two or three at a time, toward the complex's main plaza. His team also dressed in black camouflage and carrying automatic weapons, followed him as best they could. He didn't slow his pace as he ran toward the front doors.

As Wong and the team entered the lobby, three wide-eyed security guards came to their feet from behind a large and ornate reception console. Two of them, the younger guards, placed their hands on their holstered weapons. Confused, the older guard shouted, "What's going on?"

Wong pulled a picture from his vest and held it up for the lead guard to examine. "Did you let this woman in your building?"

The guard blinked twice through round glasses. "Yes. She came in about five minutes ago. Who is she?"

Ignoring the man's question, Wong asked, "Where did she go?"

The guard exchanged glances first with Wong and then the other two guards.

"Look, I don't have time to fuck with you. Where did she go?" Wong pressed.

"This is a private facility. You can't just come in here-" the guard started to protest.

With that, one of the Taipei policemen slid a blue document across the top of the dark wood covered station. "That's a search warrant! We're looking for a terrorist! If you resist, we will place you under arrest!" the officer shouted.

Wong reached across the console and grabbed the man's jacket. He almost jerked him across the top of the structure, asking, "Where did she go?!!"

Jake Harrison took the corner onto Kai Avenue at over thirty miles per hour. In doing so, he nearly took out an oncoming sedan. The other driver delivered his protest with several long blasts of his horn. Undeterred, Jake floored the accelerator, and the BMW's six-cylinder engine hurled the vehicle ahead. Beng's Golf Shop loomed ahead.

"Here you are, Mr. McGuire," Beng said as he placed a brown cardboard box into his arms.

About one meter in length, it took both arms to hold it securely. "Great!" Ben turned to his calendar, trying to figure out how to make room to debut his new clubs.

"I placed Mr. Harrison's club in the box with yours," Beng said as Ben reached the door. "And I'll have the balls ready for you tomorrow."

Ben nodded. "My wife is going to kill me," he uttered again as he exited the store.

"Edna," Wong called over the radio. "We're in the building. She's not where she supposed to be, and it's a damned big building!"

"Relax, Doll. I've got ya' covered," Edna Hennessey drawled back. She banged commands into her computer terminal as she spoke.

Anticipating the worst possible scenario, she requested the National Reconnaissance Office free up a second drone. Now under her positive control, she instructed the airborne system to send images of the Taipei Energy Corporation to her computers. With the first vehicle covering the east and south sides of the 30-floor structure and the second bird imaging the north and west exteriors, Edna predicted her machines should have enough data to provide them useful information.

A second monitor to her right displayed the results of the processed data. The image of a modern sky-rise building began to materialize as it slowly rotated in place. Windows, corners, and their surrounding detail fell into place as she looked on.

A few more keystrokes and a virtual camera whipped around the electronic structure and focused in on the computer-generated image of a blonde woman standing in an open window. The unmistakable shape of a high-powered rifle also came into view.

"Wong," Edna said into her boom microphone. "She's on the 22nd floor, Room 2209. It looks like a reception area adjacent to a maintenance office."

"Roger," was all he said.

Ben exited the store and turned to walk back up the street to his car when the sound of screeching tires reached his ears. He turned with a start to see Jake Harrison sitting behind the wheel of his BMW.

"McGuire, get in the car!" he ordered as he threw open the passenger door.

"What?"

"Get in the fucking car! Now!"

Frowning in confusion, Ben took a step toward the vehicle's open door. Ben detected the unmistakable sound of a whizzing bullet. A split second later the sidewalk behind him exploded with a loud crack. "Shit!"

He dropped the clubs and lunged for the relative safety of the vehicle. Even before Ben completely entered the car, Jake floored the gas.

"Who the hell is shooting at me?!" Ben yelped.

The rear window of the automobile exploded before Harrison could answer.

Ben yanked himself into the vehicle and slammed the door as Jake took a turn off the street. An alleyway behind the golf shop offered the first real level of safety.

Harrison brought the vehicle to stop and placed it in park. "Are you okay?" He asked as he grabbed Ben and started physically turning him from one side to the other.

"Yeah, I'm okay," Ben replied as he pulled away and slapped Jake's hands. "What the fuck was that?"

Jake sighed. "That was a Russian hired killer trying to fulfill a contract for the Chinese Government.

Ben heard the words, but they didn't make sense at first. "What?"

"Yeah," Jake replied. "Somebody on the mainland is still pissed at you about Senkaku Island."

Ben's eyes widened. "How do you know about that?"

Harrison only cocked his head to one side and opened his hands. The "you've got to be shitting me" expression spoke volumes.

Wong, in a crouch, his Glock 20 SF 10mm weapon up and aimed ahead, led the charge into the small storage closet. Ridiculously small, the room only accommodated Wong. One of his assault team members stood in the doorway behind him with his rifle leveled in the same direction.

The door burst open, and they found Galena Cheslav kneeling by her rifle and the briefcase that she reportedly carried into the building. "Please move so I can shoot you in the fucking head," Wong announced himself in Russian.

She looked up. If surprised, she didn't act so. "That would be a dreadful end to a beautiful day. Don't you think?" she asked calmly.

Wong noticed that only one of her hands was visible. He felt the hair on his neck stand at attention. "No, not really," he replied. "On the floor," he ordered.

Galena smiled. "I can't do that," she said as she pulled a grenade from behind her back. She used her thumb to pull the pin before she let the device drop in front of her.

Wong felt a tremendous tug on the back of his body-armor vest before his feet went out from under him. One of his men jerked him back into the maintenance office as the room exploded in a cataclysmic blast of fire and shrapnel.

CHAPTER EIGHT
VFA-113

Thursday, August 14th
Taipei, Taiwan
3:20 PM

"You okay?" Harrison asked Wong.

Wong sat in the rear doorway of an ambulance as a female paramedic cleaned up a cut on his forehead. He smiled at seeing Jake.

"Yeah, Boss. She gave it the college try, but she missed."

At hearing the news of Galena Cheslav's suicide bombing, Jake drove to the Taipei Energy Headquarters like a madman. Ben found himself holding on for dear life during most of the short ride.

Jake's cool exterior melted just long enough for Ben to read relief in his face. Wong, on the other hand, looked like hell. His black urban camouflage uniform was ripped and torn all over. A bloody bandage covered his left eye while smudges took care of the rest of his face.

"I'd say you were lucky, Sport."

"And it's always better to be lucky than to be good," Wong shot back with a big grin.

Jake's handheld radio crackled to life. "Jake? You there?"

He raised it to his mouth. "Yeah. Go ahead."

"You need to get down to Keelung Port Terminal."

Jake exchanged glances with Wong.

"Go ahead. I'm gonna be here a while. Take McGuire there with you."

"Jake, did you copy that?" the voice called on the radio again.

"Yeah, got it," he finally replied.

"I'll catch up to you later," Wong said as the technician began examining a large gash on his arm.

Jake nodded. "Come on, Ben."

"Thanks," Bėn said to him as he turned to follow Jake.

Wong nodded in response.

***

Chinese National Military Command Center
Beijing, China
1525 Hours

"He did what?!!" General Zhao's blood boiled. He heard the edge in his voice loud and clear. Now spending every waking moment in their command center, Zhao gave up sleeping or eating regularly. A strong brew of tea served as the only real staple in his diet of late.

"He's ordered all of the cruisers and destroyers into port, and their crews on leave, sir," Admiral Chang explained over the telephone.

"Well, stop them!" Zhao paced his expansive office to keep from throwing something. He needed to hit something.

"Sir, he's the Supreme Naval Commander. I do not have the authority."

Chang was right. "I'll have that bastard arrested-"

"Sir, even if you do, by the time we get control, it will be too late for us. We need destroyer protection now."

Zhao disbelieved his ears. Damn Sun. Damn him. He took a breath as his mind raced.

"General. Are you there, sir?"

"Another issue has arisen. The troop on-load is behind schedule. The Army commanders are bickering about who will load first. Each of them wants to claim the right to be the first into Taiwan."

Zhao let Chang's words wash over him. Placing Sun under arrest now endangered their plans. DAMN IT! Zhao suddenly remembered a course from the Command and Staff College. He stopped pacing, took in a deep breath, and let it out slowly.

"Admiral, it has been my experience that operations such as this seldom go as planned. What contingencies have you made?"

The line went suddenly quiet. Though Chang called from a hundred miles away, he almost saw him gritting his teeth in thought.

The lesson was clear; Let your subordinates use their creativity to solve problems. Let them present you options rather than them always looking to you for the answers.

"Well, Admiral?" Zhao asked after a long moment.

"Sir, I... I think we can use the missile patrol boats."

"Tell me what you mean," Zhao demanded.

"I have tactical command of several missile patrol corvettes. We can use them to screen the amphibious group."

"What is their range? Can they keep up with the larger ships?"

"Sir, we can refuel them from the larger ships, and they have twice the speed of the landing ships."

The idea had merit. "But what about the Taiwanese and American Navies? Their ships are more powerful and so many."

"We only need cover long enough to land our troops. By then, we should have the destroyers back under control."

Not what he originally planned, but it sounded feasible. "Execute your contingency, Admiral. I'll take care of the troop on-load problem."

***

U.S. Embassy
Taipei, Taiwan

Captain Pete Corrigan's eyes went wide at the sight of Deputy Chief of Mission James Dudley at his office door.

"Captain, do you have a moment?" Dudley asked. Out of courtesy and protocol, Corrigan removed his reading glasses and came to his feet. Happy for the interruption, taking his gaze away from the number of binders covering his desk was easy. "Yes, sir."

"Do you have any idea where Captain McGuire is?"

Corrigan frowned at the question. Surely McGuire knew better than to keep the Ambassador or his staff in the dark about his whereabouts. "Sir, I know he had a briefing scheduled at the Taiwanese Navy Headquarters."

"Yes, well, that ended some time ago."

Still frowning. "No, sir. Then I have no idea where he is."

"Well, we need a decision. The President's security team wants to get our assessment of the situation here. I think it's more than safe enough to push the aircraft carrier out as to not alarm the Chinese."

Corrigan sighed. "Sir, Captain McGuire-"

"Yes, yes, I know Captain McGuire expressed his views at the intelligence briefing. But I think it's time to decide what we're actually going to do here."

Corrigan grimaced.

"Captain, I think it's safe to say that Captain McGuire's time here is coming to an end. Don't you think it would be in everyone's best interests if you started your tenure on the Ambassador's good side?"

Corrigan stared blankly at Dudley for a long moment.

"Yes, sir. I do."

GENERAL QUARTERS

***

Keelung Shipping Terminal
Taipei, Taiwan
4:13 PM

"We got a hit on an NSA intercept," Jake referred to the National Security Agency. "We were able to reconstruct enough of Chinese communications code to figure out they had more than a passing interest in you."

"So you let me act as bait?" Ben McGuire asked, his anger growing with every word.

Jake sighed. "Look, all I can tell you is that there were extenuating priorities-"

"Fuck you, Jake!"

Harrison didn't respond as he drove the vehicle toward the piers.

Ben tried to remember the last time he was this pissed off. It didn't take long for the memory of his last moments on Senkaku Island to come to mind. Moments before a helicopter swooped in to rescue him, he and several Navy SEALS were losing in their bid to hold off a company of Chinese Marines with small-arms fire.

Jake stopped at a security gate and flashed his identification to a Taipei Police officer. The man examined it closely before pointing and giving Harrison instructions in Mandarin. Jake nodded, put away his wallet, and pulled ahead.

The port, large and expansive, looked full. Several ships sat at the piers and scores of metal shipping containers lined the space between the vessels and a large warehouse. As Jake made a turn in the direction given by the gate officer, several police vehicles, their lights still flashing came into view.

He saw dozens of uniformed personnel as the vehicle came to a stop. Several police officers led men and women in handcuffs away from the scene to a large bus with bars on the

137

windows. One of the prisoners, a young Asian man, leered at Ben as he walked by. What the hell was that about?

"Come on," Jake said from behind him. "You need to see this."

Ben pulled his attention from the prison bus and turned to follow Jake.

Harrison, with Ben in tow, made their way through the gathering of police and other official personnel to the inner reaches of the warehouse. Ben noticed several men wearing yellow special protective clothing, complete with masks and respirators.

Yellow police tape blocked their front. Jake stopped his advance when he reached the temporary barrier. Ben's eyes bulged when he reached the same point.

The tape kept unprotected personnel well away from several large oil barrels. Members of the HAZMAT team used stencils and spray paint to mark the barrels with "Extremely Toxic" markings. Ben, scanning the area to his right, noticed a collection of machine guns, rocket-propelled grenades, and harnesses of grenades. "Holy shit."

"Who are these guys? What is all this?" Ben asked.

"Near as we can tell, a terrorist cell. I suspect this is just one. Just like you predicted."

"Really?" Ben successfully suppressed the urge to smile at being right as he remembered his admonition to Deputy Chief of Mission Dudley.

"Somebody in China is planning something. Something big."

"This is what I meant by other priorities," Jake said softly.

Ben nodded as he continued scanning the goings-on beyond the tape.

Jake's cell phone rang, and he quickly answered it. "Harrison."

GENERAL QUARTERS

Ben switched his attention from the people in the HAZMAT suits to Harrison.

"I understand. We'll head back shortly," Jake said as he ended the call and turned to Ben. "Air Force One is on the ground We're expected back at the Embassy for the reception."

Ben nodded.

"We busted fifteen bad guys with this shit," an American agent announced to Jake. "Nice work," he added. "But not Pugachev. We've had people on him all day, but he hasn't moved or even made a phone call."

Jake gave half a smile in response to his report.

"What's in the drums?" Ben asked.

"Sarin," the same man replied.

Holy shit.

Jake leaned over toward Ben. "Are we cool?"

Ben's anger mounted again. He sneered at his colleague and stormed toward the car. As Ben brushed by others on their way toward the crime scene in the warehouse, he did not slow his pace. Jake caught up to him just as he reached the vehicle.

"Hey, McGuire?" Jake called as he tapped Ben on his shoulder.

Ben curled his right hand into a fist, whipped around, and struck Jake in the face. Jake fell backward. He sat on the ground for a long moment holding his jaw as passersby stopped to gawk.

"Now, Jake. Now, we're cool." Ben turned back toward the vehicle, leaving Harrison on the ground.

***

Taipei, Taiwan
4:15 PM

Choi Lin, with a canvas bag slung over his right shoulder, strolled into the coffee shop, scanning it closely as he entered.

He checked his watch. Perfect. The shop was full. Two employees, one behind the counter and the other cleaning tables, stood out from the bustle of the patrons. Some of the customers surfed the Web while others read newspapers and drank coffee or tea from large mugs. The shop normally buzzed with activity at this time of day. He chose it precisely for that reason.

Not far from his place of employment at the Taiwanese Presidential Mansion, the little shop featured art-deco furnishings and American jazz music. No more than 60 square meters in size with a couple of large sofas and a few tables, the little place offered a busy yet intimate setting. Choi walked past the other patrons, all of whom sat at their laptops, taking advantage of the free Internet service.

"Choi," Pin called. "What can I get for you? Your regular?"

"Yes, that would be fine. Thank you." Choi's regular was an "extra-hot" cappuccino in their best porcelain.

He slid his bag from his shoulder and took a seat as the barista began her work. The sound of the cappuccino machine filled the air. He looked over the other patrons again.

A few minutes later, his beverage appeared at the counter. Choi stood and walked over the counter. Reaching with excitement for the cup and saucer, he took a sip and spilled a good bit on his white shirt.

"Oooh!" Pin shouted back. She grabbed a towel and ran around the counter, patting at the growing stain on the otherwise pristine shirt to no avail. "I'm so sorry," the barista apologized.

"It is not your fault. I was in too great a hurry," he replied. He spied the other patrons looking in his direction.

"You should take it off and try to rinse it. The coffee stain will set if you don't," she suggested.

"Good idea. I have another shirt in my bag," Choi replied. He handed her the cup and went to grab his bag.

"Shall I make you another?" she asked as he walked toward the restroom.

"Yes, please. I'll be right out," he replied as he opened the door.

She shot him a relieved smile as he closed and locked the bathroom door.

A man drinking coffee, one of the first people Choi passed upon entering the shop, signaled him by shifting his cup from his left hand to his right and back again. A dead drop mailbox located in a recess behind a corner pipe in the restroom held a package for him. Choi changed his shirt before going over to find a small black box waiting for him. He placed the unopened item into his bag to open later, and then rinsed the coffee stain from one of his favorite shirts.

***

Office of the President
Beijing, China
4:45 PM

President Ho stood over his briefcase as it sat in his chair. He scanned his busy desk, checking off items on his mental to-do list. Ho's mind raced, trying to remember all that he needed for his meeting with the Taiwanese and American presidents. He glanced across the room at the grandfather clock occupying the opposite corner. He and his entourage planned to leave for the airport from his residence in the morning. Ending the day early allowed him to prepare and rest for the upcoming two-day summit adequately.

The intercom on his desk rang. Still distracted, President Ho reached for the button to answer his administrative assistant's call. "Yes?"

"Comrade President, Chairman Fei is here to see you," he announced.

141

The virtual list in his mind evaporated as he processed his words. Crossing his arms, he frowned at the device, "Did we have an appointment?"

"No, President Ho," he responded plainly.

What could he want? He knows I'm leaving shortly. "Very well. Send him in," he replied.

"What game are you up to, Fei?" he asked himself as the connection ended.

A few moments later, the fat man who led the People's Communist Party opened the door and marched in as if he owned the space. Still standing behind his desk, Ho watched him come to a stop just inches from the edge of the desk. Fei, rather than greet him, surveyed his desk and his bulging leather briefcase. Not bothering to wipe away his familiar sneer, he brought his eyes up to meet the President's.

"So, you have decided to go through with this lunacy?" Fei asked in a bark.

"And a good day to you, Comrade," President Ho replied as he forced a smile.

"I cannot tell you how much of a mistake this is. Going to the Americans makes us look weak, as if we are afraid of them."

"You have already explained your objections. I also have nearly two hundred messages and telephone calls that others have made on your behalf."

"And you still intend to go? How foolish you are."

"Tell me, Comrade, in 1972 when President Nixon came here to meet Chairman Mao, did he show weakness? I seem to remember the world heralded both leaders for moving the cause of peace forward."

"Yes, it did make him appear weak. And the Americans thanked their President by casting him out of office."

Ho let out a smile as he managed to suppress most of his amusement at Fei's version of history. "Chairman, don't you think his breaking their laws had something to do with his dismissal?"

"You may interpret it any way you like," Fei cut him off. "But the fact remains that he came here and now he is remembered as a man thrown out of office without honor. And that is a fate that I hope you can avoid."

"A year ago, you and the People's Congress decided to entrust me with the leadership of our people. You changed our constitution such that I could set and lead national policy. You decided I was someone whom you could trust. What has happened since then? Why will you not trust me now?"

"Because you are behaving foolishly. Ceding away our right to reclaim the runaway province is no less criminal than the deeds of the American President Nixon." He stared directly at him. "Mark my words, Comrade President, go to Taiwan, and you will regret it."

Fei turned and stormed out of the President's office. He did not bother to close the door behind him. Rather, one of Fei's security agents did it for him.

Chairman Fei Tzu noticed the sweat-soaked armpits of his tailored wool suit as he climbed into his waiting limousine. Even before his driver had closed the door, he dialed numbers for General Zhao on his secure mobile telephone. "Traitorous son-of-a-bitch!" he said under his breath as he listened to the extension ring.

"Yes, Comrade?" Zhao's deep voice answered.

"He declined my offer."

"I understand. That is unfortunate. I had hoped that this could be avoided."

"Reason seems to have taken a leave of absence," Fei Tzu replied.

"I agree."

"What will we do next?"

"We wait."

"Wait?" Fei noticed the impatience in his own voice. He wanted action, and he wanted it now. He took a breath and spoke with measured calm. "Wait for what?"

"We wait until we are ready, Comrade."

"You mean until you are ready. I am ready now," Fei shot back.

"Ready to do what? Might I remind the Chairman that any action to remove him without the cooperation of the People's Army would be rejected by the People?" Zhao's voice contained a dogmatic, almost dictatorial flavor.

Fei's stomach rumbled at Zhao's words. How dare this solider dictate terms to me?

"Chairman. We are close. We must continue to work in concert." Zhao's tone changed, too. He now sounded much more conciliatory.

"I agree," Fei forced himself to say after a long moment. "You'll pardon my anxiousness. After all, it took nearly two thousand years to arrive. What are another few days?"

"Precisely my opinion, Comrade Chairman."

The mobile telephone rang with a customized tune alerting its owner of the caller's status. A nod from the backseat was all that the driver needed in the way of an order. The thick glass partition went, acoustically sealing off the passenger section from the front seat.

"Yes?"

"Greetings, Comrade," a familiar male voice said.

"Greetings to you."

"You have the item?"

"Yes. Per the instructions, I have packed it in my baggage."

"Very good. Events have turned as expected, and your homeland may need your services. In case our primary option fails, we will need you to complete our objective."

"I am ready to serve Mother China in any way that I can."

"It may require forfeiture of your life," the Hung Yaoguai Commander replied.

His words felt like huge slabs of stone pressing in, making it difficult to breathe. He occasionally thought of dying. He knew the risks of the role. Now, suddenly, it sounded so much more certain.

"Comrade, if you are not up to the task-"

"I am up to the task."

"Good, I knew our trust in you was well-placed."

"Comrade?"

"Yes?"

"Will you look after my family, if...?"

"You shall be lauded as a hero of the People. Your family's welfare shall be the burden of our nation."

The line was quiet for a long moment. "Thank you, Comrade."

"The honor is all mine. Thank you for your service," the Commander replied as he ended the conversation.

Jung Li placed the phone back into his suit jacket.

***

PLA-N Ship Qingcheng Mountain (LSM-934)
Ningbo Naval Base
Ningbo, China
1455 Hours

Rear Admiral Chang checked his watch. Whatever Zhao said to his military commanders worked. A problem-ridden and delayed troop on-load progressed more quickly and neared completion. Now only an hour behind schedule, his force navigator recomputed the tide settings for their departure.

Chang stood on the starboard-side flag bridge of his command ship as the last of four armored tanks backed its way

145

up a large ramp into the ship's cargo area. He used binoculars to check the progress of the other two ships. Finding them in a similar state, he smiled.

"Tell the captain we should be ready to get underway very soon," he said to his aide.

"Yes, sir." The young lieutenant disappeared to carry out the order.

Chang's mind turned to his superior, Vice Admiral Sun. Under orders from Zhao, Sun remained ignorant of his actions. Normally, conducting a surreptitious amphibious operation without the knowledge of one's commanding officer usually meant an abbreviated career. Chang aimed to replace Sun as the leader of the People's Navy. If the attack met with success, Chang's future looked bright.

"Admiral," his aide announced his return.

Chang turned to face him.

"Sir, the captain is setting the Sea and Anchor Detail. He estimates taking in all lines within the next ten minutes."

Chang nodded. He took one last look across the piers before finally going inside the skin of the ship. He planned to remain in his cabin until the operation to land troops in Taiwan began.

***

Residence of the PLA-N Commander
Beijing, China
1845 Hours

Admiral Sun's residence occupied a half-acre lot on the north side of the city, almost thirty miles from his office and the Central Military Committee compound. Rather than take up residence in the traditional home of the Naval Commander, Sun remained in his childhood home. With so many years at sea, and so few left in active service, he chose to take advantage of his station in life.

The three-floor concrete block home featured three bedrooms, a formal dining and gathering area, and a library. The library served as Sun's favorite room. As a child, he spent several hours every day reading his father's unofficial, and secret collection of books. The volume of books in Sun's possession always took visitors by surprise. Bookshelves covered every bit of wall space, leaving only room for the windows and fireplace.

His decision to live in a private home, rather than government housing, required the installation of security structures and devices, and stationing of a platoon of Marine guards. Security cameras scanned both the exterior and the interior of the six-foot stonewall. Sun once cursed this intrusion into his life. Now, he praised their existence.

He carefully watched as the team of Chinese Civil Defense Police changed shifts. He noticed them the day after he declined to attend Zhao's conference. Sun knew his name, for the first time in his life, made the wrong list. He turned off the monitor as he donned his heavy coat and gold-braided hat.

"Are we going to be okay?" his wife asked.

Sun sighed. "You will."

"And you?"

"Only time and this day will tell."

She leaned in to kiss him, and he pressed his mouth against her lips. As he pulled away, he saw a tear form in her eyes. "Save those for when you need them. It is too soon yet. I have a few tricks up my sleeve," he said, forcing a smile.

She nodded and returned the same strained grin.

"Admiral," General Yau called from the doorway.

Sun pulled himself from his wife's intense gaze and turned to see the Marine Corps Commander standing in the entrance to the secret passage that once led to his father's contraband publications. He held up a mobile telephone that gave off enough light to serve as a flashlight.

"It has begun," he said.

Taking one last glance at his wife, Sun turned to enter the passage. "Turn off the lights and go to bed," he said to her. "I am hoping this is all a bad dream from which we all will awaken safely."

***

U.S. Embassy
Taipei, Taiwan
7:15 PM

"I guess we missed the reception line," Ben murmured to Jake.

"Is that a big deal for you?"

"Well, it would have been nice to meet the President," he replied.

Harrison shrugged his shoulders and pressed forward into the already crowded room.

Just like the other Embassy offices, the official reception room came from humble beginnings. Ben scanned the former conference room for anything that might give away its original intended purpose. He noted the spot on the ceiling from which a projector once hung before dismissing the thought. When he looked back, Harrison was gone.

A string quartet played classical music barely audible over the din of laughter and conversation. Ben made his way to the refreshment table passing a gauntlet of State Department and military personnel engaging in business talk while imbibing wine or soft drinks. He spotted the President and Ambassador Thomas Wooten on the far side of the room.

The densest part of the crowd, expectedly, stood near the President and the Ambassador. President Marshall Langdon busily entertained impromptu questions while his ambassador looked on adding occasional commentary.

"Ah, McGuire's here," he miraculously heard James Dudley's voice over the noise of the standing-room-only gathering.

Ben successfully fought the urge to roll his eyes at seeing the Ambassador's Chief of Staff and his favorite pain in the ass. "James. How are you?"

"Fine, fine. I'd like you to meet the President's Chief of Staff, Veronica Aldridge," he said. "And this is Special Agent Kevin Kendricks. He's the Secret Service Detail leader." Ben only counted James pushing his hair away twice this time.

Kendricks, a burly silver-haired man with a serious expression, nodded his greeting. He turned his attention back toward the President and the gathering around him before moving off in that direction.

"Very nice to meet you, Captain," she said as she extended her hand.

Ben returned his focus to the auburn-haired Government official. Holy shit. The Chief of Staff to the President of the United States. Wow. Ben grasped her hand and shook it with vigor. He tried to quit grinning but couldn't. Meeting her felt like meeting a movie star.

"Okay, McGuire. You can let go now," Dudley quipped as he threw cold water on the moment.

"Sorry," Flushed, Ben apologized.

"It's quite all right, Captain. I'm pleased to meet you, too. I've heard a great deal about you," she replied. "Jim, could you excuse us for just a moment, please."

Dudley raised his eyebrows with surprise and nodded. He slunk away a few feet, but not enough for Ben's liking.

"Admiral Kiatkowski sends his regards," she said, after Dudley granted them some space.

Ben smiled again at hearing the words. He took notice of Aldridge. She was an attractive woman in her late forties wearing shoulder-length red hair that accented blue eyes and a fair complexion. At about 5'5", she owned a trim and shapely figure.

"Thank you, ma'am," Ben replied.

"Please call me Veronica, Ben. The Admiral and I are old friends, and he says that I should count you as one of them, too."

Ben nodded his understanding and approval.

"And I should also mention that you and I will be sitting together tomorrow night at the State Dinner."

"Really? I'm looking forward to it," he lied. Ben had never planned to attend. A root-canal sounded like more fun than sitting through a three-hour meal in his Dinner Dress uniform listening to speeches.

Ben felt a tap on his shoulder. He turned to see Harrison's typical grim façade looking a little less grim than normal. "Chief of Staff," Ben began. "This is Jake Harrison. He's the—"

"Yes, I know who Mr. Harrison is, Ben," she interrupted. Aldridge extended her hand to shake Harrison's.

"Chief of Staff, I hope these two don't cause you any problems. They are quite the handful around here," Dudley tried to make a joke announcing his return.

Neither Harrison nor Ben smiled at his humor. Harrison started humming the same tune Ben had heard earlier in his office.

"Nice to meet you, Ms. Aldridge," Jake said as he released her hand.

"Same here. So how are our friends doing tonight? Nice work on the operation," she added.

"Very comfortable in the Taipei Prison," Jake replied.

"Good."

Dudley smiled and leaned in as if he had a secret. "McGuire, you should probably go check your messages."

Ben shot the skinny, dark-haired man an evil stare. "Sounds like duty calls," Ben said before shifting his focus back to COS Aldridge.

"Well, truthfully, I was coming over to pull you away. We've got some follow-up work to do," Jake said.

"Not to worry. Let's catch up later," she replied softly.

"Okay. Let's go," Ben said to Harrison.

Harrison exchanged nods with the two other civilians before falling in behind Ben as he cut a swath through the crowd.

"Oooh, I think somebody's sweet on you," Jake teased Ben as they reached the door.

"What?"

"Oh yeah, didn't you see the way she was looking at you?"

"Stick to Intel, buddy. You're nuts."

"This is Intel, pal. News you can use," he replied as he brushed by Ben to take the lead. "She was eyeing you the same way I look at a New York strip. Please don't make me start whistling that song for you."

***

Intelligence Operations Center
10:03 PM

The Intelligence Operations Center, though a long day, still hummed with activity. Someone from Harrison's team manned every workstation in the open bay area. Five raids netted almost thirty suspects. US intelligence agents smiled as they went about their work. While Jake and his team took several hours to assimilate all the new information that came from the raids, Ben used Harrison's secure terminal to check email and review new drone information on Chinese naval activity.

From the moment he pulled up the newest drone photos from his classified e-mail system, Ben knew the reason for James Dudley's buoyant disposition. Jake Harrison looked over

151

his shoulder as Ben used his computer and secure telephone to speak with his contact at NGIA.

"So, what exactly am I looking at here?" Ben asked.

Harvey Walters, located in the National Geospatial-Intelligence Agency offices in Washington, ran the brief. With tensions in the area so high, Walters felt it necessary to step out of his role as a manager. "All of their line warships are in port with the remaining two destroyers on their way there," he replied. The speakerphone amplified Walter's voice for Ben and Harrison.

Ben nodded in agreement with Walter's assessment.

"Is that normal?" Jake asked.

"No," Walters and Ben replied at nearly the same time.

Ben smiled at the coincidence.

"Frankly, we can't figure it out," Walters' disembodied voice continued. "With all of the rhetoric of the last few months, we thought more ships would come out to send a message."

Ben nodded his agreement.

"So they're standing down?" Jake asked.

And that's why Dudley was almost giddy. Ben stroked his chin.

"That would be a very pleasant hope."

"But I'm not so sure," Ben finished the sentence for him. "What about the submarines?"

"Near as we can tell, they're in port, too."

"This is very odd," Ben muttered.

"You can bet the Ambassador will want to pull the fleet back," Harrison replied.

"And Dudley will be there to egg him on," Ben chimed in.

Ben pulled up the photo for Ningbo. "Where are the amphibs?" he asked. The large troop carriers and a significant amount of material previously stacked on the piers next to them were gone.

"Not sure about that either," Walters replied.

"What the hell am I paying you guys for?" Ben quipped.

"We're thinking they're at sea."

"Without a destroyer or cruiser escort? Now that really _is_ something."

"So, where does that leave us?" Jake asked.

"I don't think for one minute this is a done deal." Ben pushed himself back from the computer monitor.

"Sucker punch?" Walters asked.

"Or bad planning on somebody's part," Jake answered for him.

Michael Wong, released from the hospital and sporting a large bandage on his forehead, entered the office carrying a folder.

"What are you going to do?" the analyst asked.

"Send my recommendations to the boss. Thanks, Harvey. Have a good night," Ben replied, forgetting the time difference.

"I think you mean, good morning. Goodnight, sir."

Ben reached the phone and ended the conversation by turning off the speaker. "How're you feeling?" Ben asked Wong.

"Good. I just wish there weren't so much work to do. My head is really starting to hurt."

"I told you, go home," Jake said as Wong handed him the folder.

"Yeah, and who's going to process these photos?"

Puzzled, Ben asked. "Photos?"

"Yeah, not all the guys we arrested have records in Taiwan. So we take their photos and run them through several databases: NCIS, Interpol," Wong replied.

Jake suddenly seemed oblivious to them as he rifled through the images. One after the other, as if he were looking for someone in particular. He stopped after the eighth or ninth one and held it up. "Who the hell is this guy?"

Wong took the photo from him and examined the back. "Oh yeah. This guy got nabbed in the downtown sting. He got caught with about his weight in US currency. Odds are he's into money-laundering."

"Shit," was all Jake said as he reached into his desk drawer and pulled out his pistol. "Come on," he said to Wong.

As surprised as Ben, Wong's eyes went wide. Out of some weird combination of curiosity and instinct, Ben quickly trailed the men out the door.

***

US Navy Fighter Attack Squadron VFA-113
Embarked aboard USS RONALD REAGAN
"The Stingers"
Ready Room

Commander Jon "Easy" Ryder sat up in his ready room chair as the Carrier Air Wing Commander laid out the next few days' plans. "You guys are in the hot seat on this one. POTUS will be on the ground in Taiwan for about two and a half days," Captain Bob Wright referred to the President of the United States.

Easy glanced across the room to see the other pilots in his squadron focused on CAG as he switched on his laser pointer.

"Now what's going to make this interesting is that the carrier will be no closer than 200 nautical miles from Taipei. Some jackass doesn't want to piss off the Chinese any more than we already have."

Easy caught himself shaking his head in disbelief.

"Skipper, this is bullshit," his wingman leaned over to whisper. Lieutenant Carla "Herman" Muenster wore the same disgusted expression.

Easy nodded in agreement.

"What's interesting is that we've seen little to no aircraft or ship traffic since we got here. The Chinese Air Force, famous for Soviet-style overflights, have been MIA so far. That's no reason to get comfortable." CAG pointed at the Chinese mainland coast as he spoke. "I smell a rat."

The Stingers would have the job of flying POTUS CAP, combat air patrols to ensure the President's safety while he was on the ground in Taipei.

"Yeah, me, too," Easy said to himself aloud.

"We'll start full-cycle flight ops in the morning. Get some sleep, folks. The next few days will be long ones," CAG warned.

CHAPTER NINE
COMPROMISED

Thursday, August 14th
Zong Shan District
Taipei, Taiwan
11:55 PM

While going through Wong's unprocessed stack of suspect photographs, one face leaped at him like a boogeyman in a horror film. The face belonged to the man that Harrison quite literally bumped into outside Ciara's apartment earlier that day.

Despite his extensive training, the urge to panic invaded his mind. Memories of Afghanistan haunted him. Her life was in danger, and he had not been smart enough to realize it sooner.

Jake Harrison checked his tie as he walked into the Londoner's Nightclub and Restaurant. The booming sound of music, thick aroma of cigarettes, and a celebrating crush of people met him at the door. He closed his jacket to keep his Glock well hidden.

Jake reasoned if Pugachev and his crew didn't know who she was, they would soon. The earlier arrests that day would cause waves in the underground.

He scanned the room and quickly located four hired guns on the bottom floor. He spotted three more watching from the balcony above. Another stood guard by a door near the rear of the club.

He scanned the room for Ciara as he took a seat at the bar. Two Chinese bargirls, attractive and scantily clad, approached him. Both wore something that looked like a cross between a negligee and an evening dress, showing off their bust-lines and legs.

"Hi, Sugar Man," the taller of them greeted in heavily accented English.

Harrison smiled at them warmly, wantonly. He sat at the bar on a stool. The shorter of them gently pried his legs apart and pressed herself against him while her partner pulled his left arm around her waist.

"Hello," he said to them.

"I'm Tina, this is Misty," the one standing between his legs introduced herself.

"We thirsty. We need a drink," the other one announced.

"I'll bet you are," Jake laughed. He signaled the bartender with a raised right hand.

With the bar so crowded, Harrison considered himself lucky to have found a seat so quickly. The barkeep, a short and stocky Russian, waddled over. He raised his head in a jerky motion.

"Whatever these beautiful young ladies would like," Jake replied to his non-verbal query.

"Gin and tonic," Misty said.

"Scotch and soda," Tina added.

The silent bartender nodded and went to work on their orders.

"You handsome man," Tina said as she rubbed the inside of Harrison's leg. "And strong," she added with a grab of his left quadriceps. The other one, Misty, rubbed his shoulders with long sultry fingers.

Jake smiled again. "So, you like me, huh?"

"Yeah," Tina replied as she pressed herself even closer.

"Well, I like you girls, too," he laughed as he took a sip from his beer.

The bartender returned with their drinks. Both beverages came in highball glasses filled mostly with ice. "Seven hundred," he said gruffly. Seven hundred Taiwan Dollars equaled about $20 US.

Before Jake could dig into his pocket, the two sirens reached for and downed their drinks in one swallow. Even if he wanted to challenge the steep price, which he did not, the opportunity too quickly passed. This club and ones like it ensured their margin by serving expensive small drinks consumed by sexy women who, with a little luck and a fair amount of skill, kept the men paying until they either went broke or paid for one of them.

Jake forked over a $100 US bill. He wanted to present himself as a successful American businessman looking for something to remind him of home. The large bill communicated his status as a player with resources. The bartender's eyes went wide with surprise and excitement. He smiled.

"Get these girls a few more," Jake said loudly, with enough volume for other girls in the bar to hear.

Tina and Misty smiled, first at the bartender and then at him. Tina pressed her little body even closer. She let her hand wander higher as she caressed his thigh.

The Zhong Shan District ran through the geographic center of Taipei. Zhong Shan North Road divided the eastern and western halves of the city. Once the commercial center of Taipei, many offices shifted to the east with bars and nightclubs taking their place. Ben thought it ironic that the city's red-light district also served as the home of the Taipei Fine Arts Museum, Xian Tian Temple, and the Taipei Children's Recreation Center.

The most arresting feature and there were more than a few in this part of the city, was the use of neon. For as far as he could see in any direction, neon signs of every imaginable color, shape, and size dotted the streets. As he drove through the city with Harrison and Wong and, a three-sectioned facsimile of a belly dancer impressed him most. Anatomically correct in every important area, the sign shimmied and shook inviting patrons into her bar.

"Wish I could see what's going on in there," Ben mused from the passenger's seat of the BMW 525i.

A small receiver broadcast Harrison's voice and those of the persons standing near him. Harrison wore a small transmitter beneath the lapel of his jacket.

Wong shrugged his answer to the question. "No worries. He'll get it done," Wong said. "That's just Jake."

"You've known him a while?" Ben asked.

"Oh yeah. Almost since joining the Agency."

"I thought you were in the State Department?" Ben quipped.

Wong rolled his eyes.

Ben smiled.

Wong did not return the grin. Instead, he shifted his attention back to the streets.

"So, he's always been like this."

"Like what?" Wong replied without looking at him.

"So intense. The guy never lets up."

Wong sat quietly for a long while. As he scanned the area near the front of the club, the goings-on inside came across the receiver in varying levels of volume. Ben wondered if he should repeat the question.

"Afghanistan," Wong said softly.

"What about it?"

"He and a new agent were there on assignment, interrogating Taliban loyalists. They dropped their guard for just a second, and one of the bastards stabbed them. The prisoner attacked Jake first. He was lying on the floor, bleeding like a stuck pig when his partner died."

"Geez."

Wong let go a loud sigh. "It really fucked Jake up for a long while. Hell, a bunch of us thought he was never coming back into the field, and then, bam. Here he is."

Ben turned and looked out toward the nightclub across the street as if he could see Harrison. "So, this is his first assignment since?"

Until that moment, Wong stared out the windshield in the same direction as Ben. The question caught his attention like a hook grabs a fish. He whipped around toward Ben. "Look. Jake's fine. He's back to his old self. Okay?" Wong asked with insistence, his voice strong and inflective.

Ben's eyes met Wong's intense glare. He nodded after a long moment. *I wonder who he's trying to convince, himself or me?*

Tina, after a sixth or seventh drink, went from tentative teasing to a full assault in her caressing. Misty, now nibbling on his neck, had her hand on his chest. Twice she attempted to unbutton his shirt and twice, Jake dissuaded her with a gentle push of her hand.

"Ladies, I'm afraid you're just not what I have in mind tonight," Jake offered apologetically.

Tina pulled back a little to look him over. "What? You want three girls?"

Jake smiled at her question. The idea flashed through his mind in a second. "No, that would be a little much," he laughed.

"What then?"

"I'm looking for a White girl tonight."

"You not like Chinese?" Misty asked as he continued kissing his neck.

"Oh, yes. I like Chinese girls just fine," he said as he put his arm around her waist and pulled her closer. "It's just that I've been away from home for a long time and I miss it. I just want to talk to an American girl."

"Just talk?" Misty laughed.

"Just talk," he replied.

Tina nodded her understanding. She pulled closer to him and placed her head on his chest. "I make you forget about America. We make you forget about everything."

Jake made his body go taught with seriousness. Tina immediately brought her face up to his. She frowned for a long second before letting it slowly evolve into a smile. She's good. A pro. If she can't make any money for the house, she'll make sure someone else does.

"You come back and see Tina and Misty some other night? Okay?"

Jake nodded as he leaned toward and kissed her on the cheek. He caught a whiff of her perfume and the name finally came to him, "Versace". She wore it well.

"I have someone for you," Tina said. "Okay? You stay here with Misty, okay?"

"Okay," Jake laughed. "A Russian girl?"

She frowned suddenly. "I thought you said you homesick? You not from Russia; you from America. Right?"

"That's right. You have an American girl here?"

"We have hot American girl. She make you very happy," Misty added. "She good talker."

They both laughed. "That's all she do... Talk, talk, talk," Misty laughed.

Jake smiled politely.

"You stay right here," Tina ordered.

Jake nodded. "I'll stay here."

Tina turned and disappeared into the crowd. Misty stopped nibbling on him and moved around in front. At first, Jake thought she was taking Tina's place. Rather, she reached for and gulped down the remainder of Tina's scotch and tonic water.

"You want another one?" Jake offered.

"Uh-huh," she nodded with a large grin. Her eyes crossed just a little as she had responded.

Jake studied her with a scrupulous gaze. Her balance fell off just a tad as she stood there. Misty, after six drinks, still stood... but not by a lot.

Jake signaled the bartender. Until now, he greeted Jake with a cheery smile when taking orders. This time, he also studied Misty. His smile diminished ever so slightly. When he came over, the smile almost disappeared completely.

He shouted something at her in Russian and Misty's bubbly disposition instantly evaporated. Her eyes grew wide with anxiety, and her body went taut. She turned toward Jake, bowed from the shoulders, and said, "Excuse me. I must be going."

Jake nodded in response. Getting drunk at work was a no-no. Her job was to get the patrons drunk. He guessed her next set of tasks included downing some water, coffee, and probably taking a shower.

Misty stumbled as she moved away from the bar. She disappeared from view as Tina reemerged with Ciara in tow. The shorter Asian woman pulled her colleague along by the hand.

Jackpot.

Her eyes went wide with surprise at seeing him. Jake casually shook his head at her. They had to play it cool.

"Sugar Man," Tina said with a laugh. "This is my friend Sierra."

"Sierra?" Jake asked. "Like the mountains?"

"Ciara," she corrected him. "C-I-A-R-A," she spelled it for him. "Your name isn't really 'Sugar Man' is it?" she smiled with red and full lips.

Jake studied her face for a long while before answering. "Jake," he replied. She gets it.

She extended her hand. He took it and brought it to his mouth and kissed it gently.

"Tina, you have brought me to a gentleman," Ciara laughed.

"And don't you forget that he's really my gentleman," Tina quipped. She leaned toward Jake and kissed him on his mouth. "You come back to see me after you not homesick," she ordered.

"Okay," Jake replied with a smile and a wink.

Tina turned, frowned at Ciara, and walked away. Jake did not wait until she disappeared into the crowd before shifting his attention to Ciara.

"What are you doing here?" she asked in a whisper.

"I think they know who you are. And if they don't, they will soon."

"What?! How!?"

"That's not important now. Just get up and follow me out."

"No, that won't work. We gotta make this look good," she replied.

"What?"

"So, I understand you're looking for a little company?" Her focus was sharp, laser-like.

He finally responded, "Yeah, I'm missing home."

She placed her hand on his forearm and gently caressed it. "Well, we'll have to take care of that," she smiled a coquettish grin. Her West Texas accent fell on him like icing on a cake.

"So, you want to get out of here?" Jake asked.

"Yes."

Jake called for the bartender. When the man arrived, he paid for the rest of Misty and Tina's drinks and tossed in another TWD 1500 to cover Ciara's bar fine.

Ciara took him by the hand and led him through the crowd of other dancing and partying patrons. Rather than go around the dance floor, she led him almost directly across it toward the club's front door.

"We should be out in a few minutes," Jake's voice said over the speaker.

Ben sat up in his seat as Wong started the vehicle.

"Michael?" Ben asked

"Yeah?"

"How do you guys get such nice cars? They gave me a piece of shit."

Wong chuckled at the question.

Ben leered at the console and leather seats. He openly coveted the vehicle in which he sat.

Alexi Pugachev wolfed down his meal of Asian noodles and clams. He tossed a newly emptied shell on a stack that easily numbered thirty or more. His jowls bulged from the shellfish and noodles as he added a sip of beer to the mix. He chewed a few bites before taking a second swig. As soon as his mouth was clear, he filled it with another fork-full of noodles. When a few of them did not make it completely into his mouth, he sucked them the rest of the way.

His mobile telephone rang just as he reached for another clam. He glanced up to see his bodyguards a short distance away, keeping vigil on him by watching the dance floor and dining area below. He picked up the device without bothering to wipe his hands or clear his mouth. He frowned at the Caller ID display. "What?" The food in his mouth muffling his voice.

"I thought you would like to know that some horny American just came in and bought one of the girls for a whole week," Vladimir's raspy voice barked into the phone.

"Is that right? That's certainly interesting but not worth interrupting my dinner," Alexi snapped as he ended the connection. He replaced the phone on the table with authority and took another drink from his beer bottle.

"Fat old son-of-a-bitch," he said to himself as he went back to his dinner.

"Hey, Boss?" Petrov called out from his station at the edge of the balcony.

"What?" he replied through another mouthful of food.

"Ciara's got herself a high-roller," Petrov said.

"What is the big deal? So she's got herself a big fat horny asshole. So what?"

"He's not fat, Boss," Petrov replied.

"So he's old."

"He's not old either."

Alexi scowled as he remembered vague warnings about the American hostess. His curiosity mounted and eventually got the best of him. He grabbed his beer bottle and climbed to his feet. Alexi Pugachev covered the meter and a half between his table and the balcony rail in four big steps. "Where is she?" he asked with his arrival.

"Over there, near the bar."

Alexi trained his eyes toward the front part of his club. He spied Ciara first and then her new acquaintance. Though he led the way, the man moved with confidence and purpose. A knot grew in his stomach. He knew the man's face—American CIA.

"Get down there. Stop them."

"What?" Petrov replied with breathless surprise.

"Move, damn you!" Alexi shouted as he shoved the larger man.

The bulky man's eyes widened as he stumbled to regain his balance. He turned and headed down the staircase to the floor below.

Alexi kept his focus fixed on the pair until they disappeared from his view. He turned and walked back to the table and his phone.

The rear passenger door opened, and a red-haired woman piled into the darkened vehicle. Ben, usually too polite to stare, could not take his eyes away from her. Perhaps it was the gold, form-fitting silk dress, or her radiant face. Ben concluded Jake failed to describe her because he did not have the words to do so.

"Wait," a male voice called as Harrison was about to close the door. Ben whipped around to see a tall, muscular white man coming out of the club door toward them.

"Yeah?" Jake replied.

"My boss wants to see you."

Ben and the man delaying their departure exchanged glances through the passenger side window.

"I don't think so," Jake said with ease. He nodded at Wong, and his partner floored the accelerator.

The man reached for the door but missed. Tires squealed against the pavement as the car pulled away in a cloud of smoke.

Jake closed the door as the car gathered speed. "Go, Michael, go!" Jake ordered.

Wong pressed on, making his way down the street, occasionally swerving to avoid slower-moving vehicles, and pedestrians.

Ben finally turned in his seat toward the rear of the vehicle. Lights from a car behind them simultaneously blinded him and illuminated his face.

"Hi. What's your name?" she asked.

"I'm Ben."

They reached across the seat and shook hands.

"Get us to the Embassy," Jake said to Wong. "Fast."

"Got it," the younger agent replied.

"The Embassy?" Ciara asked. "Why are you taking me there?"

"You'll be safe there. They know where you live, too," Jake almost whispered as he spoke.

"We've got company," Wong announced from the driver's seat as he peered into the rear-view mirror.

Ben, Jake, and Ciara turned to look through the rear window at the large black sedan moving up their left side.

While not as congested as mid-day, more than a few scooters, motorcycles, and vehicles dotted the streets. Wong zigzagged his way around with expert skill. In some cases, only inches separated them from safe-passage and collision. Ben cinched his seat and shoulder belt tighter.

Their pursuers pulled alongside on the left. Ben glanced at the speedometer to see the needle pushing past 150 kilometers per hour. He looked back up in time to see a large white man hanging out of the passenger window gesturing toward the right side of the road.

"I think he wants us to stop," Wong laughed.

"Yeah, well tell him hello," Jake replied.

Wong gave the man the finger and pressed the accelerator. Their car lunged ahead.

Ben winced. This BMW was fast. Ben knew it well as his civilian boss, John Castlebury, owned the same model. However, the Russians drove a Benz E55. Bigger, faster, and more powerful, Ben knew the bad guy's car could eat their lunch. "We're not going to outrun these guys," he said to Wong and Harrison.

Before either of them could respond, the Mercedes dove toward and slammed into them. Their car jumped a foot or so but kept its footing.

"I know!" Wong snapped.

When they pulled away and back to the left, Wong returned the maneuver, ramming the Russians. It felt like they tried to nudge a mountain. The larger vehicle hardly moved. Wong kept the car against them. Tires screamed in protest as smoke billowed behind the two vehicles. Ben found himself bracing with his legs and freehand.

A large white van loomed ahead. Moving at a much slower pace, it favored the left side of the one-way street. Wong alternatively shifted his gaze from the demolition derby to the vehicle in front of them. In the backseat, both Harrison and Ciara transfixed on the black sedan and its occupants.

The distance to the van closed quickly. The Russians, not completely consumed in the vehicular shoving match, must have noticed it too. They began pushing back by turning into them. Wong surprised Ben and held firm. The Russians turned away for just a second and then back toward them with teeth-jarring ferocity. Still, the BMW held its place on the road. Wong managed to time his course corrections with theirs by turning into them at just the right moment.

The van came up quickly. At the last second, the big black sedan slammed on its brakes, but too late. They rear-ended the vehicle in a fiery crash as Wong tore to the right and away from the scene. Before he could hit the gas, two motor scooters got in their way. Rather than wait for them, he jerked the wheel again and sent them onto the sidewalk.

"Shit!" Ben shouted.

Screaming pedestrians dove out of the way as the automobile bulldozed down the sidewalk. A street vendor's cart of watermelons, pineapples, and bananas exploded as a result. Wong stayed on the smaller thoroughfare long enough to get past the dawdling scooters. As soon as he could, he careened back into the street. Once there, he floored the accelerator.

"Nice job--now get us out of here," Harrison ordered.

A second later, the sound of shattering auto glass filled the air. Ben looked behind to see the blown-out remnants of the rear window. Beyond the end of the car, the black sedan weaved back and forth as the same man leaned out the passenger window with a machine gun. The unmistakable rapid thumps of automatic weapons fire knifed the night air. A portion of the dashboard in front of him exploded in a cloud of black plastic and leather.

Ben went breathless at the sight and sound. He wanted to cower behind the seat but knew it would do no good. The seats, while among the most comfortable in the world, were not known for their ability to withstand bullets. He reached for the pistol in the holster beneath his arm.

"Get down!" Harrison shouted to Ciara.

The woman, wide-eyed in terror, instantly followed his order.

Harrison, his weapon already up, aimed out the back window and fired. Ben, his weapon now out of its holster, could not get a clear shot off for fear of hitting Harrison.

The Russians turned to the left again, giving them a clear shot for a moment. The gangster let go of a burst as Harrison took what cover he could below the trunk line of the vehicle. Ben, still looking to the rear, followed Harrison's lead as best he could in the confined space.

The sound of several rounds hitting the car interior reminded Ben of popcorn in a metal pan. Sparks flew as bullets impacted metal. The sound of the vehicle engine declined as Ben felt a warm sensation on his neck and face.

He looked up from the floorboard to find himself covered in a red fluid. He first checked himself. No wounds.

Horror replaced confusion as he looked to his left. Michael Wong slumped to his left as half of his skull fell open. Ben gagged as he fought the urge to throw up. The sensation of the vehicle slowing, and the sound of Jake shouting woke him from a daze.

"McGuire! Grab the wheel! McGuire! Wake the fuck up! Grab the wheel!"

Ben felt as if he moved in molasses. He forced himself to turn back to the front of the car. He reached for the wheel with his left hand. Wong's hand was still pulling the vehicle to the left. Ben stretched the rest of the way across the console and knocked it loose as he pulled the vehicle back into the center of the street.

"We're slowing down!" Jake shouted.

Ben nodded as he removed his seatbelt and climbed part of the way over the center section of the car and pushed the dead man's limp appendage away from the floor controls. Ben jammed his left foot against the accelerator, and they picked up speed.

The sound of Jake firing at the Russians, the slippery-with-blood steering wheel, and the dead body pressing against him finally overloaded Ben's brain. He regurgitated his lunch in one large retch.

The firing from the other vehicle stopped, at least for the moment. "What are they doing? Why'd they stop shooting?" Ben yelled.

"Reloading! Turn up there!" Jake shouted.

"Where?" Ben used his shoulder to wipe his mouth.

"There!"

Ben noticed an alley coming up quickly.

Is he nuts? I can't make that!

"Turn, damn it! Turn now!"

Ben jerked the wheel as he reached between his legs and pulled the handbrake. The battered BMW groaned as it twisted toward the side street. Again, the sound of squealing rubber filled the air, a welcome change over the gunfire. The auto careened off the building's stone wall in a shower of sparks and the sound of grinding metal.

The Russians tried to negotiate the turn, too, but could not. Ben snuck a glance in a bullet-battered rearview mirror. Their vehicle, much larger and with more momentum, sailed by with screeching tires. Smoke billowed behind them.

The alley was full of garbage. Ben floored the accelerator, smashing anything in his way. Crates, garbage cans, and a parked motorcycle all fell victim to the charging vehicle's front end. A cross street and the end of the alley loomed ahead.

The glare from unseen streetlights gave the image of the light at the end of a long tunnel. Ben focused on driving the car and tried to ignore Wong's cooling body.

"Is he...dead?" Ciara asked.

No one answered.

"Stop at the end of the alley," Jake said quietly, almost as if he were praying.

Ben could not believe what he had just heard. "What?"

"Stop at the street," Jake said again.

This time Ben turned around in his makeshift seat.

Jake nodded. His eyes were as cold and lifeless as Wong's body. He was deadly serious.

Ben braked and brought the vehicle to a noisy stop. The nose of the car poked from between the two buildings guarding the alley, giving him a clear vision of the street. As soon as the car stopped, Jake hopped out and went around to the rear of the vehicle.

Ben dislodged himself from his awkward position and climbed out the passenger side as Jake opened the trunk. Ben watched as he eyed Wong's body for a moment on his way toward the street.

Harrison emerged from the vehicle rear with a long black case with him. Ben could tell from the way it hung at the end of the government agent's arm that it held significant weight.

"What's that?" Ben asked. About four feet long, the handle at the midpoint allowed Harrison to handle it with relative ease. He placed the case on the ground as he reached the street.

Jake did not reply. His face took a stone-like façade to match the deadness in his eyes. Rather, he opened the black case and extracted an olive-green tubular-shaped device. Ben instantly recognized it as an M72 Light Anti-Tank Weapon rocket launcher.

The sound of the car door opening pulled Ben's attention back to the vehicle. Ciara was halfway out of the car and showed no intention of slowing her exit. "Get back in!" he ordered.

Her eyes, already wide with excitement and fear, opened wider still. Her mouth dropped open to make her face the picture of shock and dismay. She instantly halted her progress and edged back into the darkened vehicle.

"Close the door."

Again, she did as he commanded.

Ben returned his attention to Harrison as he placed the weapon on his right shoulder and keyed a couple of buttons on the handset. He stood as the sound of an approaching vehicle pulled their attention to the right and up the street.

The Russian's sedan made the turn toward them and gunned its engine as it increased speed. The same shooter's thick head came into view as he hung out of the passenger window and leveled his machine gun in their direction.

Jake pulled the device's scope to his right eye and pointed at the advancing car. Ben estimated the car sped toward them at over 80 MPH covering thirty yards in seconds.

As the sound of the Russian gunman firing the machine gun reached their ears, the green tube on Jake's shoulder belched flames. A black object darted from the tube and toward the car. A split-second later, the advancing automobile exploded. The sound and accompanying shockwave knocked Ben backward, almost off-balance. The battered but beautiful luxury automobile morphed into an airborne blob of molten metal and flames. The vehicle's momentum continued to carry it forward for a few more yards.

Jake watched as the flaming mass came to rest on the far side of the street as if he were watching a boring movie. Ben, ready to breathe a sigh of relief, watched Harrison drop the spent launcher, pull out his pistol and march up the street.

As Harrison neared his destination, Ben realized someone had been ejected from the car. Ben moved away from their battered BMW to get a clearer view of a man's twisted and bloody body on the right side of the street.

As Jake advanced on his position, he pointed his pistol at him.

"Poor bastard," Ben said to himself when he caught a glimpse of the injured man's head.

Jake came to a stop, pulled back the slide on the automatic pistol, and fired. The sound of the pistol expelling four rounds cut through that of the burning vehicle a few yards away.

Jake turned and walked back toward him. He put the weapon's safety back on and slipped it into his holster. "Let's go," he said as he arrived.

Ben instantly remembered Senkaku Island and catching up with Dr. Deitrich after the traitor shot one of his men. Only the presence of the Chinese Navy and their imminent invasion of the island kept Ben from acting similarly.

Ben looked over his shoulder to see Ciara's face. She looked stunned, as if in a state of shock.

"Come on. I need your help, please. We need to put Michael in the trunk," Harrison asked.

Ben frowned as the tone of his voice sank in. He asked, not ordered. Ben nodded, realizing he just heard Harrison use the word "please" for the first time since their meeting.

CHAPTER TEN
THE LIMELIGHT

Friday, August 15th
USS Princeton *(CG-59)*
Northern Taiwan Straits, Steaming in company with:
USS William P. Lawrence *(DDG-110) &*
USS John Paul Jones *(DDG-53)*
0100 Hours

The *Princeton* crew knew Lieutenant Commander Paul Daniels' habit of roaming his ship in the dead of night all too well. One of his junior officers once quizzed him about it, asking whether he trusted them or not. In response, Daniels quoted President Ronald Reagan, "Trust but verify, and don't be afraid to see what you see."

No one ever knew where he would show up: Engineering Control, Combat Information Center, Crew's Galley, or the Bridge. Since his meeting with Captain Nation, Daniels found sleeping difficult. Rather than his usual hour or so, the nocturnal tours took almost three. Daniels considered it a key part of being a good Executive Officer.

Near-complete darkness engulfed the bridge as he entered from the ladder passageway, the bridge instruments giving off small pinpoints of red, green, or blue light. The watch team masked the other instruments and any producers of white light to minimize the effect on their night vision. Daniels squinted as he looked around. The watch team and their equipment appeared as shapeless figures in the darkness.

"The XO is on the Bridge," the Boatswain's Mate of the Watch announced in a quiet, but just loud enough voice.

"Good evening, sir," Lieutenant Jefferson, the OOD, greeted him.

"Good morning," Daniels replied, correcting him. "How's the watch?"

"Quiet, sir. Like a graveyard."

Daniels nodded in the darkness making his way to stand adjacent to the radarscope between the OOD and his assistant, the Junior Officer of the Deck, or JOOD. Both officers, dressed in the camouflage Navy Working Uniform, wore the ship's baseball cap with binoculars draped around their necks. Ensign Hansen, only a few months out of college, was the JOOD tonight. He pulled his binoculars up to his eyes as Daniels arrived.

"Good, let's keep it that way," Daniels finally responded.

He examined the radar picture and compared it to the plot he had just seen in the Combat Information Center. Everything synched. Good.

"Mister Hansen," Paul greeted.

"Good morning, sir."

"Mr. Hansen, what is your primary contact of interest?"

"Sir, I have one contact, SKUNK Uniform," the officer replied using the naval acronym for an unidentified surface radar contact. He lowered his binoculars and pointed at an echo on the surface search radarscope with his right index finger. "It has a slow but steady right bearing drift. It should pass us on our starboard quarter at a range of about six miles." A grease-pencil line gave evidence that Jefferson and Hansen were closely monitoring the contact's progress.

"All the others are past CPA and opening. No threat, sir," he replied, referring to their closest point of approach.

"What's our screen station?"

"Sir, we are to be between a bearing of 010 and 060 True, and between four and ten miles from *William P. Lawrence*."

"Very well, Mr. Hansen. I'm comfortable that you won't kill me tonight. Carry on," Paul replied with a smile.

Hansen had promise. Daniels, just for a moment, let himself wonder how well the young officer would develop after his departure.

"OOD, I'm gonna go have a cigar out on the bridge wing."

"Aye, sir," LT Jefferson replied.

Daniels turned toward the port side of the space and the door that led to the open area adjacent to the Pilot House. "How are you guys tonight?" he asked as he passed the enlisted watch team members.

"Great, sir. Fine Navy evening," the Boatswain replied.

The others gave similar responses.

Daniels smiled as he zipped his jacket closed.

He opened the door and stepped out into the cold night air. He guessed the temperature was no more than fifty degrees. His breath fogged momentarily before the wind blew it away. Daniels made his way to the port bridge wing and climbed into the Captain's Chair. As the Executive Officer, he had Nation's permission to usurp the privilege of using her chairs, provided she was not doing so.

A full moon cast everything around him in dull gray light. A few stars filled a cloudless sky. The sounds of jet aircraft in the sky occasionally interrupted the wind whistling through some of the standing equipment around him. He reached into his right pocket and pulled out his gloves. Rather than put them on, he placed them on his lap.

He reached into his left pocket, withdrew a Partagas maduro and his cigar torch. After a pull on the torch trigger, the cigar lighter threw a powerful half-inch high flame. Daniels held it against the cigar, rotating them both until the tip glowed uniformly red. He shut off the lighter, pulled the stogie to his mouth, and took three powerful drags. Daniels put the lighter away and pulled on his gloves, reclining in the chair. He closed his eyes for a moment as he longed for the taste of scotch whiskey. The breeze quickly carried away his exhaled smoke.

"Sir, you told me you were going to quit smoking those," he heard Juanita Juarez' voice from behind him.

Daniels smiled. He took another drag from the cigar, pulled it from his mouth to knock off some ash. He made a point of not turning to face her. "You really shouldn't sneak up on me. It could be dangerous," he replied. He placed the cigar back into his mouth.

He heard her footfalls as she came around and into view.

"You didn't answer the question, sir."

"Was that a question?" Daniels asked. "It sounded like a statement to me."

Juarez shook her head as she frowned at him.

Daniels brought his gaze to meet hers. They stared into each other's eyes for a long while. Daniels was first to look away. When he did, he turned toward the lights of one of the Aegis destroyers sailing with them some six miles away. USS *John Paul Jones* was recovering aircraft. Another helicopter passing overhead pulled his attention upward. Daniels followed it until it disappeared into the night sky.

"There's a rumor running around the ship," she said plainly.

"There are lots of rumors running around this ship," he said with feigned laughter.

"So, is it true? You did request a transfer?" she asked.

Daniels used his free hand to open the pocket of his jacket. He dug for and retrieved the small box. Once he had it, he pulled the cigar from his mouth and sat up.

"Nita," he began. "I'm a fool."

She frowned. "I don't understand," she almost whispered.

"I'm sorry. I think I may have killed my career and yours. I honestly thought I could keep how I felt about you to myself."

"You have never had a poker-face, at least not in the time I've known you."

He nodded in agreement. Daniels pulled the cigar back to his mouth. "It would appear that this ship is not big enough for both of us."

"I'm sorry, Paul. I know how much you love this."

"So, what now?"

"Now, I hope the Captain gives me a good FITREP, and I move on. Hopefully to another ship. If that doesn't work, I can make some serious money. I've already gotten a job offer from the company that makes our weapons system."

She nodded. He looked up to see her gazing off into the distant darkness. "And us?"

He sighed. "How I feel hasn't changed. But while we're on this ship--" he paused. "While we're on this ship, we are not a 'we.'"

"I'm getting tired of this, you know?"

"What do you want from me? I'm the XO of this ship. Even this conversation is wrong," he protested. He heard the irritation in his voice.

"I," she began. "I should have never taken orders to this ship."

He sat up in the chair. "No, I should have turned them down. I had more latitude than you."

Silence.

"Look. I'll be out of here in a few weeks. This will all blow over," Daniels mumbled.

"And I'll have to deal with the CO. She'll be pissed because I cost her a good XO."

"No. Nation's not like that. I think she gets it."

Juarez took in a deep breath and let it out. "I'm glad you have more faith in her than I do." She turned and walked away.

"JJ," he called after her quietly. But she kept moving.

Daniels slowly returned to his cigar and watching the sea.

***

US Embassy
Taipei, Taiwan
4:45 AM

When Ben, Jake, and Ciara arrived with Wong's body, the Marine guard was ready. Two camouflage-clad enlisted men helped remove Agent Wong's body from the car and another escorted Ciara Edwards to an interview room. A few moments later, the first Marine returned and presented Ben with a khaki shirt and a pair of their serge-green trousers.

When he returned from a quick shower and a change of clothing, he found a single armed Marine standing guard outside the interview room door. Jake Harrison stood in front of a plate-glass window, his arms crossed, wearing a contemplative frown. Ben went over to him and spied Ciara sitting alone at a long white table.

"Has she said anything?" Ben asked Jake.

"No. Not a word."

He nodded.

Jake winced as he held the edge of a file folder to his mouth.

Ben's gaze flashed to the folder in Jake's left hand. "What's that?"

"A file on Alexi Pugachev," Jake replied. "Ben, we need to chat," Jake said softly as he looked around to ensure their privacy.

"Yeah?"

"Ciara, she's not just a contract agent," he said as if he were confessing to a crime.

Ben, confused, caught himself frowning.

"She's more than just a contract agent," Jake added. He brought his gaze even with Ben's.

"Oh," Ben replied as he realized their status. "Is this serious?"

Jake sighed. "You know if anyone but you had asked me that on any other day, I think I could have said 'no.' But, it's not just any other day."

Ben nodded. "So what are we doing here?"

"Finding Alexi Pugachev. She's been undercover in his club for months."

Ben nodded before he turned to walk into the room. He stopped short of turning the knob when he felt Jake's hand on his arm.

"Are we cool?" Jake asked.

Ben raised his eyebrow in confusion. "What? What are you talking about?"

"Am I going to have to worry about you filing a report on me?"

Ben stared back at him for a long while before answering. "Wong and I talked about Afghanistan."

Jake's eyebrows went up.

"He was a good guy. And he didn't have to die so young," Ben added. He took a long, hard stare at Jake. "About tonight... I don't know what you're talking about."

Jake gaped back for a minute before he nodded.

Ben turned and opened the door to the interview room.

The unremarkable room featured banks of fluorescent light tubes that cast it in harsh white light. The light color complimented a beige table, walls, and floor. A black multi-line telephone on the far end of the table away from the door stood out as the only dark object in the room.

Ciara's green eyes came up to greet Jake's as they entered the room. She looked small and frail, not like the bawdy young woman who bounded into their vehicle earlier that night. Jake closed the door behind them as Ben moved to an empty chair on the opposite side of the table from her.

She stood and ran into Jake's arms. Ben almost felt embarrassed at being there. He did his best to look away.

"You're okay," Jake said.

"I can't believe they killed your friend," she replied as tears rolled down her face. "That was terrible!"

"I need some information from you. I need you to get a grip," Jake said as he pulled her face up to his. "Can you help us?"

She nodded as Jake walked her over to an open chair.

Jake sat on the edge of the table rather than take the last chair. "Alexi's in the wind," he started. "We've had people watching his house and his cottage out in the country. He hasn't shown. Any ideas where he could be?"

She shook her head. "No. I'm sorry, I don't. Have you checked all his clubs?"

"Yeah," he replied as he eased into a chair.

"Shit."

"He's got warehouses all over town. You know that," she explained.

Jake nodded with reluctance.

"Have there been any new faces around this week?" Ben asked.

"No, same old crew."

Ben hoped for something else, but it was what it was. They were running into a dead-end.

She took a deep breath and sighed. "You got a cigarette?"

"Sorry, there's no smoking in here," Ben replied.

"Have you seen any of these people?" he opened a file folder and spread several color images of Asian and Caucasian men in front of her.

Ciara carefully scanned each of the photographs. When she reached the third man, her eyes went wide.

"Something?" Jake asked.

"Yeah. This guy was hanging out in the club a few days ago." The man was Asian, probably in his late thirties.

"Who is he?" Ben asked Jake.

"Song Fann. He's a Chinese Military Intelligence officer," Jake said plainly. "Damn. He's definitely here."

"So?"

Jake started to pace, brought his hand to his chin. "So, that means these guys are definitely up to something." He came back to the table and stared at the photograph. "Where the hell are you?" he asked Song's image.

"What was he doing at the club?" Ben asked Ciara.

"He rented property from Alexi."

"Property. What property?"

"He owns a townhouse down by the waterfront in Keelung."

Jake grabbed the file and rifled through it to find Alexi Pugachev's property listing. He scanned the list with his finger twice. "There's no waterfront townhouse here."

"Sorry, but he has one," she replied with certainty.

Jake stood. "We've gotta get going." Jake pulled out his mobile telephone and began dialing.

"Ok," Ben said as he stood.

"This is Jake," he said into the phone. "I have a location. We're going to check it out."

***

Keelung District
Taipei, Taiwan
5:20 AM

Clad in a Marine Corps-issue khaki shirt and green trousers, Ben rode in the passenger seat, this time in a blue and white bread truck. Jake Harrison drove this time. Back at the consulate, Ben watched in awe as the senior CIA agent wielded his influence to commandeer the bakery delivery vehicle. Ciara

182

stood in the space between the two seats. She gave verbal directions to get them across town from the embassy to a modern and upscale area sitting against the Straits of the Taiwan coastline.

As they drove east, Ben caught glimpses of the dark seascape and spots of light from the ships at anchor or those in passing. Sunrise still an hour or so away, blue hues began pushing away the black sky. The rooftops of businesses and apartment homes still resembled dark boxes more than architecturally pleasing shapes.

"Turn right at the next intersection," Ciara instructed.

"How far after that?"

"Less than a block. The apartment is down on the right. Why?"

Harrison nodded and then slowed the vehicle. The last turn loomed ahead. He made the turn slowly and stopped at the top of the street. An empty parking spot beckoned. Harrison pulled the vehicle into it and parked. He left the engine at idle.

"What are you doing?" Ben asked.

He selected a parking place at the top of a hill that provided an elevated view of the street down to the waterfront. Due to the severity of the incline, Ben felt as if he might fall out of his seat.

"Well, if the Russians are there, it wouldn't make any sense to drive up right in front of them, would it?"

"Ah, the sarcastic edge that I've grown to love," Ben quipped.

Harrison smiled.

Ben laughed as he turned his attention to the street in front and below. Ciara, still wearing her evening dress, came to the front part of the vehicle and squeezed herself onto the seat with Ben.

"Which one?" Jake asked her.

"Third one on the right."

Ben leveled his focus on an empty driveway about seventy-five yards away. The street looked as sleepy as the rest of the neighborhood. A barking dog cracked the silence. Ben estimated, from the echo, the animal called out from streets away.

He studied the apartment building. At an awkward angle, he only made out one lighted window. From this vantage point, he found it impossible to see any others. "Looks quiet enough," Ben said.

"Yeah." Harrison scanned the street in silence for a long moment.

"What are you thinking?" Ben finally asked.

"That we should take a look. C'mon," he said as he went to open the door.

Just as the vehicle's door came open, the sound of approaching vehicles reached his ears. "Wait!"

Harrison and Ben quickly pulled their doors shut and slunk down in their seats. Ciara squatted below the dashboard level until the last of three dark sedans went by.

All three cars, though black in color, represented different BMW models. As the vehicles came to a stop in front of Alexi's bayside abode, the three observers peeked over the dashboard. Jake shut off the engine.

Four men poured out of the first vehicle. Even in the morning light and from a distance of thirty yards, Ben easily saw the sub-machine guns slung around their bodies. The first four guys guarded the lower reaches of the street. Two more men climbed out of the car nearest them. Just like the first group, they pulled out pistols and pointed them towards the top of the hill.

"Get down." Jake slouched in the chair as to not draw their attention.

Following his lead, Ben and Ciara took on similar postures. One of the guards moved toward the truck, and Ben thought his heart might leap from his chest. The man stopped just a few feet from them to examine a car. All three breathed a collective sigh of relief, as the guard looked the vehicle over and turned back to rejoin his partner.

"That's Alexi," Ciara whispered. She pointed at a stocky blonde man getting out of the middle vehicle's back seat.

Alexi looked fit. He almost marched rather than walk as he exited his vehicle for the apartment. His guards followed him toward the front door as their boss went inside.

They scanned the group of armed men for the elusive Chinese Intelligence officer.

"Damn it. No Song Fann. He's not with them."

Ben watched in wide-eyed concern as Jake pulled his pistol from its holster and flipped off the safety. "What are you doing?"

Jake didn't respond. His entire body looked like a flexed muscle. His attention seemed fixated on the squad of well-armed Russians just yards away.

Ben glanced away from Jake for a moment then back. "Listen, man. We need help to take on this many. I know you want Pugachev to pay for killing Wong, but you might get us killed in the process. You might get her killed in the process."

Jake kept staring at the Russians. After a long moment, the tension in his face eased. He finally brought his gaze to meet Ben's, then Ciara's. He nodded his concurrence with Ben's admonition.

Ben gave a half-smile. "So, what's the new plan, Boss?"

Harrison returned his gaze to the street. The sky was much lighter now. Venus stood out in a dark blue sky.

"Is this truck going to keep us hidden for much longer?" Ben worried.

"I think we'll be ok. Bread trucks make deliveries all over the place in the mornings here. We'll follow him until he settles. Then we call in for backup. Okay?"

Ben nodded. "Okay."

The entourage emerged from the apartment driveway. The two rear guards fanned out toward them and their truck. Ciara moved into the vehicle's rear area. Ben and Harrison kneeled at the dashboard and watched as Alexi came out of the building. One of his guards carried a couple of suitcases that he loaded into the middle car. As soon as the middle car's last door shut, the other men piled back into their respective vehicles.

Harrison started the van's engine from his concealment. He climbed into his seat as the convoy pulled away. Ben made his way back to his place in the passenger's seat as Harrison slammed the truck into gear and pulled into the street. He kept the headlights off as he pulled away from the curb to follow the Russians.

Ben laughed. "So, we're following Russian gangsters and Chinese spies in a bread truck? No one is ever going to believe this."

"That's ok. You won't be able to tell anyone about it anyway. This is classified." Jake shot back with a grin.

Harrison hung back almost a full block. When the convoy of sedans turned left, Jake floored the accelerator to get to the intersection as quickly as possible. When he made the turn, Jake handled the vehicle as if he were carrying a cargo of eggs. This thoroughfare ran along the waterfront.

Ben spotted the vehicles ahead of them suddenly slow and turn right.

"Where are they going?" Harrison asked Ciara.

"Don't know," Ciara replied.

Harrison pulled the vehicle over to the right and parked it. As soon as Jake set the brake, he hopped out the driver's side. Ben climbed out his side of the van. "You stay here," he said to Ciara as she prepared to join him.

"What? Why?" she asked.

"Too dangerous. You stay here."

"No way." She continued exiting the truck.

Harrison trotted away toward the small alley where the sedans turned. Ben wanted to shout, "Wait!" However, they were too far away and the risk too great.

"Come on," he said in a burdened manner.

Ben jogged after Harrison. Ciara Edwards yanked off her high-heels and ran barefoot to catch the two men.

Harrison reached the corner and peered around it. Rather than give the bad guys two targets, Ben waited until Harrison pulled back around. "They're down at the pier," he reported.

"Shit."

"Yeah," Harrison agreed.

Harrison looked past Ben and Ciara and toward the building behind which they hid. He blew past Ben and Ciara to a gate.

Harrison gestured with his head for them to follow. Once again, Ciara moved first. Ben gently closed the tattered door behind them.

Light, what there was of it, streamed in through partially broken windowpanes of a large warehouse. Crates of varying sizes lay in uneven stacks all around them. Last to enter, Ben looked over to see Harrison and Ciara climbing a scaffold-style stairwell to a higher floor. He made his way as best he could in the darkened space, wondering how they could have gotten away from him so quickly.

By the time he reached them, they were on the top level of the facility looking out of the corner of a window. "Damn it," Harrison spat.

"What?"

Ben did not wait for him to respond. Rather, he ignored safety and common sense by going to stand in front of the window. Dirty, the glass had an almost translucent quality. Ben hoped that it would only be the by greatest of chances that the men standing on the dock would look up to see him.

Alexi and one of his men stood at the end of a long pier. An elegant and shiny black motorboat rumbled to a stop in front of them. The guard jumped in first. Alexi Pugachev handed him the suitcases and climbed in afterwards. As soon as he was aboard, the boat backed out, turned for the harbor, and accelerated away.

"Son of a bitch." Jake hit his leg with a fist.

"Any ideas where he's going?" Ben asked Ciara.

Curiosity got the best of her, too. She stood with him in the window, observing the happenings below.

"No. I didn't even know Alexi had a boat," she replied.

They continued watching the small craft's progress. It traveled in almost a straight line. Ben mentally estimated the boat's speed—about ten knots. As the boat moved further into the channel, it slowed to negotiate waves. Small whitecaps formed further out in the channel.

The boat suddenly turned left toward a large and anchored yacht. Almost a mile away now, the small boat approached an accommodation ladder and stopped. Someone jumped out onto the pitching platform and tied off the boat. A few seconds later, another man assisted Pugachev out of the boat and up the stairs. The three watched until Pugachev boarded the craft and disappeared below decks.

"What now?" Ben asked.

Harrison looked at his watch. He finally took a seat on the warehouse's dirty floor. He motioned for Ben and Ciara to do likewise. Harrison pulled out his mobile telephone and dialed. "Patch me through to the NRO Liaison," he said a few moments later.

Ben, hungry and tired, still had enough of his faculties to realize his partner in this adventure was on the phone with the "Home Office." He watched silently.

"Triangulate on my position," Harrison said to someone on the other end of the connection. He looked at Ben. "My telephone signal is locatable down to the square foot."

Ben nodded. He once worked with a client some number of months ago to make use of a technique called Time Delay of Arrival to determine a mobile telephone user's location. The method uses multiple antennas at a base station to determine the incident angle of an arriving signal. If a handset transmitting a signal is within line-of-sight, the antenna array can determine the direction from which the signal came. A second base station also locates the handset and compares it with data from the first base station to pinpoint the caller's location. But why did he need someone to do that?

"Got it?" he asked the person on the other end. "Good," he said after a moment.

Harrison stood and walked back over to the dirt-covered window facing the ocean. "A green and white hundred-foot yacht bears 034 degrees from me. I estimate the range at about two and a half miles."

"Of course," Ben said to himself. He watched as Harrison provided someone at the National Reconnaissance Office the necessary information to use a drone to observe the ship.

"Okay. Thanks," Harrison said, ending the conversation. He came back over to them.

In silent mode, Ben's phone alerted him to an incoming call. "McGuire," he answered.

"Ben? Where are you? All hell is breaking loose around here," Corrigan asked.

"What? What's going on?"

"You're supposed to be here briefing POTUS not playing spy with Harrison. The President just ordered the *Reagan* Battle Group out to five hundred miles."

Shit. Despite his recommendations, someone in the Ambassador's inner circle was feeling comfortable.

***

Central Military Committee Command Center (CMCCC)
Beijing, China
0901 Hours

General Zhao Chin Lee turned on the lights in his Command Center office located deep within the bowels of China's armed forces nerve center. His aide, Brigadier General Pan, followed close behind. Direct control of all military units—Air Force squadrons, Army brigades, Navy ships and submarines, and Civil Defense commands emanated from here. As he drew back the curtains to the window that overlooked the operations center floor, he mused about their victory.

"A greater China is only a few hours away," he said to Brigadier General Pan.

"I cannot believe we have come so far."

"I cannot believe we have been able to keep it secret until now. Chairman Fei has not been at all helpful on that front."

Zhao nodded as he lit a cigarette and took a long drag. "Yes. I quite agree."

The General of China's Army folded his arms as he studied the six large projection screens on the farthest wall. A sea of green uniforms with red epaulets moved with ordered intensity. Almost one thousand military personnel sat at or worked around stations on the floor below.

"Has General Yang communicated his status?"

"Yes, General. He is ready."

Zhao nodded. "And Admiral Chang?"

"His amphibious fleet is at sea, General. Their last position report placed them six hours north of Taiwan."

"Be sure that we keep close tabs on Admiral Sun. As soon as the signal is given, I want him arrested with the others."

"Yes, General."

GENERAL QUARTERS

As he continued watching the goings-on below him, Zhao's mind flashed back to the meeting just days before. So much had happened, so much hung in the balance. Would it all come together? So many things could go wrong.

"What will be the signal?" Lieutenant General Weidong, the Air Force Commander, had asked.

"The American news media will trigger our action with a report. Something tragic will happen to our President on their soil. We will, of course, act to prepare ourselves for an attack."

"Something tragic," Lieutenant General Cui mused with an open grin. Cui, the only person in the room more hardline than Zhao, was known for his open disdain of China's President.

"Admiral Chang, the East Sea Commander, will have the job of getting our Army to Taiwan. He has been able to place three amphibious ships at sea for exercises. He has also been able to ready a submarine and two missile patrol boats to protect the amphibious force."

"General, a few days ago you mentioned two submarines," General Pan noted.

"Yes. Mechanical issues will keep these ships in port."

The men nodded their understanding.

"And me, my General. How can I be of assistance?" Yang asked. He stood as he spoke, puffing out his chest with pride.

Zhao sighed as he pondered the Strategic Missile Commander's question. "It is my hope that you will not be necessary."

Zhao's mind returned to the present. Zhao personally made the calls to his generals. "A greater China" was not far away. He knew his place in history, both if they were successful, and if they failed.

He checked his watch. Chairman Fei should arrive soon. "Where is the Interior Minister?"

"At last check, he was in his residence."

"Good. Be prepared to bring him here at any moment."

Pan frowned. "Sir, I do not understand. With Chairman Fei here, there should be no need for the Interior Minister. He will assume control of the government."

Zhao did not verbally respond to his former aide's statement. Rather he only turned and brought his gaze to meet Pan's.

Pan's eyes went wide with surprise. "General."

"Chairman Fei Tzu means to take power for himself, not for China. We cannot return to despotism."

Pan, still wide-eyed, nodded slowly.

"Not to worry, Pan. I will take care of it myself." With that, Zhao reached into his top desk drawer and removed a Tokarev TT33 pistol. He checked the magazine and chambered a round. After engaging the safety, he slid it into his inside jacket pocket.

The buzzer on his desk intercom sounded. He leaned forward and pressed the microphone button. "General Zhao."

"General," a young woman's voice called. "Chairman Fei is here to see you."

"Very well. Escort him to my office."

***

Taoyuan Airport
Taipei, Taiwan
10:00 AM

Ben McGuire's first brush with an historic moment came when he was in grade school. He had crystal-clear recall of the night he and his older brother watched astronauts Neil Armstrong and Edwin Aldrin bounce around on the moon's surface in 1969. That night, billions of people all over the world shared that moment. Ben came away from the experience with a desire to do more than watch history on television. Fulfillment of that hope and the desire to fly propelled him toward the Naval Academy, and beyond into his current life.

"Be careful what you wish for, you might just get it," served as his watchwords. Such was the case with his heroic actions aboard the USS DEVON. That adventure had brought him the fleeting spotlight of notoriety and his first realization that participating in history was dangerous, and the Senkaku Island affair served as a reminder of the same.

Ben, attired in his full-dress white uniform, stood in a loose military formation with other US Embassy personnel. Compared to their ROC counterparts on the other side of the red carpet, the Americans stood "very loose." Ben smiled at the dichotomy.

Gathered to greet the arriving President of the People's Republic of China, the senior staff of the American Embassy stood in four ranks across a red carpet from the President's cabinet, lawmakers from the five branches, or Yauns, of government, and senior military staff. Ben exchanged nodding greetings with Admiral Lu, the leader of the Aegis Cruiser negotiations until the first strains of the PRC's national anthem started. Ben and all the other military personnel: Chinese, Taiwanese, and American, came to attention and saluted.

On Ben's left and at the end of a long red carpet, the PRC President's airplane and a long gantry struck a historical scene. President Ho and members of his entourage stood at attention while a military band played his country's anthem. The 40-piece unit stood in ranks near the opposite side of the carpet.

On his right, President Liu Chao-hsuan stood at attention. Immediately behind him, the flags of the ROC, PRC, and USA, held by a sturdy metal stand, billowed in the warm summer breeze. The President of the United States stood to the left of President Liu.

Ben's arm ached as he held it in place during the long salute. Nearly every part of him ached. He couldn't remember the last time he felt this tired. He closed his eyes every few seconds or so to ease the burning. He spent the bulk of his energy fighting the urge to yawn.

The music finally ended and Ben, almost in unison with the other military personnel, lowered his salute. The urge to yawn came again, and this time, he couldn't fight it. Rather than raise his hand to his mouth, he kept his mouth closed, making a moaning noise that drew the attention of those around him.

"Sorry," he apologized to those around him. "Long night," he said in a whisper.

The leaders of the two Chinas approached each other as news crews beamed the first-ever meeting between the leaders. The two men stopped in the middle of the carpeted walk. They bowed to each other and then shook hands. President Ho was the first to smile. President Liu finally relaxed enough to do the same.

"Anybody care to take bets that we'll be at war within the week?" one of the Americans murmured just loud enough for Ben to hear.

"You won't find any suckers in this crowd," another of them said.

"Dinner ought to be interesting," the same person said.

That's a fact. Once this event came to an end, Ben planned to go home for a long nap. He knew the hours between now and the evening's State Dinner would pass like minutes.

***

Republic of China Presidential Building
Taipei, Taiwan
11:45 AM

US Presidential Chief of Staff Veronica Aldridge stood across the reception room from her boss. She and her aide,

Jane Plesums, studied the three heads of state as they each drank a soft drink and conferred through their translators. From a distance, the first hour of the historic summit seemed to be going well. The three men at the center of the world's angst behaved more like long-separated fraternity brothers at a reunion than heads of state on diametrically diverging courses.

While the Presidents of Taiwan, the United States and the People's Republic of China gave the appearance of finding common ground, their staffs remained segregated, huddling in different parts of the expansive room. Each group of five or so persons occasionally caught the probing and unapproachable glances of the other. Veronica found this troubling because the real work and progress in this type of meeting usually occurred at their level. She further predicted failure until and unless they built some bridges.

"Come on," Aldridge said to her aide and interpreter as she started walking toward the PRC Delegation.

Plesums and her interpreter fell in behind their boss.

"Look, Ho's Chief of Staff didn't make the trip," she said to Plesums. "Introduce yourself to his aide. He's the tall skinny guy in the middle there."

"Ok, Boss."

"His name is Jung Li Chan. Just try to get him talking, about anything."

She nodded her understanding.

Aldridge noticed Jung Li was the first of his delegation to spot them. He gestured toward them to his colleagues as they closed. All the Chinese representatives turned to face them as they arrived.

"Hi," Jane said as she bowed at the shoulders. "We are so happy that you are here. How was your journey?"

None of them spoke.

Veronica and Jane, after a long moment of uncomfortable silence, shifted their attention to the interpreter. The young woman, a bookish Asian woman in round spectacles, spoke to Jung in Mandarin.

Rather than respond, the young man peered back at her as if he did not understand a word. The interpreter finally turned to Veronica and shrugged in frustration.

"Tell him that I am the President's Chief of Staff," Veronica said with authority. "Tell him that I would greatly appreciate a few moments of his time."

The interpreter nodded her understanding and began speaking to Jung again.

"We understood your words," one of the other men said softly as he interrupted the translation. His English was quite clear and understandable. Veronica was sure that she had detected a British accent.

Surprised and a bit put off, Veronica tried to regroup. "Um, so, you do speak English?"

"Quite so. We will not respond or engage in negotiations with you. We are under a directive from our government to leave that work to the President."

"But won't that make things just a bit difficult?" Veronica asked.

"If you will excuse us," the man said softly as he raised his hand and gracefully pointed the Americans away from them.

I'll be damned. He's dismissing me. After a long while, Veronica shook her head in disbelief. She finally turned and walked away. The others followed closely after her.

"How rude," Jane Plesums complained.

"No, not rude. It just means Ho is in this on his own, without the backing of his government. That's a problem for us."

She needed to get to the President.

***

GENERAL QUARTERS

USS Princeton *(CG-59)*
Captain's At-Sea Cabin
Western Pacific Ocean
1150 Hours

Captain Nation studied a message, trying to read between the lines. The order from COMSEVENTHFLT was as distinct as it was cryptic:

TO: COMMANDING OFFICER, USS PRINCETON (CG-59)
FM: COMMANDER, SEVENTH FLEET
MAKE BEST SPEED TO TAKE POSITION NO CLOSER THAN 150 NM FROM THE TAIWAN STRAITS BY AS SOON AS POSSIBLE. UPON ARRIVAL, STANDBY FOR FURTHER TASKING.

"What the hell's going on?" she asked herself as an expected knock came at the door.

"Enter," she ordered.

Lieutenant Commander Daniels opened the door and marched in as much as he could on the pitching deck. "Yes, Captain?"

"New orders, XO," she said as she handed him the document.

Daniels scanned it. "Hmm. Mysterious."

"Yes."

"I'll get the Navigator working on it. Meanwhile, I'll order us northeast?"

"Yes. And order up a full-speed bell."

"Refueling, Skipper?"

"Order the bell. And get me some UNREP options."

"Yes, ma'am," Daniels said as he turned to depart.

"XO?"

"Ma'am?" He stopped in his tracks and turned back to face her.

"I assume you and Ms. Juarez had a conversation?"

"Yes, ma'am. I don't think you'll have any issues out of her."

"Paul, I know this must be tough for you. I appreciate your attitude," she said.

Daniels swallowed hard before answering. "Yes, ma'am."

"I've sent a note to NAVPERS recommending you for command at the earliest opportunity. I didn't say anything about the details of the transfer, just that you had some personal things going on and that it was for the good of you, and the Navy."

Daniels' heart skipped a beat. "Thank you, ma'am."

"You've been a great XO. I think you'll make a fine skipper. And I'm sorry our time together is ending so soon."

"Yes, Captain. I understand."

She held up yet another message document. "Your relief will be on the pier when we next pull into port."

***

The Presidential Office
Chieh Shou Hall
Taipei, Taiwan
1:45 PM

Chieh Shou Hall serves as the official reception and dining area, within the Presidential Office Building. Blood red carpet covered the floor of the expansive gathering space. Half-meter high wood-panels enclosed the lower levels of the wall and eased the transition to the taupe-colored walls. Well-lit by three chandeliers, thirty round tables with ten chairs each took up most of the main floor.

Choi stood behind one of the tables at the head of the room on an elevated dais. Two tables, one on each side of an oak lectern, stood ready to receive guests. He examined his work carefully. His job of preparing the Presidential table setting neared completion.

He looked up to see his fellow staff members, nearly thirty of them, moving about the tables, readying them for the evening's meal. He also took notice of the equal number of security personnel that walked among them, scrutinizing their every move.

The Presidential Office's normal routine disappeared after the announcement of the Chinese State visit. Almost immediately, US Secret Service and PRC State Security personnel joined the Republic of China Secret Service agents as they descended on the facility. Over the last few days and hours, the three teams worked together to isolate and eliminate physical security threats as well as investigate and interview hotel personnel who might encounter any of the chief executives.

Choi checked his watch as he monitored the security teams. At each main checkpoint, an American, PRC or ROC Security agent checked identification with great scrutiny. As he had prepared to enter the dining area, yet another agent guided him through a metal detector and checked his pockets for contraband.

The security teams rotated in sections. A casual observer might believe their rotation interval happened at random. However, Choi considered himself anything but a casual observer. He smirked in self-congratulations at calculating their routine. He went back to his work as he arranged the last of the settings. He heard the footfalls of an agent as he placed a third saltshaker near the President of China's seat.

The security agent, a brawny American with a clean-shaven head, came over and examined his surroundings carefully. "So what's up with the salt?" he pressed.

"It is a salt-substitute. President Ho has hypertension, and his physicians have advised him to reduce his salt intake. I am to make sure he uses this instead of real salt."

"But why so many shakers? You've got three of them there."

Choi shrugged. "Just following instructions."

The American took his focus from the shakers and leveled it like a gunsight at Choi.

Not intimidated, especially by this minion, Choi stared back. "Is there something else?" he finally asked.

The agent raised his hand and signaled one of his colleagues over. When the second man, slightly shorter but just as burly, came over the first agent reached over and picked up one of the saltshakers. He emptied some of the contents into his hand, brought it up to his mouth, and tasted the granules. He nodded slightly, more to himself than anyone else before reaching for the other shakers, one at a time. He repeated the action. Satisfied, the American finally turned away and walked toward the far part of the dais, carefully scanning the area as he moved.

Choi sighed with relief. His work in this adventure was done. Only one task remained—serving food to the Presidents of Taiwan and the United States, and President of the People's Republic of China.

As soon as the room was set, the security teams would lock it down by posting guards at all entrances. No one would enter it again until the first of the food servers arrived for last-minute preparations.

*****

Intelligence Operations Center
US Embassy, Taipei Taiwan
4:45 PM

"I just heard you're not coming tonight. What's up?"

"Not my kinda deal," Jake replied without looking up from his computer.

"Come on, man. This is history in the making. How often do you get a chance to see that?" Ben pressed his point.

"More often than you can ever know," Jake shot back. He smirked as he continued his work. "Besides. I've gotta take Ciara to the airport. She's going home."

Ben noticed Jake stopped smirking and his serious, business-like demeanor returned almost as quickly as it disappeared. He seemed to tense as he mentioned the woman's name.

"Home, huh? Texas, right?"

"Yeah."

"So, what's gonna happen with you two?"

Jake stopped typing and looked up at Ben with a frown. He looked as if he had just been insulted. "What can I do for you, Captain? I'm kind of busy here."

Ben instantly realized he had crossed some invisible line. Over the last few months, the two men had drunk, smoked cigars, and golfed together. In the last few days, gangsters and spies shot at them during a high-speed car chase. However, Ben realized at that very moment while they shared a friendly discourse, they were not friends, and probably would never become so. He took a breath. "Nothing," Ben finally said. "I guess not. Sorry for the interruption. I need to get going. Have a good evening, Jake."

Harrison didn't respond. He went back to work on the computer. Ben took one last glance at the man who in effect, made history possible by breaking up the cell that planned to kill any chances of peace in Asia. Jake Harrison, and men and women like him, never seek the limelight. Their work needed the seclusion and relative safety of anonymity.

CHAPTER ELEVEN
A GREATER CHINA

Friday, August 15th
Presidential Office Building
Chieh Shou Hall
Taipei, Taiwan
6:10 PM

Veronica Aldridge clenched her teeth in frustration. This evening's event belonged to the Taiwanese. Relinquishing control was an abnormal and unnatural act. While her boss had undeniably set the process in motion to make tonight possible, it was also an irrefutable fact that now he only served as an actor in this play. Success, and she defined success as peace in the region, clearly lay in the hands of the Presidents of the Republic of Taiwan and the People's Republic of China. She watched the goings-on with wide eyes and a taut face.

President Liu, President Ho, and President Langdon entered the room as the band played their respective honors. "Hail to the Chief," signaled the arrival of the last head of state. During their entrance, all three leaders waved to an applauding crowd of over 300 guests who stood out of respect for their station. Especially excited attendees sounded out cheers and shouts above the already deafening ovation.

The only item under Veronica's purview was the US seating chart for President Langdon's guests. Langdon, through Veronica, made sure his rivals on the Senate Foreign Relations

GENERAL QUARTERS

Committee sat as close to the media section as possible, near the exact rear-center of the large ballroom. Five tables provided seating for top television, radio, and newspaper reporters from all three countries. A smaller contingent of camera-people stood with their equipment at the rear of the room. Marshall Langdon didn't want the historical significance of this moment to escape anyone.

After meeting at the foot of the dais, the three leaders shook hands and walked slowly across the raised floor to their table. Liu led the way, followed by Ho, then Langdon. The applause grew in intensity as they each took their place behind their respective chair. The three dignitaries posed for a photo opportunity, and a melee of flashes lit the room. Even media-savvy Marshall Langdon found himself squinting against the small explosions of light.

Located just to the right front of the dais, Veronica Aldridge shared her table with Secretary of State Hugh Standish, National Security Advisor Nelson Schroeder, Ambassador to the Republic of Taiwan Thomas Wooten and Ambassador to the People's Republic of China John McNamara. In keeping with her promise to Admiral Kiatkowski, Captain Ben McGuire, looking quite handsome in his naval Dinner Dress White uniform, sat at her right.

President Liu raised his hand, signaling for quiet. He bade the other two leaders sit by gesturing toward their chairs with an open hand. On cue, the American and Chinese Presidents took their seats, as did the rest of the gathering. Electric intensity filled the air as President Liu walked with purpose to the lectern on his left. Again, the cacophony of shutters and auto-winders filled the air as camera flashes illuminated the room.

The podium, a plain oak stand with a microphone, seemed almost naked as it lacked any national emblems or crests. Having decided to go without teleprompters for tonight's event,

Liu picked up a hardcopy text of his remarks. An interpreter came to her feet and eased her way over to a microphone stand located on the floor at the far right of the dais.

China's delegation, what there was of it, sat adjacent to Veronica's table. Jung Li Chan, President Ho's aide, sat with several nameless Chinese State Security personnel. To prevent any embarrassment, members of the PRC's aircraft crew filled in the rest of the seats at the table.

Since Ho's Chief of Staff did not make the trip, Veronica found herself focusing on fostering a relationship with the Chinese President's young aide. Before meeting the man, she looked forward to working with him. However, after their initial lukewarm greeting and more than five hours of constant contact, Veronica was more than ready for him to go home. While their bosses seemed immersed in a "love-fest," she and Jung Li seemed to share a profound dislike of each other.

Veronica glanced across the room at the head of the President's Secret Service Detail. Kevin Kendricks was speaking to one of his agents over his wrist radio. When the burly, dark-haired man finally looked up, he nodded his head in reassurance.

"Thank you for coming tonight," President Liu's translator said as the Republic of China's chief executive finally began. "We are fortunate to lead great peoples. Aside from our political differences, our nations are comprised of honorable, courageous, and generous men and women who look to us for leadership and wisdom."

Veronica scanned her table and then the room. Everyone sat riveted. Stop it, she told herself. Enjoy this moment.

Liu continued. "Tonight as we dine, our warships and warplanes keep an anxious watch on one another. Collectively, we have the resources to destroy the world several times over. I wonder if we have the collective wisdom to keep it and our peoples safe. It is my great hope that tonight we will begin a new tomorrow."

The gathering applauded his words. President Langdon and President Ho clapped as well.

President Liu bowed from the shoulders, first at the audience and then at President Ho. Ho, in turn, stood and returned the genuflect.

President Langdon came to his feet. The American President made his way to replace President Liu at the lectern as the President of Taiwan took his seat.

"Let me join my good friend, President Liu, in welcoming you all tonight. And I especially welcome our new partner in peace, President Ho."

Applause.

"I often give the press in my country a hard time because they sometimes have issues getting the story right. Well, tonight I'd have to say that I am in complete agreement with their assessment: This is an historic moment. President Ho, on behalf of the world, welcome. I hope that your visit will be fruitful," Langdon said as he turned to face him.

The President of China smiled widely and bowed his head in agreement.

The crowd applauded lightly.

"We hope that China, Taiwan and the United States of America are all committed to the safety and security of the world and that our nations can join together in making the world that much safer by pledging to allow the people of the island nation of Taiwan to choose their own path."

The audience broke out into open applause yet again. The demonstration turned into a standing ovation. President Langdon extended his right hand toward President Ho.

President Ho stood, bowing to the gathering for a short while before coming over to replace Langdon at the lectern. The gathering continued its applause as the President of the United

States first bowed and then shook hands with President Ho. The two men hugged warmly before President Langdon took his seat.

Ho acknowledged the crowd with several bows of his head before gesturing for them to take their seats. "Thank you for your truly kind welcome. President Liu, thank you for allowing me to visit you here, in your very wonderful country," he said in Mandarin.

The crowd came to its feet in applause once again, even before the translator finished communicating his words. The standing ovation continued for just over a minute.

Ho smiled at the reception of his words. As the audience again took their seats, he continued. "President Langdon, I also thank you for coming so far in the name of world peace. I also hope that we can lead the way in bringing peace to a troubled world."

The audience again applauded his words, albeit with less enthusiasm than the last demonstration. Ho and Langdon acknowledged each other by nodding their heads before he turned to continue his address. "My country has made its entry onto the world stage and does not plan to retreat. As all nations who take on the challenge of expansion make missteps, so have we, and so will we. Our great philosopher Confucius said, 'By three methods we may learn wisdom: First, by reflection, which is noblest; Second, by imitation, which is easiest; and third by experience, which is the bitterest.'"

"And that's as close as we'll ever get to an apology for the North Korean thing," Veronica murmured to Ben McGuire who nodded in agreement.

"To answer my new friend, President Langdon's, question," this time President Ho spoke in English. "Yes, we stand ready to ensure peace. Again, it is my great honor to represent my nation here tonight. Several days, perhaps even hours ago, I thought tonight I would be sitting down for dinner with an adversary. I had hopes. I harbored fears. Tonight, my hopes have been met, and my fears assuaged. I am sitting down tonight to dine with friends."

A standing ovation met President Ho's comments. A few of the more vocal members of the gathering threw in the occasional "Bravo" and "Yahoo."

He took a bow and made his way to sit beside the President of Taiwan. Liu, still on his feet from applauding his remarks, pulled out the chair on his left for his new friend, the President of the People's Republic of China. Ho thanked him with a bow of his head, a smile, and a handshake.

After the head table took their seats, the rest of the dinner guests followed their lead. Food servers emerged from their stations, each carrying a large tray hoisted in the air with one arm.

As the wait-staff served the appetizer, Veronica continued surveying the other dinner guests. The gathering mainly consisted of Taiwanese and American politicos. American Democrats and Republicans, international media, and a few Hollywood notables all laughed, drank, and talked as the evening progressed.

Ben McGuire hated wearing neckties. One of the major factors in his decision to join Information View was their "business casual" dress policy. In his civilian job, he could easily count the number of times in three years that his work required a business suit. With six months behind him at the Embassy, those days seemed a million years in the past. He tugged at his bowtie and tight-collared ruffled shirt in vain. Dinner Dress White, regardless of its relative splendor, at the end of the day was just another suit.

Ben couldn't help noticing that of all the other embassy employees in the room, he was the only one seated at the same table as the Secretary of State, National Security Advisor, and the President's Chief of Staff. Occasionally, he caught the jealous glances of some of his associates. If the relatively hardwood chairs had made it possible, he would have slumped in his chair—they did not. However, when he caught Deputy Chief of Mission James Dudley's eye, all discomfort suddenly faded. Ben even went so far as to hoist his glass in a taunting toast. Dudley did not return the gesture.

"Having fun?" Aldridge asked.

Ben, his focus elsewhere, flinched with a start at the question. "Yeah. This is great."

"Uh, huh." She smiled knowingly.

As a food server placed his appetizer in front of him, Ben used the diversion as an excuse to turn from her probing, yet amused, stare.

The menu, as well planned as the rest of the event, offered something for everyone. The meal started with grilled calamari stuffed with feta, arugula, and orzo cheese appetizer. Ben dug into his meal like a starved man as soon as the others seated at his table received their plates.

Ben read the rest of the menu as the first course did its job. The main course offered a choice between prime rib and sea bass. Ben weighed his decision with every bite of calamari. Somehow, he found the presence of mind to momentarily take his attention from his meal back to Chief of Staff Aldridge.

Rather than take pleasure in what he considered one of the best meals he had ever consumed, she made deep study of the PRC table. Ben shifted his focus in the same direction to understand her intrigue with Jung Li Chan.

The man looked "pissed." Like Veronica Aldridge, he busily observed others instead of eating his meal. He seemed locked in on his President. After watching Jung for a long moment, Ben finally turned toward the dais. What was so compelling?

Ben looked up to see President Liu and President Ho, chatting over their meal. Both men seemed genuinely taken with each other. Liu whispered something that Ho found humorous as he burst out laughing. Liu smiled at the effect of his words on the PRC President.

"Mr. President!" one of the reporters called out.

President Ho covered his mouth with a napkin as his laughter subsided. He took a swallow, sipped some water, stood, and walked over to the microphone. "Yes?"

"Did the President make a joke?"

Ho looked at President Liu for permission. Liu smiled and bowed his head in agreement.

"Yes. He told a very funny joke. He asked if I had heard the latest definition for International Diplomacy," Ho said as he paused for dramatic effect.

"And the answer?" the same reporter asked.

Ho started laughing again as he was about to speak. "The ability to tell a person to go to hell in such a way that they look forward to the trip!" He laughed even louder.

Ben smirked at hearing the quip. "Old joke," he mouthed more to himself than anyone else.

Where Ben found the joke only mildly amusing, the rest of the audience let go a mutual guffaw. Even Aldridge stopped her surveillance of Jung Li long enough to laugh aloud at the Asian leader's humor.

Ho, after laughing at President Liu's joke again, returned to his seat. As the laughter and applause subsided, Ben watched Aldridge turn her gaze back to Jung. Drawn by her interest in the man, Ben studied him, too. Rather than a smile, the man wore the same foul grimace as before as he sat on the edge of his chair.

Tradition and duty set the path of Jung Li Chan's life before his birth. Both sets of grandparents had marched with Chairman Mao. Both sets had spilled blood in the name of the

Cultural Revolution. His place in the Hung Yaoguai, like his parents', was his for the taking at birth.

He, like them, lived to serve China. His life was inconsequential to the life of Mother China. His mission was clear this night. No matter the difficulty, President Ho Lin Shih must die, and he must die on Taiwan's soil. Whether it was by "the weapon" or by his hand, it did not matter. The Chinese People would never believe in Taiwan's innocence. The story in Mother China would be simple: Either Taiwan conspired to kill Ho or did not offer adequate protection. China would hold Taiwan, and America, responsible.

From his seat only a few steps away; he contemplated "the item," a thousand-year-old wooden knife hidden in his jacket. Covered with a quick-acting poison, if the nanites did not finish the job, he knew he must.

Jung watched the dais with laser-like focus. He looked up in time to see President Liu reach for the saltshaker to his left, the one nearest President Ho.

Jung suddenly felt as if someone had placed a ton of bricks on his chest. He labored to take a breath as he helplessly watched the President of Taiwan use the wrong saltshaker as he liberally dusted his food.

Jung suppressed the urge to shout "NO!" as President Liu placed a fork-full of sauce-covered fish into his mouth. Jung slumped in his chair.

Stella Chamblis, the Ambassador's administrative assistant, a thin, red-haired woman with a long face, sat two tables away, on the far side of the press table. She suddenly let out a scream so piercing and horror-filled that Ben's skin crawled. He flinched as plates, glasses, food, and utensils all went flying from the area immediately around President Liu. Ben jumped to his feet for a better view.

GENERAL QUARTERS

Paralyzed with shock, Ben watched in wide-eyed awe as President Liu convulsed uncontrollably. His arms, torso, head, and legs flailed and flopped like a shaken rag doll. Blood spewed from every visible orifice as the rest of the dinner set in front of him flew from the table in a shower of food, porcelain, and silver. The table at which the men had just been sitting also flew from the raised platform onto the floor below, giving all clear sight of the horrid spectacle.

The melee was in full form now. Ben, like everyone around him, clamored to their feet. Those not trying to help President Liu tried to pull away from the bloody and horrific scene. Secret Service and Chinese Security Agents, their guns drawn, froze in manic consternation. The President of Taiwan was obviously under attack. However, from whom, or what?

Most of the State Department personnel moved back from the gory scene while the media pressed forward toward the dais. Ben finally felt his mind engaging. He looked to his left to find Veronica Aldridge missing. He looked back toward the head of the room to see her pressing through the reporters and camera operators, occasionally shoving them as she made her way.

He shifted his attention back to the stage to find Liu's bloody body still in distress. President Langdon tried to grab hold of one of the man's thrashing appendages but to no avail. Langdon, still in possession of the physique that he once owned as college football all-star, fell back as if a lineman had hit him.

President Ho, a man of a far slighter build at less than a hundred and eighty pounds, even tried to help. When he grabbed Liu's arm, the Taiwanese President's involuntary response was so strong that it almost threw him headfirst off the dais.

Three Secret Service agents charged the dais and manhandled Langdon away. Four ROC security personnel made their way to the dais, weapons drawn took position around their fallen leader. With no one to guard him, Chinese President Ho pulled himself from the platform and backed away. He stopped just a few feet away from Liu. None of his entourage came to his side.

Ben glanced back at the PRC table. All of them, including men he assumed as guards, stood motionless. All of them but one.

Aldridge made her way through the crowd to her boss' side. They stood back as the Taiwanese security agents tended to President Liu.

A few of the women wept openly at the gruesome sight that had just moments before been a celebratory setting. The sounds of a dying man's body flopping on the platform mixed with their yelps.

Ben's heart pounded. He finally allowed himself to take a breath when he noticed Jung Li moving up the right side of the room. He was holding something in his left hand as he continued toward the blood-drenched dais. "What the hell?"

Ben turned to get on the other side of the table, but awestruck onlookers stymied him. He pushed as best he could, but the sea of humanity was just too great. The crowd suddenly shifted toward him. As Ben felt the crowd ready to trample him, he once again spied Jung on the other side of the tables. The object in his hand was visible now. Ben's resolve stiffened.

He fell back from the crowd, and with one powerful leap, jumped from the floor to the top of the table at which he had sat moments before. Plates and glasses broke beneath his weight. His eyes caught the surprised gaze of a few of the other guests.

Ben regrouped and turned his attention back to Jung Li. The knife in his left hand looked ancient but still deadly. He scanned the room for the nearest Secret Service Agent. His eyes fell on Kendricks. The Presidential Detail Leader was pushing his way toward President Langdon.

"Kendricks!" he shouted above the riot as he pointed at Jung.

The Secret Service agent looked up with anxiety-filled eyes.

"Knife!" He pointed toward Jung Li again. "Knife!"

Kendricks shifted his gaze toward the Chinese aide. He tried in vain to change his direction as he struggled against the mob.

Damn. He doesn't have a shot.

Ben crossed the table in two steps. He leaped over the heads of several panic-ridden guests onto the table at which Jung had been sitting. Jung Li's back was to him now as he closed on the scuffle near the Presidents.

Liu's body suddenly went limp. Now only a few feet from the dais, Ben could make out black and blue bruises covering most of Liu's bloody face. President Langdon stood with Aldridge on the left side of the platform while President Ho watched on from the right side.

Ben brought his focus back to Jung as he edged with increasing speed to the left side of the stage. My God. He's after Ho.

Ben took one last look at Kendricks, who was still shoving his way through the crowd. He inhaled a deep breath as he took two powerful strides across the table toward President Ho's aide. Ben dove through the air toward the attacker. Unfortunately, Ben poorly timed and executed his leap through space. Ben felt the man fall forward as his weight landed on him. He landed on Jung's right side before he eventually hit the floor. A loud popping noise and searing pain informed Ben that he probably broke his hand in the attempt.

The Asian lost his balance, but only for a second. Staggering to regain composure, he turned to see Ben lying on the floor. He brought the knife up to strike Ben. "Arrogant and stupid American," was all he said before his chest exploded to the sound of gunshots. A red vapor engulfed his chest as Jung Li fell dead at Ben's feet.

Ben cradled his hand as Special Agent Kevin Kendricks kicked the wooden knife away from Jung's still body.

"This is Kendricks," the Secret Service agent said into his wrist-radio transmitter. "Lockdown the facility and get 'Buckeye' ready to move. And tell Air Force One to standby. We're on our way."

***

Central Military Committee Command Center (CMCCC)
Beijing, China
1825 Hours

Chairman Fei sat across the desk from Zhao. Since the fat man's arrival, they had hardly spoken. Fei smoked a cigarette that Zhao had offered. Zhao alternated his focus from the computer monitor on his desk to the man sitting across from him and back. Fei took a long drag and blew it out heavily.

"Funny, isn't it?"

"What?" Fei asked gruffly.

"How slow the waiting is. It was like this in Tiananmen that day."

Fei's eyes narrowed. He took another puff.

"We knew it would come, the order to act. But the wait, it was interminable."

Fei did not respond.

"And when that little bastard stood in front of my lead tank, I thought we would go then. But no. We had to wait."

The telephone on Zhao's desk rang. As he went to answer it, he also heard a surge of noise from the operations floor. He stood as he picked up the telephone.

"General, this is the CMCCC Watch Officer. There has been an incident in Taipei," he heard the Army colonel on the other end say. Zhao turned to look out his windows at the Watch Floor below. Each of the large display screens now displayed the American CNN news network.

Zhao shot Fei an excited glance. "I'll be right down," he said to the watch officer.

Fei took one last drag and extinguished his cigarette.

The General put down the phone, picked up his hat, and walked around his desk. He bowed to Fei in traditional style. "Comrade Chairman, we are only a few moments away from a greater China. I am honored to serve her with you."

Fei bowed in return. "We shall make history today, General."

Zhao smiled as he reached to shake Fei's hand. When he did, the concealed pistol's hardness reminded its owner of its presence. Zhao, with the Chairman's permission, led the way out of the room and into his nation's history.

***

Taipei, Taiwan
6:45 PM

"What about him?" Song asked Guo. The landlord's body lay in a crumpled heap just a few feet away. Even in the low evening light, Song could see the exit wounds from two bullets and the landlord's blood-soaked and otherwise light-colored shirt. Song tried to look away but kept finding his attention drawn to the graphically violent scene.

"What about him? He's a stupid ass. He should have minded his business," Guo retorted.

The lack of remorse in his tone only punctuated the shock of the last few moments. The older man had surprised them as they moved the last of their equipment onto the roof. While he had left them no choice, Guo had taken great pleasure in eliminating him from the challenge completing their mission.

"Just do your work. We are almost out of time."

Song nodded his acknowledgment of his superior's orders and turned to finish assembling the missile launcher. The only remaining components were the night scope and the BGM-71F missile.

For the last three months, he and Guo had trained extensively on the assembly and employment of the American-made M220A1 TOW weapon system. Originally designed for battlefield use against Soviet tanks, the weapon featured a tube-launched, optically tracked, wire-guided missile. The entire unit weighed almost three hundred pounds when fully assembled. Consequently, he and Guo found it necessary to split the unit across three cases.

As Song snapped the night scope into place, Guo's mobile telephone rang. He aligned it with the markings he had made the day before.

"Yes, sir. I understand. We will not fail," his partner said into the phone. He turned to Song as he ended the call and placed the device back into his pocket. "We have a mission to complete. Are you ready?" Guo asked.

"Yes," Song said as he placed the first of two high-explosive missiles on the launcher and snapped it into place. He next connected the missile guidance kit to the canister containing the projectile and the wire spool through which commands would guide the missile to its target.

Guo took a moment to scan the skies above them with his naked eye. He then brought up a pair of binoculars and turned toward their target.

"Almost ready," Song announced as he knelt on the gravel and brought his right eye to the night scope viewfinder. He adjusted the crosshairs and sighted-in on the first of their two targets. Air Force One sat under guard at Taoyuan International Airport. Their second target, PRC Alpha, the Chinese President's aircraft, sat only a few degrees away from the primary target.

"Ready," Song said softly. An invisible infrared beam now connected the fuselage of the large blue and white Boeing 747 jet with his launcher. His missile would use that beam of light as input until it reached the targeted aircraft.

"Fire," Guo ordered.

Song pulled the trigger and five-tenths of a second later, a gyroscope in the missile guidance system spun up to 42,000 rpm. Once there, it sent an electrical current to the launch motor, and it fired. A blue shaft of fire expelled from the launcher to Song's rear as the missile exited its tube. The wire spool made a snake-like hissing noise as it dispensed its contents in the missile's wake.

As long as the missile was in flight, Song would maintain his position at the night scope's viewfinder. As the missile flew downrange, the infrared beam entered the receiver on the projectile and reflected on a spinning mirror called a nutater. The missile's motor cut off a second a half later and started coasting the rest of the way to its target. Two seconds later, a tremendous explosion rocked the airport.

As the fireball from the fuselage reached the fuel in the large aircraft's wings, a secondary and fiery explosion fully engulfed the airport terminal and many of the buildings and vehicles near the aircraft. The ground shook beneath Song's feet as the fire and sound lauded the death of the aircraft and any crew members still aboard.

"Aiyee!" Guo shouted. "Aiyee!"

Song wasted no time. He stood, disengaged the first missile canister and tossed it aside. The guidewire from the first missile ran from the canister into the distance in front of them. Speed was now of the essence as that wire would also serve to lead security personnel to their location.

"Ready," Song announced after he had turned the night scope to his right by four degrees and sighted in on the PRC President's aircraft.

"Fire," Guo replied with a lilt.

Again, Song pulled the launcher trigger. The missile made its violent ascent into the now fire-lit sky with the same snake-hissing noise from the wire spool. Song, once again, skillfully guided the high-explosive projectile to its target some three miles away. The apartment building shook with the sound and light from the explosion's fury.

Song came to stand next to Guo as he examined his handiwork. His heart sank at the sight of the two burning aircraft. Killing Americans was one thing. However, he had just slaughtered several of his fellow countrymen who were guilty of doing nothing more than their jobs. He felt as if he were in a bad dream.

"Beautiful," Guo said.

Song turned to see his partner smiling widely. Song's hand eventually found his pistol-holster. He unsnapped it and slowly removed the weapon.

Song's orders had been clear: Eliminate the Presidents' aircraft and thereby their means of leaving the island nation and do not allow yourselves to be taken prisoner.

"Let's go," Guo said. The sound of approaching helicopters almost muted his anxiety-filled voice.

"There's no place to go," Song said as the first of several aircraft-mounted searchlights turned night into day. A second and third security aircraft zeroed in from opposing sides of the building.

"Put your hands up!" an amplified voice shouted at them.

"What do we do now?" Guo asked.

Song took one last look at the death and destruction he had just caused. In one smooth motion, he pulled the weapon up and pointed it at the first helicopter. Their lives ended in a loud burst of automatic weapons fire.

***

GENERAL QUARTERS

Sitting alone in a sea of empty chairs near the center of the room, Ben watched with morbid curiosity as emergency medical personnel attempted to revive President Liu. Three male and one female paramedic, all wearing protective clothing, exchanged troubled and anxious glances as their leader pronounced the President of the Republic of China dead on the scene.

Security personnel had cleared the room, moving nearly everyone into the main foyer for questioning. Secret Service agents had brusquely removed President Langdon from the area just after their team leader verified Jung Li was dead. Presumably, Langdon either was stashed away somewhere in the building or on his way to Air Force One.

Only a few people remained in the hall. PRC President Ho, the Taiwanese Vice President, and their respective security details all watched the same sad scene from the other side of the room. Taiwanese Secret Service and their PRC counterparts kept an anxious watch on their protectees, as well as each other. Vice President Isaac Chin stood close to his president's side.

Now they show up. This was a coup. Ben shook his head in even portions of disbelief and disgust. Fucking cowards.

"How's that feel?" yet another medic asked Ben as he finished binding his broken hand.

Immobilized, it still hurt like hell. "Not too bad," he lied. Ben had refused any pain medication. He needed a clear head.

Ben returned his attention to the team attending President Liu. The lead paramedic, an older man with a thick mop of gray hair, stood and went over to Chin. They spoke for a moment before the Vice President nodded. Two of the medics stood and started packing their gear while a third unfolded a stretcher and placed it near Liu's battered and bloody body.

"Captain McGuire," a PRC State Security agent said to Ben with a thick accent.

He had not seen the man approach him. Ben, slightly startled, jerked around to see the muscular young Asian man looking down at him. "Yeah?"

"The President would like to speak with you."

Ben looked at the PRC's leader and then back at the agent. He managed to swallow his disdain. He nodded and stood.

Ben followed in the agent's wake, occasionally looking at the dais area. They gently loaded Liu's body onto the stretcher and carried him out. Ben shook his head in disbelief at what had just transpired.

"President Ho," one of the Taiwanese agents said as Ben arrived. "This is Captain Ben McGuire, the American Naval Attaché' here in Taiwan."

Ben came to a halt and stood at attention.

The PRC President shot the agents a glance, and they backed away to give the two men some privacy. When it appeared that they were out of earshot, Ho turned his gaze back to him.

The PRC President drew near, giving Ben a close view of his face. He looked tired as if he had just run a marathon. "Captain, are you the same Benjamin McGuire from Senkaku Island?" he asked with a direct tone. His dark brown eyes were piercing.

Ben felt the weight of his stare. As much as he wanted to lie to protect the secret, he knew it was pointless. Besides, as the leader of the PRC, he probably had access to the information anyway. "Yes, sir. I am."

Ho shook his head as he grunted. "It would appear that I am in your debt, Captain."

"No, sir. I was just doing my job."

"There are men in my country who would like to see you dead."

"I know. One of them tried to kill me just yesterday," Ben retorted.

Ho's eyes went wide with surprise.

"You didn't know," Ben said noting the astonishment in his voice.

"No, I did not." Ho frowned. The PRC President took a deep breath. "You will no longer have reason to fear anyone from China again." He extended his hand.

Ben, after a long moment, took hold and shook it with his left hand. Feels awkward.

The door to the room suddenly swung open, and an American Secret Service Agent entered in a rush. He pushed past the Taiwanese and Chinese agents towards Ben. His face wore an anxious and pained expression.

"President Ho, Captain McGuire. There's been an incident at the airport."

***

USS Princeton *(CG-59)*
Northern Taiwan Straits
1910 Hours

"Enter," Nation answered her door.

"Ma'am." Petty Officer Freeman, normally one of the most upbeat members of her crew, sounded almost somber. His face finished painting the picture of a tense and worried young man. "Your flash traffic, ma'am." His speech was disjointed and ill cadenced. He handed her two sheets of paper.

She frowned at him and then the message. Her heart sank as she read the text. Nation reread the document several times to be sure.

She reached for her intercom and dialed the bridge.

221

"Officer of the Deck," the person on the other end answered.

"Mr. Jeffers."

"Yes, ma'am?"

"Have the XO meet me in Combat," she ordered.

***

Operations Center
1st Information Warfare Brigade
Beijing, China
1911 Hours

To the casual observer, the IWB's Operations Center gave the same appearance as a western-style network operations center. Sixteen technicians sat at workstations guarded by chest-high cubicles. At the front of the room, a 13-meter-high wall held several video screens. Three larger screens, arranged horizontally, depicted the status of China's telecommunications networks for Civil and Military services. Eighteen smaller screens, arranged in two rows of nine each, displayed other critical operations data. At the rear of the room, an elevated dais provided General Pan an overall view of the entire center. The commander's stations looked very much like his operator's locations: two screens and two telephones, one each for classified and unclassified information. However, General Pan's telephone had speed dials for the highest of China's officials.

"Are we ready?" Pan asked the watch supervisor over an intercom headset.

"Yes, General. All stations are standing by," a young colonel replied from his station on the operations floor.

Pan checked the digital clock on his workstation desk. As the second hand clicked over to the number "12," he took a deep breath. "Proceed," he said with the same level of casualness that he might use to order a cup of tea.

GENERAL QUARTERS

Seconds later, the top rows of smaller screens flickered, and Taiwan's critical infrastructure appeared on them. The air in the room soon filled with the sound of 32 sets of hands working computer keyboards. Within moments, red icons began to appear on the screens. Each blimp represented a node in the electronic systems keeping Taiwan functioning. On the other side of the Straits, the country of Taiwan was going dark.

CHAPTER TWELVE
A NIGHT OF TREACHERY

Friday, August 15th
50 Nautical Miles North of Taiwan
5000 Feet
2110 Hours

On the night of April 14, 1865, the night of President Abraham Lincoln's murder, conspirators tried to destroy the US government. Historians call it "a night of treachery." In addition to John Wilkes Booth's successful attack on Lincoln, fellow plotters had tried to kill Vice President Andrew Johnson, Secretary of State William Seward, and General Ulysses S. Grant.

Ben's sense of history compelled him to draw a parallel between that fateful night and this one. Somewhere, probably in a dark room, men and women schemed to kill at least one of three national leaders, maybe all three, and in so doing, destroy peace in the region. The destruction of Air Force One and the Chinese President's aircraft gave merit to Ben's evolving theory.

As with the planners of that night so long ago, the people behind this plot accomplished only a marginal job of their homework, at least as far as the Americans were concerned. The US Secret Service, after 103 years of protecting Presidents and other dignitaries, had learned its lessons well. Contingency planning, although not usually necessary, was always a part of their work.

As the Naval Attaché, Ben McGuire had helped develop the contingency plans to ensure the President's safety in case something "unusual" happened. In case of an emergency that required the President's departure, Ben secured the means and resources to deliver him to the closest US sovereign territory as quickly as possible. In this part of the world, this translated to another Embassy or a US Navy ship.

Two hours earlier, four Navy SH-60 helicopters touched down in the expansive and darkened courtyard in front of the Taiwanese Presidential Building. The aircraft sat on the ground, rotors still spinning, less than four minutes later they took off again. When they departed, they carried the key members of the President's entourage and staff, and the US Naval Attaché to Taiwan.

Wearing night-vision goggles, Navy pilots flew their aircraft away from the city. A sea of darkness dotted with fires, lay below them where a vibrant and brightly lit metropolis usually existed. Ben knew this was no coincidence. An attack was well underway.

Appropriately, President Langdon flew with the National Security Advisor in "Navy One" en route to the USS *Princeton*. Based on pre-visit questions from the Presidential Staff, Ben knew the President was in constant communications with the Pentagon. The people behind tonight's events were obviously also behind a coup in China. Until President Ho resolved the situation in his country, the threat of war was palpable and more imminent than ever before. Just before taking off, Ben listened in as the President placed US Forces in the highest state of readiness. The threat of a rouge group taking charge of China's nuclear arsenal called for suitable escalation: DEFCON ONE.

Secretary of State Hugh Standish flew in a second aircraft. He, along with two members of the Senate Foreign Relations Committee, headed for the USS *William P. Lawrence*, one of the ships steaming in company with *Princeton*.

Back in Taipei, the Secret Service, the Taiwanese and the remaining members of the Chinese Security team protecting the PRC President permitted the press to run with the inaccurate story that President Langdon was hunkered down inside the Taiwanese Presidential Building. They hoped it would buy them the time they needed to get the President of the United States out of harm's way and allow the President of China the opportunity to regain control of his country. The electrical outage hampered the news crews' normal efficiency—a plus in this situation.

"Captain," Chief of Staff Veronica Aldridge called as she leaned toward him.

Ben successfully fought the urge to laugh. Wearing a white safety helmet and goggles, Aldridge's long auburn hair caused her headgear to sit at an odd angle. She sat next to him on the left side of their SH-60 helicopter as it made its way to the USS *Princeton*. "Yes, Ma'am?"

Ben frowned in confusion as he watched her survey the relatively crowded cabin before speaking. In addition to the Navy air crewman, a couple of congressional representatives flew with them. She pulled Ben even closer and brought her mouth up to his ear.

"I have read the reports from Senkaku Island, Ben."

He nodded his understanding.

She continued. "That event may remain classified for quite some time to come. However, tonight you distinguished yourself. Your days of being a nameless sailor are over, again."

Ben turned to face her as she raised a serious eyebrow.

"I don't know if you have a political party but get ready for the pressure. It's coming. Your life just changed."

Ben took a deep breath and let it out. "Great."

***

GENERAL QUARTERS

Central Military Committee Command Center (CMCCC)
Beijing, China

"Comrade General," the watch officer called with a trembling voice. A taut face spoke volumes of the officer's angst. "I have a message from our liaison in Taipei." He handed Zhao a single sheet of paper.

Zhao read the communiqué before handing it to Fei. He placed his hand on the young colonel's shoulder. Zhao gripped his muscular frame as he brought his gaze to meet the Colonel's eyes. The general smiled, and the officer instantly relaxed his shoulders.

"Now," General Zhao said softly. "Turn off those television monitors and give me the microphone so that I can address the center."

"Yes, sir." Colonel Mulin directed the technician at his right to do as the General ordered.

Fei stood to the right of Mulin's watch console. He crossed his arms as he watched the goings-on around him.

When the screens went blank, the technician handed Mulin a small microphone that the colonel then gave to General Zhao.

"Comrades," Zhao began. "Our beloved president has fallen to American treachery. He has been killed while serving Mother China. I believe the Americans mean to take advantage of us during our moment of grief and despair."

A hush went over the center. Every person within Zhao's sight ceased moving. He had their complete attention. Their faces, some wide-eyed, some with mouths agape, all looked to him and his next words. Zhao knew the look of fear. He knew the word they feared most was "war." He would play on this fear to obtain the rest of his aims.

"The Americans will not dare come here. But they will dare to occupy the runaway province. We must act now to secure it. Are you with me?"

No one answered. Instead, they exchanged uneasy glances with the persons nearest them.

"Chairman Fei Tzu has come to support us. He is the head of our government now."

With that, Fei raised two beefy arms into the air. The crowd of officers and enlisted personnel slowly began to applaud. Sparse at first, it slowly moved across the tiers of workstations and tables. It finally began to grow in volume and intensity.

"Are you with me, Comrades?" Zhao asked again.

Cheers rose as the applause reached its crescendo. Zhao and Fei exchanged confident and joy-filled glances, each applauding the others. Zhao again placed his hand on the shoulder of a now-smiling Colonel Mulin.

***

Presidential Office Building
Taipei, Taiwan
9:15 PM

The knot in President Ho Lin Shih's stomach grew with each unanswered telephone call. The list of the hundred or so failed call attempts read like a who's-who of Chinese Government and Communist Party officials: the Prime Minister, the Foreign Minister, and, of course, the Chairman of the Party. All and many others did not answer or take his call. With each moment, Ho felt like a man without a country.

The telephone rang, pulling Ho from his thoughts. His assistant answered for him.

"Sir?" Liling Chi asked. The interpreter from the ill-fated state dinner occupied the other desk in the small office provided him by the new President of Taiwan, Isaac Chin. How ironic, he thought, that a Taiwanese national was his most able assistant in getting his country back under his control.

"Yes?"

"Sir, it is President Langdon."

Ho nodded as he pressed the button to connect the line and picked up the phone. "Yes, Mister President?" he answered.

Liling stayed on the line. "Any news yet?" she translated the US President's question.

"No. I have not made contact with anyone."

Silence. The line crackled.

"I will be landing aboard one of our ships soon. I will call you back then," Liling translated President Langdon's words.

"Very well, Mr. President. I will wait to hear from you then."

"President Ho. This is an extremely dangerous situation."

"Yes, Mr. President. It is."

Silence again.

"I will talk to you soon. Good luck," the American President said as the line went dead.

Ho put down the telephone receiver and reclined in his chair. After a short while, he looked up to find Liling's probing eyes. They exchange a long quiet glance. "Tell me, Liling?"

"Have you ever been to China?" he asked.

"No, sir. Never."

"China is a good country," Ho added. "Full of good people."

Liling did not respond.

"This is not one of our better moments, I'm afraid."

She nodded.

Ho picked up his telephone book and started dialing again.

***

Aboard Sapphire One
Northern Taiwan Straits
2115 Hours

Ben peered out the helicopter's cabin window to watch Navy One land on USS *Princeton*'s flight deck without issue. Thanks to a bright moonlit sky, he watched windblown spray fly up

229

from the ocean surrounding the stern of the Aegis-class cruiser, but quickly fade as the aircraft reduced its rotor speed.

Ben's helicopter hovered off the ship's starboard quarter, providing them a stunning view of one of his favorite ship classes. Sleek, deadly, and beautiful, USS *Princeton* (CG-59) glistened in the moonlight.

"Captain McGuire, you look like a kid in a candy store," Veronica Aldridge shouted above the aircraft noise.

"Can't help it. I miss this."

"So, why'd you get out? It fits you."

Ben wished he had a dollar for every time someone asked him that question. He could probably buy a ship like *Princeton.* "Long story," was all he said.

From their vantage point, they watched as men and women with white vests offloaded three Secret Service agents, National Security Advisor Schroeder, and finally President Langdon. The President followed the others into the ship's hangar deck.

"It sure is big," Congresswoman Anders commented as she looked over Ben's shoulder at the ship below.

"Yeah."

"How fast is the ship?"

"Just over thirty knots," he replied as he gave the Unclassified version of the answer. "A little over thirty-six miles per hour."

"Really? Is that all?" she remarked with disappointment.

Ben smiled at her ignorance. "Most ships barely travel faster than fifteen miles per hour," he added. "She's plenty fast enough."

"What is that John Paul Jones-quote you guys like?" Aldridge asked. "Something about a fast ship."

"'Give me a fast ship for I intend to go in harm's way,'" Ben assisted her. "That there is what good old Captain Jones was dreaming of when he said that," Ben replied as he pointed toward the ship.

The helicopter formerly designated as Navy One lifted off and rose away from the deck on the starboard side of the ship. Moments later, their pilot began his approach. From a hundred yards off the ship's stern, *Princeton* barely looked big enough to accommodate the aircraft. Ben remarked to himself that the ship did not appear that much larger as they flew closer.

"Are we gonna fit?" Congressman Jones asked as he clenched his seat.

"That's why the Navy calls their pilots 'aviators.' Anybody else would be crazy to try this," Aldridge retorted.

Ben smiled as he saw the Chief of Staff place a death-grip on her seat.

The SH-60 hovered over the deck's center. The pilot sat it down gently and reduced the power. The sound of metal-on-metal clanging announced the flight deck crew securing the aircraft to the ship's. Soon the familiar sway of a ship at sea made its feeling known to him. "We're here," Ben said to the others, still grinning.

With the power off the rotors, the pilot engaged the brake, and the blades churned to a rapid stop. After getting the flight crewman's okay, Ben led the others out of the aircraft by bounding out of the open cabin door onto the *Princeton*'s deck. A bright full moon and the ship's lighting provided more than enough light to safely make their way forward to the hangar.

"Captain McGuire, sir?" a tall dark-complexioned black lieutenant commander, flanked by two other officers, asked as he saluted.

"Yes."

"Sir. I'm Lieutenant Commander Paul Daniels, Executive Officer. It is an honor to have you aboard, sir."

The other officers followed Daniels' lead, stood at attention, and saluted with him.

If Ben could blush, he would have. Ben returned the salute. "Good evening, XO," he replied above the helicopter and ocean noise. "This is Chief of Staff Aldridge, Congresswoman Anders, and Congressman Jones."

Daniels and the other officers, all dressed in standard camouflage Navy Working Uniform, lowered their salute and returned to the best form of attention possible on a pitching deck. LCDR Daniels greeted them in the same well-practiced and respectful manner and then turned to Aldridge. "Ma'am, the President has been escorted to the Flag Stateroom. He requests the Chief of Staff join him there."

Ben turned to Veronica Aldridge, who nodded her understanding.

"This is LT Pickens. He will escort you to the President," Daniels added.

The short and stocky reddish-blonde haired man took a step forward. "If you'll follow me, ma'am."

Aldridge patted Ben on the shoulder. "Talk to you in a bit," she said as she fell in behind the lieutenant.

Daniels turned his attention to the two congressional representatives. "We have set up some refreshments for you in our wardroom. Lieutenant Jefferson will escort you there," Daniels added.

"Thanks for the ride, Captain," Congressman Jones said as he brushed by Ben. Congresswoman Anders took large steps to catch up to her colleague.

Daniels finally turned to Ben. "Sir, the Commanding Officer sends her compliments and requests that you join her in her cabin."

"Very well. Let's go see Captain Nation." Ben gestured for the young officer to proceed. "After you."

This was not a moment that Ben sought or even thought would occur. It had been almost four years since his last meeting with Captain Nation. The image of the tall blonde woman chewing him out aboard the USS BLUE RIDGE flashed into his mind. If they ever decided to put a picture of a hard ass in the dictionary, Ben was sure they would use Beth Nation's photo. "And the hits just keep on coming," he said to himself.

The first thing that Ben noticed was the ship's cleanliness. Perhaps it was the years of standing watch as the USS DEVON's Command Duty Officer that conditioned his scan. Whatever it was, the first thing he now noticed whenever he visited a Navy ship was her outward material condition. Long ago when he was a junior officer, someone once told him, "You can learn a lot about a ship by its cleanliness." If true, this ship was ready for anything. She was spotless.

As they made their way up a ladder, the officers and crew stopped their routine making way for them. The number of female personnel onboard also captured Ben's attention. Even as late as 1990, during Desert Storm, no US warship included women officers or enlisted personnel assigned. The Navy had changed.

Ben instantly remembered discussing the feasibility of women on warships at dinner one night at sea during his first junior officer tour. His XO, a brutish Bostonian, ended the conversation by telling him and the other officers that only certain subjects were appropriate for the wardroom, and the subject of women in warships was not one of them.

Ben did not consider himself a sexist; he knew from both his civilian and Navy Reserve careers that competence came from attitude and education rather than gender. Nevertheless, he found himself amazed at their prominence.

Ben trailed directly behind Lieutenant Commander Daniels as they reached the O-3 Level. Two junior officers, a male junior-grade lieutenant and a female lieutenant stepped to the side of the passageway to make way for them. The female officer, an attractive Latin woman, and Daniels exchanged heavy glances as he strode by and on toward the forward part of the ship.

"Good morning, sir," she said to Ben as her gaze finally shifted to him.

Ben nodded in response.

"So, sir. How do you know the Captain?" Daniels asked Ben as he followed him up the passageway toward another set of doors.

"We've served together before."

"Really? Where, sir?"

The doors led to yet another ladder. Ben followed Daniels as he started climbing.

"Seventh Fleet. I was part of their Reserve Component."

Daniels nodded his understanding.

As Ben made his way toward Captain Nation's at-sea cabin, he began rehearsing his greeting. It mattered little that they both held the same rank now. Not only was she senior to him, but she also commanded one the Navy's premier warships.

They arrived outside of a lone gray door. A painted label read, "Commanding Officer." Daniels knocked and then turned the knob to open the door.

"Ma'am, Captain McGuire."

Ben stepped in, marching with some difficulty, on the pitching deck. He came to attention as he stopped, making sure to face her. "Captain Ben McGuire reporting as ordered, ma'am."

The tall blonde woman wore reading glasses as she sat at her desk. She looked up from her work casually. An eyebrow went up as she examined Ben. He knew he must look a sight attired in Dinner Dress White aboard a ship at sea.

She shifted her gaze to Daniels. "Thanks, XO. That'll be all," she said pulling the glasses from her face.

Daniels nodded and backed out of the room. He closed the door on his way out.

Almost as soon as the door closed, Nation came to her feet. In the years since their last meeting, Ben had almost forgotten

Nation's 6'5" imposing physique. The former Olympic skier still looked fit and confident. "Ben, it's damn good to see you," she said with an extended hand. "But you didn't have to dress up to come see us," she laughed.

Shocked, Ben hesitated a moment before he returned the gesture. They shook hands warmly. He anticipated a different persona. She actually made a joke. Standing in front of her wearing dinner dress blues made the moment even more uncanny. "Thank you, Captain. You look well. Command suits you," he said forcing a smile.

"And O-6 suits you. I was happy to see your name on the promotion list. Congratulations, you deserve it."

Ben shrugged for the second time in less than fifteen minutes. "Deserve it or not, I'll take it," he laughed.

She backed away to her chair. "Have a seat."

"Thank you, ma'am."

"The President is safely onboard. As soon as we secure from flight ops, we'll head east to rendezvous with the carrier."

Ben nodded. "And the President of China. Any news?"

"Still trying to reach someone in China. We're still at DEFCON ONE. A coup in a nuclear-capable state kind of gets people hopping."

"Yeah. No doubt."

"We will rendezvous with *Ronald Reagan*. Some fool ordered her five-hundred miles out."

Ben smiled to himself at hearing her analysis of Deputy Chief of Mission Dudley's blunder. It might someday become public knowledge that moving the ship was Dudley's call against Ben's recommendation, but that was for historians to publish.

"So, can I bother someone for some clothes? We left in a hurry."

"I'll have someone bring something to you. You look like hell. Try to get some sleep."

Ben nodded. "Good idea, ma'am. Thanks again. And I'm glad it was you that picked us up."

CHAPTER THIRTEEN
VAMPIRES

Saturday, August 16th
POTUS Combat Air Patrol
Stinger Zero One and One One Four
Approximately 200 NM North of Taipei
0537 Hours

"Stinger Zero One, Raven One Two Six. Multiple surface contacts approximately 150 miles from you. Vector 017, 210 for intercept." Ryder listened to the radio call from the Navy E-2 Hawkeye airborne early-warning aircraft. From an altitude of 35,000 Feet, Raven One Two Six had the job of watching the waters north of the Taiwan Straits.

"Stinger Zero One," Ryder responded as he and "Herman" Muenster turned their F/A-18's north.

PLA-N Guided Missile Patrol Boat Houjiang (PGG-770)
Northern Taiwan Straits

Lieutenant Commander Liang Tau walked the bridge of his 215-foot vessel. Ready for battle, he and his crew of fifty-five wore combat helmets and flash gear, fire retardant clothing to protect exposed skin. Ordered to probe south, Liang and his crew cleared the way for the amphibious ships. Somewhere out there, a Wuhan-class submarine shadowed them, assisting in keeping their amphibious strike force safe.

Liang harbored concerns. Why did such an important operation merit only two small ships as escorts? While his ship's formidable armament consisted of cruise missiles and torpedoes, it lacked the abilities of a frigate or a destroyer. He scanned the pre-dawn horizon with binoculars and tried to push his away his anxiety.

"Captain?" his radar operator called. The younger officer barely kept his composure.

"Yes, Mr. Tong?"

"Multiple radar contacts. Bearing 178 degrees. Range is 94 kilometers."

Liang covered the two and a half meters to the radar station in two large and anxious steps. "Course?" he asked.

The operator drew a couple of grease-pencil lines on the screen and turned a couple of dials on the scope. "They are on a course of 358. Speed is 40 kilometers per hour."

"Damn," Liang murmured. He pulled his glasses up to see if he could spot the advancing craft. "They're coming right at us."

"Electronic Warfare Officer!" Liang bellowed.

"I am already looking at it, sir."

"Well. What is it, damn you?"

"One moment, Captain," the EWO replied from his station at the rear of the bridge.

This officer's equipment allowed him to analyze the electronic emissions of other vessels. Once collected, he would compare them to entries on file in an electronic database. They should be able to classify the distant surface contact quickly.

"Captain. There are three American warships, Aegis class."

A chill ran through Liang as he reached for the radio transmitter. "Go to Battle Stations. Prepare to attack."

"HYDRA, this is ANDROMEDA," he said into the microphone as he placed a call to the flagship.

GENERAL QUARTERS

USS Princeton *(CG-59)*

Captain Nation arrived to find the normal CIC crew plus a few visitors. Two of her enlisted personnel happily provided Congresswoman Anders a lecture on the air and surface combat stations. Nation smiled at her crew's enthusiasm. She then exchanged a smiling nod with Captain McGuire.

Captain McGuire, Chief of Staff Aldridge, and Congressman Jones, all wearing borrowed blue coveralls, stood near the surface status radar display. Only McGuire's uniform had any rank insignia. He wore borrowed Captain's eagles, her eagles, on his collar.

"Good morning. You folks are up awful early," Nation greeted as she approached the first group of visitors.

"Couldn't sleep," Congresswoman Anders replied cheerfully. "I simply had to see more of your wonderful ship, Captain."

Nation's face felt flush. "Thank you, Congresswoman. I'm sorry that we couldn't have arranged a tour under better circumstances."

"So, Captain," Congressman Anders began. "What is it like being a career woman in the Navy?"

"Why, Congresswoman, I would assume it's like being a career woman anywhere else," Nation laughed. "Full of opportunities and surprises."

POTUS Combat Air Patrol
Approximately 100 NM North of Taipei

"Boss, are you seeing this?" 'Herman' Muenster called over the secure radio.

"Affirmative." Shit. Ryder's heart pumped a tad faster as he spied two Chinese patrol boats leading three troop transports, all southbound, towards the straits and the President's location.

Ryder keyed his radio microphone, this time to call their REAGAN. "Rawhide, Stinger Zero One. Spool up the Surface Strike Package. I think we've got a problem. Over."

***

Chinese Marine Mobile Command Post
Beijing, China
0545 Hours

They parked the dark green trailer in the alley of one of Beijing's many slums. Marine General Yau's contacts inside the Army headquarters proved reliable. With so many military personnel suddenly in the streets, one green vehicle tended to look very much like another. As well as his mobile unit, he also was able to quietly insert two companies of Marines into the city without raising suspicions on the part of the plotters.

"Now what do we do?" Yau asked Sun.

They watched the Chinese State news broadcast with dismay and a growing sense of fear.

"Our breaking news story once again... The President of the United States and the President of China have been poisoned and are feared dead. Sources present at the state dinner tell us that both executives were present, celebrating the President of China's visit when they were stricken. Details are sketchy at this hour..."

"We save as many of our people as we can," Sun replied.

"I don't understand."

"The men who are here at our orders are all in danger. We must order them back to their posts. Immediately."

"Admiral!"

"We gambled and lost Yau. I did not think that Zhao would be so bold as to kill our President in a foreign land. This is truly a nightmare."

GENERAL QUARTERS

***

PLA-N Guided Missile Patrol Boat Houjiang (PGG-770)
Taiwan Straits

"Houjaing, this is Task Group Command," the secure radio in the patrol boat's pilothouse crackled. "We are being overflown by two American aircraft."

Liang's blood ran cold as he ran to the starboard side of his small ship and out onto the observation wing. He peered upward to find the source of the jet engine noise that already reached his ears. Once spotting a silver glint in the sky, he pulled up his binoculars to see an American Navy F/A-18 Hornet turning toward his ship. Lieutenant Commander Liang steeled his nerves as he ordered the craft to full speed.

"I have a firing solution on the American warships," his weapons technician called.

In Liang's fifteen years as a naval officer, he conducted nearly a thousand exercises. In each of those, he had been able to complete his attack unscathed successfully. However, he also conducted those attacks in concert with several other ships and never against such an advanced platform as an American Aegis cruiser.

He labored to ignore his fear.

USS Princeton *(CG-59)*
0550 Hours

LT Juarez stood the watch as the ship's Tactical Action Officer. Lieutenant Commander Paul Daniels sat at his station just a few feet away monitoring their progress. Since their last conversation a few nights earlier, Daniels presented only his most professional demeanor. He seemed so far away, even cold.

Captain Nation sat at her station, occupying the space between them. Juarez made several attempts to engage her

241

skipper but to no real avail. The senior officer barely gave her any notice; rather, Nation studied the displays in front of her with laser-like intensity.

"TAO," the Electronic Warfare Technician called from his station.

"TAO, aye," Juarez replied into her headset.

She scanned the surface, air, and sub-surface large screen displays in front of her. Since arriving in the Taiwan Straits vicinity, the surface and air picture were awash with contacts. Keeping track of them all proved more than a full-time job.

"I've got a weird-looking radar signature over here, ma'am."

"What do you mean?"

One of *Princeton*'s most vital sensors was her AN/SLQ-32, or Slick 32, Threat Emitter Analyzer. The system provided the operational capability for early warning of threat weapon system emitters and emitters associated with targeting platforms. It also provided the ship the ability to jam aircraft, ship, and missile-borne radars.

"I've got something showing up as weird-looking surface search/Square Tie variant."

"Discrimination on?"

"Yes, ma'am."

She looked over at Daniels. He was on the telephone with someone. Her first impulse was to ask him for guidance. Then the memory of his attitude over the last day or so played back in her mind.

A Square-Tie signature usually indicated a missile-targeting radar system. Juarez also recalled the intelligence reports on the location of Chinese vessels she had reviewed before taking the watch. All missile-capable ships were accounted for and reported in port.

The thought of asking Captain Nation for her advice quickly coursed through her mind. Juarez quickly weighed her skipper's mood over the last hour or so. JJ decided just to handle it herself. "Classify it as a merchant ship. Keep an eye on it."

"But it's coming from…"

"Look, Olson! I'm busy here! If something else pops up, like another Square Tie, call me!"

"Yes, ma'am."

JJ's response drew a glare from Nation. She had violated one of her Captain's cardinal rules: "No shouting or raised voices in CIC unless it's an emergency."

JJ finally found the courage to find Nation's gaze. "Sorry, Ma'am," she muttered.

Nation shook her head as she finally looked away.

JJ was sure she read "disgust" in the senior officer's eyes and gesture. Juarez blew out her anxiety as he returned to scanning the displays.

***

Central Military Committee Command Center
Beijing, China
0551 Hours

"Colonel, we have a task force en route to Taiwan. Two patrol boats and a submarine are providing escort. Can you find some other ships that can assist them?"

"Yes, General. I will contact the Fleet Headquarters. Admiral Sun-"

"Admiral Sun is indisposed," Zhao interrupted. "Make the call to his duty officer instead. I'm sure they have heard about the emergency by now."

"Yes, General," Mulin replied as he picked up the phone.

Zhao turned toward Chairman Fei in time to see him pulling out his mobile telephone.

"That will not function in here," Zhao admonished.

Fei frowned in confusion.

"We have an electronic blanket covering the building to keep American eavesdropping at bay."

"Of course," Fei replied. The fat man eyed one of the telephones on the console in front of him.

"And I'm afraid that we must keep all lines open for the present. Several key commanders will need to contact us with their status."

Fei nodded as he eased his phone back into his pocket.

As Zhao moved his gaze from the fidgeting politician, one of the telephones on the desk rang. The General watched as a member of the watch team answered with professional military precision. The officer's eyes went wide as he listened to the person on other end speak.

"Who is this?" he asked.

Zhao grimaced at the young man and the phone against his ear. "What? Who is that?"

"Sir. They're asking for you. It is a man," he stuttered. "He claims to be the President," he continued.

Zhao exchanged a tension-laced and troubled glance with Fei as he snatched the receiver from the young officer. "Who the hell is this?"

"General Zhao. This is President Ho," the voice said.

His heart almost stopped at the sound. He knew it to be him. He had heard his voice too many times. Zhao quickly recovered his composure. "This is General Zhao Chin Lee. This is not the time for pranks. I will find you and have you arrested!"

"General. This is no prank..."

Zhao slammed the phone down onto its carriage. "Damned fools. How dare they play games at a time like this?!"

The watch officer who had taken the call cowered in his chair. All color had drained from his face.

"We will ignore any more calls claiming to be the President!" Zhao ordered.

"Yes, General," Colonel Mulin replied.

Zhao maintained a stern front. He did not dare look at Fei for fear of giving away his newest secret. *Damn him! He's alive! He's fucking alive!*

***

Combat Information Center
USS Princeton (CG-59)

"That's affirmative. They're headed in your direction. I estimate you're inside of their missile engagement envelope now," the pilot's voice boomed over the speaker."

"Fuck." Paul Daniels' stomach went taut. "Roger," he managed to say into the radio's microphone.

"Take the ship to General Quarters," Nation said to Juarez. "XO, get the President below decks."

Daniels nodded turned to Chief Guerette. "Go. Take POTUS to DC Central. And get your ass back up here!"

The Operations Specialist Chief Petty Officer was already up and moving before Daniels finished speaking.

"What's going on?" Aldridge asked.

"Chinese warships are closing on us."

"We're moving the President to the safest place on the ship," Ben explained.

POTUS Combat Air Patrol
Approximately 100 NM North of Taipei

"Stinger Zero One, Hammer Four Zero," the surface strike leader called. "We're two minutes out."

The tension in Ryder's stomach finally eased a bit, but only for a second. The surface ship strike aircraft, a flight of four F-18's armed with laser-guided bombs, were only minutes away. Ryder had a bad feeling, and it grew worse by the second.

"Four Zero, roger. Hurry," Ryder said with as much succinctness as he could muster.

PLA-N Guided Missile Patrol Boat Houjiang (PGG-770)
Taiwan Straits
0555 Hours

"Shoot," Liang ordered.

The fire control technician pressed a single red button on his console, and the craft shuddered for a long moment as six C-801 cruise missiles leaped into the air. He watched each booster lift its 165 kilograms of high-explosive payload into the air until they disappeared against the gray horizon.

"We'll keep the ship turned toward the American vessel. If they survive the shot, they'll be looking for us. We'll present a smaller profile at this angle, and we'll be ready to fire another shot," he reassured his crew.

Liang hoped he was putting up a brave front. He knew from his training that if the American Aegis Cruiser survived the missile attack, they would hunt him down like a dog. He hoped that his men did not know that they might have just signed their own death warrants.

POTUS Combat Air Patrol

"Holy shit," Ryder said to himself as he watched the patrol boats launch missiles. "Herman, fight's on!" he shouted to his wingman over the radio. He pushed the stick forward and to the left to place his aircraft in a steep dive toward the missiles and flipped the toggle arming his weapons.

"Roger." Herman was on his right-wing, right where she was supposed to be.

"*Princeton*, this is Stinger Zero One. You have six vampires inbound. I say again, you have six vampires inbound. POTUS CAP is engaging." Ryder, his heart raging, congratulated himself for keeping a calm voice during his call.

The self-adulation lasted only seconds as the first missile fell into his HUD's targeting reticle. Ryder "got good tone" as his first missile locked on to the target in his display. "Fox Two," he called while launching an AIM-9 Sidewinder missile off his left wing.

Seconds later, Muenster followed her commander's lead. Two explosions punctuated the end of two Chinese cruise missiles.

Ryder checked his radar display. USS *Princeton* and her two escorts were looming into view. They were out of time. "Herman, break off," he ordered as he sighted in on a third target.

"Fox Two," Ryder called again as he fired the last missile and pulled upward and left, away from the US Navy ships. A third explosion ended the third of six missiles.

"Breaking right," Herman responded as she pulled her aircraft into a steep climb.

Ryder pulled his aircraft up and to the left away from the friendly surface ships. He and Muenster flew inside *Princeton*'s missile engagement envelope. They cleared out to avoid *Princeton* mistaking them as missiles.

"*Princeton*, we got three of them. You have three vampires inbound," he called over the radio.

"SUCAP," Ryder called the strike team lead. "Your targets are the missile patrol boats leading the amphibs. They just fired on POTUS."

USS Princeton (CG-59)
0601 Hours

"VAMPIRE! VAMPIRE! VAMPIRE!" the Electronic Warfare Operator shouted. His voice cut the air in the Combat Information Center like a razor-edged sword. They were under missile attack. Seconds before, the speaker in CIC had crackled with the same warning from the two F-18 Hornets flying combat air patrol.

Ben's heart nearly jumped from his chest as his mind flashed back to the past for a split second. There he was again, back in the CIC of the USS DEVON under attack from a Libyan Styx missile. A half a thought later, the horror of the moment chased memories from his mind and the breath from his lungs.

"What's going on?" the President's Chief of Staff asked with fear growing in her eyes.

"CHAFF! CHAFF now!!!" the female officer sitting in the TAO chair shouted at the top of her lungs.

"Slick's already doing it!" the technician shouted back referring to the ship's SLQ-32 system.

Everyone's eyes went wide as the dull sound and vibration of the launchers sent a cloud of aluminum foil into the air over the ship. If it worked properly, the metal strips would fool the missile into exploding early and thereby save the ship.

"We're under attack," Ben said, not believing his own words.

"Hard right rudder! All ahead, flank!" Nation shouted into the 21MC intercom to the Bridge.

"My rudder is hard right. No course given," the Officer of the Deck replied. "Engines ahead, flank."

"CWIS is in full automatic," Juarez reported, referring to the ship's Close-In Weapons System.

The ship listed heavily as the rudder bit into the ocean below the waterline. Ben grabbed hold of an equipment cabinet to keep his balance. Chief of Staff Aldridge anchored herself by holding onto the back of LT Juarez' chair.

"What are we doing?" Chief of Staff Aldridge asked.

"Giving the Close-In Weapons System a clear shot at the missile."

"Steady as she goes," Daniels said into the 21MC. He glanced at the gyrocompass display for a course heading. "Steady up on one five zero, true."

"Steadying up on one five zero, true. Aye, sir," a young voice replied over the intercom.

"What is a SEAWIZ?" Aldridge asked.

"Close-In Weapons System, C I W S. It's a high-caliber machine-gun with a radar system attached to it. There's one on the back of the ship and one on each side. If a missile flies within its engagement view, it should shoot it down," Ben explained.

The unit consisted of a 20mm Gatling-gun attached to a closed-loop radar system so precise that its depleted-uranium rounds even attacked the remains of a target once attaining the destruction of its main body.

Aldridge nodded. "Does it work?"

Ben turned to see Aldridge's taut-faced expression of concern. "Yeah. It works," he said as he turned to face the large screen displays. "Most of the time." The sound of the CIWS engaging the incoming missile sounded like a dull jackhammer thumping against the ship's superstructure. Ben instinctively looked up as if he would be able to see the CIWS firing.

A loud BOOM sounded. Vibration emanated from the rear of the ship, causing everything to rattle violently for a long moment. The silence of the CIC's routine made a triumphant return.

"Enemy missile destroyed," Juarez announced loudly.

The CIC watch team exploded in cheers and applause.

"Shut up, damn it! This isn't a fucking ballgame!" Daniels bellowed.

A graveyard-like silence returned to the space. Ben mentally smiled at Daniels' command style.

Seconds later *Princeton* shuddered like a tin shack in a tornado as a cruise missile detonated. The sound was deafening. The shockwave threw lights from the overhead and sailors from their chairs. Ben, and everyone near him who had been standing, found themselves on the deck. A fireball blew the door to the forward passageway off its hinges, filling the Combat Information Center with thick, gray acrid smoke.

Lighting in the space first flickered, and then went out, casting it into complete darkness. All around him, electrical equipment arced to illuminate Combat like a lightning storm.

Ben coughed as he gasped for air. Through ringing ears, he heard the muffled noises of others in the dark struggling to breathe. Disoriented, he felt for the deck. Some of the blue florescent lights in the overhead flickered back to life.

A woman's shriek cut through the ringing in Ben's ears. The heart-wrenching sound came from the direction of the command console, and the ship's captain and executive officer's stations. He struggled to peer through stinging eyes and smoke to make out the reason for the matter but to no avail.

Fire engulfed several consoles. Crew members quickly grabbed fire extinguishers and attacked the flames. Ben climbed to his feet as others around him did the same. As his head cleared, he helped Veronica Aldridge stand. Her normally well-coiffed hair, now a disheveled mop, and soot covered her face. Muffled voices murmured "Oh my God" and other shock-filled expletives. Ben pushed his way toward the direction of the crew's angst.

He fought back the urge to regurgitate when he saw Captain Beth Nation's caved-in skull. Her tall torso lay almost headless in an expanding pool of thick red blood. The Chinese missile's explosion turned one of the overhead-mounted monitors into yet another but an interior missile. The screen lay near the edge of the blood pool; an unmistakable piece of Nation's skull and brain-matter adhered to its edge.

Lieutenant Commander Daniels knelt by her body, his eyes and mouth agape. The TAO also stood in silent disbelief.

Memories of his time on the USS DEVON flooded Ben's thoughts again. They had suffered a missile strike, seriously injuring the captain and killing the executive officer. The third in command, the Operations Officer panicked, leaving Ben with one choice: take command. Only this time, the Executive Officer survived the attack. Daniels needed to take charge.

"Come on," Ben said as he grabbed Daniels by his collar.

"What?"

"Get up."

"Have some respect here!" the ship's Executive Officer screamed back through tearing eyes. He sank back down to his knees in front of Nation's broken corpse.

Ben grabbed Daniels again, this time hoisting him completely to his feet. He threw the taller officer against the Captain's chair and seized him by his uniform collar. "Pull your head out of your ass! You've got a ship to save! She's dead! We're not, and I've got a family to get to! Now move, damn you!" Ben shoved Daniels toward his station and shot the TAO an equally stern glance. "Move, damn it!"

Daniels stood for a long moment. He slowly scanned his ship's shattered CIC and then McGuire. He nodded slowly and took his station. Members of the Combat Information Center team stared at Daniels for a long moment, waiting for his orders.

"All hands, this is the XO," Daniels finally spoke into the 1MC intercom.

Ben looked up at an overhead speaker. He was astonished to find it working. He heard Daniels' amplified voice.

"Make Damage Control Reports to DC Central. Let's get these fires out."

On closer examination, Daniels had a deep gash on his forehead. Blood ran down his face, pooling at his chin. He swiped at it, making it worse.

"Phone. I need a phone," Aldridge demanded.

Daniels pointed at his console.

"How do I dial the President?" she asked as she pulled the receiver from its holder.

"0304," Daniels replied as he scanned his damaged ship.

She punched in the numbers.

Ben sat on the edge of his seat as he waited for her to speak.

"Mr. President?"

Ben felt himself relax a bit.

"Are you okay, sir?"

Ben tuned out the remainder of the conversation as the Naval Officer part of his psyche completed taking him over.

The TAO, now in her chair, still wore a dazed, wide-eyed quality. She wavered in her chair for a moment or two before eventually putting her head down on the console and passing out.

"What happened?" he heard Congressman Jones ask from behind him.

The congressman stood holding his arm. Pain racked his face. A disheveled Congresswoman Anders stood next to him.

"We were almost hit by a missile," Ben replied.

"Almost?" Jones asked.

"Yeah. If it had hit us, we'd be dead now."

Ben turned his gaze back toward the female representative. She looked like hell, pallid, sweaty. "Congresswoman, are you okay?" he asked.

"Yeah, yeah. Just need a minute to catch my breath," she replied.

Suddenly, the sound a man screaming in deadly agony reached Ben's ears. His stomach turned at the intensity of his distress. Ben turned toward the direction of the cry to see several crewmen in blue uniforms running through the blue smoke toward one of their shipmates.

"Cut the power!! Cut the power!!" an unidentified female voice shouted above the din.

Ben's gaze finally fixed on large muscular man convulsing against a gray-colored console. Sparks flew from his shoulders and arms as he screamed. Several of his crewmen stood by in desperation, all looking for something to use to knock him loose from the malfunctioning equipment.

A portion of the compartment went dark as an unseen technician pulled a switch to secure electrical power to the console. The afflicted crew member fell lifelessly from his chair onto the gray deck. Two other crew members immediately began performing CPR on their fallen comrade.

"Who is it?!! Daniels shouted to the gathering.

"It's the Senior Chief!" a young voice shouted back.

Daniels turned to TAO. "Get the corpsman up here! Now!"

"Yes, sir."

At that point, Ben and Daniels' eyes locked. Both then turned to face the broken doorway leading to the passageway and the ladder to the bridge. "Oh God."

Both men charged through the still smoky space for the door. When they reached it, Daniels forgot all military courtesy and cut in front of Ben. Even more smoke-filled than the CIC, they had to feel their way along until the light from the morning sun cut through the haze enough for them to see.

Fires still blazed on the bridge. Equipment, rubber, and fabric components were all engulfed by flame. The breeze caused by *Princeton*'s forward speed fed the fires with fresh oxygen. Ben and Daniels each grabbed an extinguisher and began knocking down the flames.

Smoke billowed through the broken bridge windows. It occasionally broke enough for Ben to see outside. He strained through stinging eyes to see a large column of black smoke on the ship's starboard horizon. "Holy shit!"

"What, sir?" Daniels asked over the sound of his CO2 extinguisher.

"Is that one of the escorts?" Ben asked as he pointed.

Daniels craned to look in the same direction. "Damn. It's *John Paul Jones*."

Two halves jutted above the water while the middle section appeared fully ablaze. Ben immediately knew the ship and her crew were lost.

As the fires started dying, the odor of burned and charred flesh reached Ben's nostrils. Making his way toward the center of the bridge, he tripped and fell over something bulky and relatively soft. He sat up to regain his bearings and found himself near two dead and severely burned bodies. The remains of several crewmen lay all around him, smoke still rising from them all. For the second time in as many days, he threw up at the sight of violent death.

"Captain." he heard Daniels shout from the other side of the space.

Ben wiped his mouth with the back of his sleeve. Reeling, devastated with anguish, he climbed to his feet. "Yeah. I'm coming," he replied.

POTUS Combat Air Patrol
5,000 Feet above the Taiwan Straits

"Hammer Four Zero in hot," the surface strike leader announced over the radio as he led three other bomb-laden F-18's into a steep dive.

"Zero One, roger," Ryder replied. Orbiting the area, Ryder flew in a perfect location to observe the attack. His wingman, 'Herman' Muenster, was a few miles away taking on fuel from an aerial tanker. She would return to the area afterward to allow Ryder to refuel.

Laser designators, invisible to the naked eye, illuminated the two patrol boats below. Ryder carefully scanned his electronic warfare sensors to determine if the amphibious ships to the north were targeting them. Nothing. The screen was clear. He frowned at his analysis. Something didn't fit. Three troopships escorted by only three patrol boats. "Somebody really screwed up here."

GENERAL QUARTERS

He leveled his gaze at the scene below in time to see the fighters pull out of their dives. Seconds later, five explosions of yellow and orange fire engulfed the Chinese missile patrol boats. Dark-colored debris of varying shapes and sizes flew outward from the blasts' center. Ryder's aircraft buffeted slightly as the sound and shockwave finally reached his location.

"Splash two," the strike leader reported the destruction of the Chinese vessels.

"Roger," Ryder replied as he acknowledged the report. "Weapons status?" he asked the Hammer Four Zero, inquiring his ability to attack the remaining Chinese amphibious ships.

"Got plenty more where that came from."

Ryder chuckled at the response. "Roger. Standby." Ryder switched the channel on his radio to the maritime VHF channel that the Chinese ships below should have been monitoring. "Southbound Chinese warship, side number 934, state your intentions, over." Ryder's current rules of engagement only allowed them to attack vessels that had fired on US assets or posed a threat of firing on US assets.

Ryder waited thirty seconds or so for a response. As he prepared to key his microphone to repeat the hail, he scanned the Chinese ships below. He nodded to himself, confidently at seeing the unmistakable bend in the ships' wakes as they turned to reverse their course. They were heading home. "I thought that might be your answer."

***

Chinese Marine Mobile Command Post
Beijing, China.
0605 Hours

Yau, despite his protestations to Sun, stood over his communications operator. He held a hastily written message per Admiral Sun's instructions. A lump formed in his throat as he prepared to take the station to make the transmission himself. The Marine Commander took a last look over his shoulder at Sun. His friend and mentor sat quietly at a small table on the other side of the van. A loaded 9mm pistol was in front of him. He knew that as soon as the transmission was over, Sun would act to save his family by ending his life.

The sound of a ringing mobile telephone intruded into the noise of military transmissions. Yau watched as the sound seemed to pull Sun out of his death-like trance. The four-star admiral at up, reached into his jacket, and withdrew the ringing phone. He stared at the display intently before finally pressing the button to speak.

"Hello."

Yau watched as Sun's eyes narrowed.

"How do I know this is not a ruse?" Sun asked the person on the other end.

Yau backed away from the telecom console and walked toward Sun.

"What is the code?" Sun asked the person on the other end.

Sun gestured for Yau to come closer. The Marine officer placed his ear near Sun's to hear the caller's voice.

"I don't know the code. My assistant destroyed the codebook before he was killed."

"This is some trick. I am not falling for..."

"Admiral. When you took command of the People's Navy, your wife was with you," the man interjected.

"That's no secret. Anyone could tell you that."

"But can anyone tell you that she was happy to be coming home to Beijing after all these years?" he asked.

Sun's eyes went wide again, but his back stiffened.

Yau could not believe his ears. Was he really alive? How? How could they determine if it was Ho? Like Sun, Yau was unconvinced.

"I gave you a book on the day you took command," he tried yet again.

Sun's demeanor softened. He let his shoulders slump. "Yes. Yes. I received a book from the President. And what was that book?" he asked.

"Comrade Admiral, it was the Art of War," he replied.

Still not completely convinced, he asked one last question. "Was there anything else?"

"I marked a special passage for you, advice for your trials to come."

Sun stood suddenly. Yau changed his posture to keep his ear near the phone.

"And?" Sun asked.

"It was the passage entitled 'Fight Only the Battles One Can Win.'"

Sun again took on a rigid posture. Only this time, he stood at attention. "Comrade President, how can your Navy be of assistance?"

"I am not sure, Admiral. What is your status?"

Sun reached for and put away his pistol. General Yau shot him a smile as the two men bowed to one another with their heads.

***

USS Princeton (CG-59)
0608 Hours

By the time Ben returned to CIC, the space was coming back to life. With all the fires extinguished, a thin haze had replaced the thick cloud of smoke. While many of the equipment cabinets looked lifeless, several more remained operative. Two of the three large screen displays projected the air and surface picture for the XO and the TAO. Finally, only a large pool of drying blood remained to mark the place on the deck where Nation's body laid.

"What's the status of our weapons systems?" Ben asked Daniels.

"Looks like we've still got everything except the forward missile magazine, sir."

"What happened up there?" Veronica Aldridge asked as she came over.

"The missile exploded near the bridge. The bridge crew is dead. And we lost one of the escort ships, Ben replied."

She took in a deep breath and let it out slowly.

"That's not the worst of it. Congresswoman Anders had a heart attack," the TAO added. "They just took her down to Sick Bay. It didn't look good."

Aldridge turned toward Ben. "So, what now? Who's in command?" she asked.

Ben gestured toward Lieutenant Commander Daniels with his head. "He is."

Her eyes bugged. "But he's only a lieutenant commander-"

"He's the Executive Officer of this ship," Ben shot back.

"Maybe so, Captain. But you out-rank him. You should take command."

"No, he should know more about this ship than anyone. Including me."

Aldridge shifted her eyes from Ben back to Daniels. The young officer stood at his console with his hands on his hips, watching the goings-on.

"I don't think he knows what to do," Aldridge observed.

She was right. This was no time for him to shut down as his Operations Officer did so many years ago. Ben turned to the TAO. Her face wore a listless gaze as she seemed transfixed on the portion of the console immediately in front of her. He scanned her nametag. "Ms. Juarez? Are you okay?"

She did not answer.

"JJ?" Daniels called.

She finally turned to face Daniels. Her eyes started welling with tears. "I fucked up."

"What?" Daniels asked.

"I misread the radar threat. I thought it was a surface search radar. I'm sorry. I'm so sorry," she blubbered.

Daniels only frowned in disbelief at the woman. He finally turned to Ben. "Sir, I could use some help here."

Aldridge shot Ben a supportive glance and nod.

"Yeah," Ben replied. "What about the active sonar?" Ben asked. "Is it up?"

"Sir?"

"Turn it on," Ben ordered. "Go active. Now."

Juarez also turned to face Daniels. Her face, still wet with tears, now had the added dimension of a confused frown.

"I don't know what the hell is going on between you two and frankly, I don't care," the tone of Ben's voice grew firmer and louder with each word. "The President of the United States is embarked in this ship, and we're still in a fight out here! Now turn on the damned sonar!" Ben ordered.

"But why active, sir?" the TAO asked.

"How else are you gonna find a diesel submarine out here?" Ben shot back.

Daniels nodded at Juarez, and he picked up the microphone for the 1MC. "This is the TAO…"

"Now," he said to Daniels. "Show me on this thing where we were when we got hit," he said, referring to the surface display.

Daniels used a trackball on his console to highlight the position on the ship's track to indicate *Princeton*'s position at the time of missile impact.

Ben nodded as the sound of the huge transducer located in *Princeton*'s hull, sending a pulse through the ocean reached their ears.

"Sir, we checked the Intel reports. All of their subs are accounted for," the TAO inserted.

"Maybe. But it's their doctrine to always attack a surface vessel with back up from a submarine," Ben replied. "Now, what was the bearing line of that radar intercept you misread?"

Juarez took control of the screen from her console. She used the instrument to draw in a line leading from the impact point out on a bearing of 305 degrees.

"Sir, *William P. Lawrence* is on the move," one of the technicians in the space called out.

Ben looked at the tactical display to see the remaining AEGIS Destroyer taking up position on *Princeton*'s port bow.

"What's she doing?" Juarez asked.

"Giving us cover. Putting themselves between us and another missile," Ben replied.

"Sir, how do you know-?" Daniels began to ask.

"I don't, Mr. Daniels. This is a game of seconds and not second-guessing. Your ship has taken a missile hit. We won't survive another one. Right now the guys that just shot you are getting ready to finish you off."

"Sonar Contact!" Juarez reported.

Ben, while he expected it, he had hoped he would not hear those words. "And the hits just keep on coming."

"Bearing 297, range fifteen thousand yards."

Ben turned to face Daniels.

"Yes, sir. I've got it. Developing a firing solution," the TAO interjected. Ben nodded.

***

Vicinity of the Central Military Committee Compound
Beijing, China
0614 Hours

"Yes, I understand," Yau said into his mobile telephone.

GENERAL QUARTERS

Sun observed his subordinate and friend as their limousine came to a stop around the corner from the expansive compound. Sun played a hunch that the Civil Defense Police stationed outside his house were looking for him by now. A call to his wife would have answered the question. However, it also would have incriminated her as his accomplice. In case this gambit failed, he wanted to make sure that he would not inadvertently make her life any more difficult.

Yau ended his call and lowered the small phone from his ear. "You were right. General Zhao has issued a warrant for your arrest."

Sun nodded. "Well, at least some of my instincts are still good," he joked. "What about you?"

"No. I am still looked upon with favor."

"Good. Good." Sun sat up in the vehicle. It was time to go.

"Are you certain that we should go forward with this?" Yau asked. He crossed his arms and grimaced.

Sun sighed heavily. The plan was dangerous. Zhao undoubtedly knew that President Ho was still alive. Whatever he was up to, it was unraveling ever so slightly. He would be a volatile adversary. Still, China's future was at risk. "Yes. We will proceed."

"Good luck, Admiral," Yau said as he bowed his head.

"And the same to you. You have been a good friend," Sun replied. He smiled and climbed out of the vehicle.

***

USS Princeton (CG-59)

"Sir, I've got a firing solution on the submarine," Juarez announced.

"Two torpedoes, Lieutenant. Engage the target."

"Aye, sir. Underwater Battery, Tube Two, two torpedoes, shoot," she said into her headset.

A closed-circuit television camera displayed compressed air ejecting two Mark-48 torpedoes toward their target from the triple torpedo tube on *Princeton*'s port side.

"TAO," the Sub-Surface Warfare console operator called. "Two fish, running hot straight and normal. Time to target, two minutes."

"TAO, aye."

***

Central Military Committee Command Center
0617 Hours

"What is happening?" Fei asked Zhao under his breath.

The tempo of activity in the center had increased in the last few minutes. The invasion fleet's escort had engaged American warships. The patrol boat's commanding officer claimed to have scored two kills and was maneuvering for another attack. Zhao now waited to hear from Lieutenant General Weidong Mauo, the Air Force Commander. The invasion fleet needed air cover, and now.

"Be still," Zhao shot back quietly, intensely.

Fei's eyes grew wide as blood rushed to his face. He drew even closer to Zhao. "What are you doing, General?"

"Trying to win this. Now shut the hell up and be still," he snapped back. Zhao looked down suddenly to see Colonel Mulin and two other watch-standers at the main console closely observing them. Once noticed, all three turned away quickly to face their consoles, the main view screens, or any direction except the two politicos.

"Do not press me, General. I am the Chairman of the People's Party," he whispered.

Zhao did not respond. Rather he focused on the weapon in his jacket pocket and how it seemed to push against his ribs with growing concentration. Taking it out now would provide relief on several levels.

CHAPTER FOURTEEN
HONOR AND GLORY

Saturday, August 16th
USS Princeton (CG-59)
0627 Hours

"TAO, loud underwater explosion! I have buckling metal," the Sub-Surface sensor operator announced.

Ben slapped Daniels on his back. "Shit hot."

Daniels nodded in agreement.

"TAO, I have no other contacts," Sub-Surface reported.

"Now, let's get the hell out of here. Signal *William P. Lawrence*," Daniels ordered. "We'll hold 12 knots until we're past the continental shelf and in deeper water."

Ben wanted to breathe a sigh of relief but knew it was too soon to do so. They had too far to go for that.

***

Central Military Committee Compound Entrance
Beijing, China
0630 Hours

Groups of soldiers, sailors, and airmen made their way up and down the thoroughfare and sidewalks approaching the compound entrance. Officers and enlisted personnel alike, saluted him with wide-eyed surprise. Sun smiled as he returned each salute.

His limo dropped him almost a block and a half away from the gate. Sun scanned the streets as he watched for Civil

Defense or Police vehicles. There were none, as he had hoped. He suspected that this was the last place his adversaries, whoever they were, expected to see him. The main gate loomed ahead.

As he approached the main gate, Sun spotted four soldiers on duty. Each wore a holstered pistol and a rifle slung over their left shoulder. Two inspected the identification cards of those persons in vehicles or on foot while the other two provided them cover.

Digging into his pocket for his identification card, Sun marched right up to the guard standing closest to the sidewalk and presented himself to the sentries. "I am Vice Admiral Sun Xueliang," he said to a young Army guard. He held out his credentials as he came to a stop and stood at attention.

The guard, a baby-faced corporal, came to attention and saluted him smartly. After Sun returned the salute, the guard took his identification card and inspected it. He looked up suddenly and called his partner over to him. The second guard examined the card and then Sun.

The fourth soldier was a short, burly man with thick eyebrows. When he walked, he marched with purpose. Though muscular, his uniform was well-tailored. He saluted Admiral Sun when he arrived. He waited until Sun returned the salute before turning to inspect the identification card.

The sergeant looked up from the plastic card and turned toward Sun. "Sir, I regret to inform you that I must place you under arrest," he said respectfully.

Sun smiled. "Of course. May I ask the charge?"

"Sir, I have no information on the charges."

"Can you tell me who has preferred charges against me?"

"Yes, Admiral. The order comes from General Zhao."

Sun's limousine pulled up to the gate. Two of the guards came to attention and saluted. A third went around to the driver's side.

"Admiral. I have orders to take you to General Zhao," the sergeant added, bringing Sun's attention back to his pending arrest.

Of course. Zhao is a megalomaniac. He needs to see his vanquished foe. "Really. Where is he?"

When the driver passed two credentials through his window to the guard, Sun reached up and pushed his hat back on his head.

General Yau, from the relative cover of the vehicle's darkened windows, watched the goings-on outside the car. He held an open briefcase on his lap to give the appearance of a busy military executive. His stomach tightened when he watched sergeant of the guard take Admiral Sun into custody. In their nearly fifteen-year relationship, he had never seen Sun slump as he stood. His friend normally presented the picture of military bearing and deportment.

When Sun reached up and adjusted his hat, Yau's anxiety subsided somewhat. Per their pre-arranged signal, Sun signaled he was on his way to Zhao. His part of the plan, if successful, would help save his country and, hopefully, his friend and commander's life.

"Good morning, General," a guard greeted as he returned his identification to his driver and saluted.

Yau looked up when the guard spoke. He nodded and returned to feigning work.

***

Presidential Office Building
Taipei, Taiwan

"People of China, a terrible crime has been perpetrated on our nation," Ho Lin Shih said into the camera. "But this crime was not committed by the United States or Taiwan; it was committed by our fellow countrymen. Unfortunately, the President of Taiwan is also a victim of this conspiracy. Tonight, he gave his life in defense of his country, and ours."

CNN's Jack Mitchell had introduced the President of China to his country and the world. Now he stood by as he transmitted his history-making address.

"I have every reason to believe that members of our Government and our military are seeking to take control of our country, if they have not already done so. I urge you to disbelieve the news of my death. I am quite well and am anxious to return home. Please do not allow this tyranny to stand," the President pleaded.

He nodded, and the camera operator swung the lens toward Mitchell. "This is Jack Mitchell for CNN reporting from Taipei, Taiwan. This transmission will be repeated by our network for as long as it takes to determine...to determine," he stopped himself. "We will continue to repeat this transmission for the next hour."

***

Central Military Committee Command Center
Beijing, China
0635 Hours

Two guards escorted Admiral Sun into the command center. From the moment he entered, Sun started reading the status boards. Occasionally, a passing Navy person greeted him respectfully, breaking Sun's concentration and causing him to note that more than just a few people knew of his plight.

Chang. You fool. He quickly surmised that his East Sea Commander was part of the coup. At that very moment, he commanded a small and poorly defended task force en route to Taipei. Worse yet, the American navy had already destroyed two missile corvettes. It was little wonder that the CMC had redoubled its focus on developing a professional Navy. Army officers did not understand war at sea.

"Admiral," Zhao hissed as the guards delivered him. "I understand you surrendered yourself."

Zhao switched his gaze from the screens to Admiral Sun. His eyes were wide and full of life. He almost laughed as he spoke.

"Yes, General. That is correct," Sun replied.

Zhao smiled like a hungry tiger before a meal. "That was probably the wisest action you have taken in the last two months. Unfortunately, it is probably too little, too late."

Yau made his way down the fifth flight of stairs two steps at a time. His breathless state surprised him as he passed a sign that read "Sub-Level 3." Yau started each day with a three-mile run in full-combat gear including a rucksack and boots. For extra measure, one of his junior officers usually accompanied him. He knew he was in the best of physical condition.

Damn, I'm tired. Thisis what no sleep will do.

As tired as he was, he knew Sun was that much more so. He and his friend were on their fortieth hour without rest. He smiled at both his arrival and no further steps lay ahead.

He pulled a pistol from his pants pocket as he placed his hand on the door handle. Yau listened intently for the sound of the patrolling sentry. He took note of the cool dampness that seemed to cover everything. Drops of moisture occasionally fell from the ceiling to the concrete floor. He stood deathly still for almost four long minutes listening and reaching out to detect the presence of another human being. Finally, slowly, he twisted the latch and pulled open the door.

The space on the other side was warmer and drier than the stairwell. He knew instantly his information had brought him to the right place. He looked to his left and right. On both sides, a long narrow passageway with fluorescent lighting beckoned.

He mentally pictured the floor plan and turned left. Yau lowered the weapon and proceeded down the corridor. He walked as swiftly and as quietly as possible. Speed and stealth were of the essence. He repeatedly pushed thoughts of Sun's well-being, or lack thereof, out of his mind. If he was okay, then this gambit might pay off. If not, he might find himself in similar circumstances facing Zhao with little to no chance of survival.

The door to an electrical wiring room loomed ahead. Yau paused to listen. He trembled at the sound of approaching footsteps. He swallowed hard as he focused on the door. He needed time to open it, but knew there was no way. His options flashed through his mind as he looked down at the gun in his hand. The thought of killing another loyal comrade was as abhorrent to him as failing Sun. The footsteps drew nearer.

Sun turned and looked into the glaring eyes of the Chairman of the People's Communist Party, Fei Tzu. They had met once before when he was a staffer working for Zhao's predecessor. The men exchanged a long cold stare before either of them spoke.

"Chairman Fei. I must say that I am surprised to find you a part of this."

Fei smiled a jowly grin. "I'm surprised to find you on the wrong side of history, Admiral Sun. I have watched your career for some time. I had hoped better for you."

"Save your hopes for yourself, Chairman. When the People find out what you have done, there will be--consequences."

"The People will laud us as heroes, Admiral. And denigrate those who stood against us."

Sun checked his watch. It was almost time.

"Have you an appointment?" Fei asked.

"In a manner of speaking, yes."

"Take him away," Zhao said to the guards. "He is to be placed in solitary confinement until his trial."

The guards placed heavy hands on Sun's uniform. He knew immediately that Zhao had moved up his timetable. "PRESIDENT HO IS ALIVE," Sun shouted.

The guards loosened their grip. Fei's eyes bugged. Zhao whipped around toward him with so much anger in his eyes that he looked like a wild animal.

"General Zhao. I place you under arrest. I charge you with treason and the attempted assassination of our President."

Zhao walked over to him and stared into his eyes. After a long while, he smiled. He eventually started laughing. "You will say anything to save yourself, won't you?"

"He's alive..."

"That is a lie! The Americans killed him!" Zhao shouted.

Yau lay prostrate on the cold floor, his face away from the sound of the approaching footsteps. He positioned himself to look as if he had fainted, his left arm and legs at odd angles. He lay on his right hand, which still held the pistol.

As the sound drew nearer, it first slowed, then quickened. He mentally smiled. There was only one sentry.

Yau felt the sentry's body heat as he knelt beside him. "A general," the sentry said to himself but aloud.

Yau held perfectly still. Soon there was the unmistakable sound of heavy metal coming into contact with the concrete floor. The sentry had laid down his rifle. When the man rolled Yau over to examine him, he leveled his pistol at the head of another loyal countryman.

"Do not move," Yau ordered.

The guard was a young man, barely eighteen. His eyes were wide with fear and confusion. Yau was glad that he did not have to kill him. He did not know how he knew, but Yau was sure that too many had already died that day.

"Back away," he ordered.

The child wearing a uniform too large for him did as the general ordered.

Yau climbed to his feet and picked up the rifle.

The disarmed sentry's eyes widened even more.

"Turn around," Yau ordered.

He slowly turned to face away from Yau. Once the young sentry faced away, Yau took two steps toward him, raised the butt of the pistol and slammed it against the back of the young soldier's head. He fell to the floor in a heap.

Concerned that he might have hit him too hard, Yau kneeled to check for blood and a pulse. The blow had rendered the soldier unconscious without breaking the skin. Yau checked his watch. He was late and knew his friend was in trouble.

He placed the pistol back in his pocket and aimed the business end of the rifle at the doorknob. He fired once and the metal shattered, leaving the door to swing away and open. The lights in the switch room were off. He reached for and found the light switch as he entered the cramped space.

Sun looked away from Zhao's piercing glare for only a second; long enough to see that he had an audience. He came back to the seething General of the People's Army. "He's alive."

"Take him away," Zhao ordered.

"Switch the big screen to the outside news network if you do not believe me," Sun shouted as the guards turned on him again.

His last statement got Fei's attention. The fat man's confident composure seemed to go limp before Sun's eyes. He shifted his glare toward Zhao, seemingly for reassurance.

"Call him, General. He's on his mobile telephone waiting to speak to you," Sun said as he pointed toward the desk.

Fei's eyes went wide. He crossed and uncrossed his arms several times. He looked at Zhao, then Sun and then back to Zhao again, and he finally turned to walk toward the desk.

"Stop," Zhao ordered him.

Fei ignored the General's command.

Sun reared back in shock when Zhao pulled a pistol from his jacket and pointed it at Fei. "I said stop, damn you."

The Colonel and the two technicians sitting at the central console scrambled away from danger. Even the guards, who themselves were heavily armed, pulled back, leaving Sun standing on his own.

"I am the Chairman of the Communist Party. Are you mad?" Fei asked with a laugh as he picked up the phone.

A single gunshot rang out. Fei Tzu's heavy body fell forward onto the console. A large puddle of blood oozed from beneath him, onto the console and then the floor. Sun's heart pumped wildly as if trying to beat itself out of his chest while his armpits and the bend of his knees ran with sweat.

Zhao stared at Fei's body for a long while. He seemed transfixed on the huge lump of flesh sprawled before him. The room, except for the sound of radio calls, fell as silent as a graveyard. Sun--unarmed and unsure if Yau had come through, stood in silent trepidation.

The next sound that came was almost as sweet as his wife's voice. Electronic and persistent, it confirmed that even if he did not survive the next few moments, China would. The sound grew in number and intensity. The sound of human voices started blending with the sound of ringing mobile telephones. Yau had done his part.

Sun watched the faces of the officers and enlisted personnel around him. They were getting the news from loved ones and friends from the outside. He smiled as his eyes met those who now knew the identity of the real traitor.

Someone switched all four of the large screens to an outside source. President Ho's image filled each screen. He spoke, but no sound matched his lips. An interminable few moments later, Ho's voice boomed from large speakers perched in the corners of the cavernous room.

Zhao broke his focus from Fei and turned toward the screen. His face took on a new expression, almost studious, as if he just learned something new.

"This is President Ho. I have been the victim of an assassination attempt. Please stand down our military. I am well. I am waiting to hear from you," he pleaded.

The American news organization beamed his image and voice to the entire world. Per their quickly devised plan, the word would get to his people and hopefully to President Ho's military in time to stop whatever plans the plotters had placed in motion.

Zhao turned away from the screen and the repeating message, and brought his attention to Sun. He shook his head as he reached into his pocket with his free hand, pulled out his mobile phone.

"General. Once again, I must place you under arrest," Sun said softly.

Using his free hand, Zhao punched several keys before finally hitting "Send". "In my office, you will find evidence that General Weidong Mauo has sold secret material to the Russians for sexual favors. He deserves whatever form of justice is meted out to him."

"General. Give me the gun," Sun said softly.

"I am afraid, Admiral, that is impossible."

Zhao turned his focus toward the screen and President Ho's image. He looked at it for a long moment before turning toward the large map of China on the adjacent wall. He seemed to study it before gesturing toward the lower right corner of it with his head. "If we cannot have her, then none shall." General Zhao placed the pistol against his head and pulled the trigger.

"Are you okay?" Yau asked the young man as he stirred. The soldier that he had incapacitated regained consciousness slowly. Yau took a seat next to him on the cold floor as the young man instinctively reached for the sore place on the back of his head.

Still rubbing his head, the soldier sat upright. He looked around as if he did not know his whereabouts. He frowned when his eyes landed on the Commander of China's Marine Corps. "Sir. Why did you hit me?" he asked in a dazed voice.

"I apologize for striking you. It was the only way to keep you from sounding the alarm."

Yau slid across the floor to put his back against the wall. He dug into his coat pocket and pulled out a pack of cigarettes. When Yau offered one to the soldier, the young man declined. The General took one for himself, pulled a lighter from his trousers, and lit up. He took a long drag and blew it out slowly. "What is your name?"

"I am Corporal Shin," he sat upright as he answered.

"Corporal Shin, I did not hit you."

He looked confused.

"You came to the rescue of your nation. You acted heroically today, and your country is in your debt."

"General. Now I really do not understand."

Yau smiled. "You will."

Six Army security personnel worked to place Zhao and Fei's bodies on stretchers. While two young men grabbed General Zhao's corpse by the feet and shoulders, it took four to hoist Chairman Fei's considerable mass. Their blood marked the consoles, chairs, and floor where they fell. Sun reached across a six-inch pool of blood to pick up a telephone.

"President Ho, this is Vice-Admiral Sun. I have assumed command of the CMCCC and military forces under its purview."

"Admiral, it is good to hear from you. Where are Chairman Fei and General Zhao?"

"Comrade President, they are dead." Sun kept his tone succinct. While he was happy to be alive and that his country was safe, General Zhao's life had been one of service. His loss would be long felt.

"I understand," Ho replied after a long moment. "The Americans tell me that there is an invasion force at sea. What can you tell me?"

"Comrade President, I have already recalled them. Admiral Chang claims he was following General Zhao's orders. He is now following mine."

"Very well, Admiral. Admiral Sun, your service in this crisis has been exemplary..."

As he listened, Sun scanned the operations center. The chaos that had moments before gripped China's military command center was finally fading into the center's normal business-like buzz. The noise level in the space dramatically decreased as normal speaking volumes resumed. Sun let out a cleansing sigh as the President droned on about his status as China's newest hero.

"Thank you, Comrade President. But I must point out that General Yau acted with equal heroism, if not greater." Sun, continuing to examine the room, finally let his gaze drift upward toward the large screen monitors. A small green symbol in the top center of the left screen caught his attention.

"AIYA!" he said more to himself, but aloud.

The horror of the symbol's meaning seized him. He momentarily lost the ability to think or even speak. Sun first forced himself to breathe, then to speak.

"Colonel!" he shouted. "Get the data on that contact! Is that real?!" he shouted at Mulin.

Mulin, who had stood only a few feet from the failed coup's fireworks, looked considerably older than the nominal forty-six years for men in his rank. The army officer turned first toward Sun then directed his attention toward the screen which was the Navy Admiral's focus.

His eyes went wide in abject horror for the fourth time in less than an hour. He immediately began barking commands at his duty team. Sun noticed nearly everyone in the room tasked with managing China's airspace viewed the same image on their computer screens.

"Admiral. What is happening?" the President asked.

The icon tracked across the screen. A small window appeared on the screen. The information indicated the missile's origin, a silo in western Manchuria, its altitude, thirty thousand kilometers, and its speed, nearly Mach 2.0.

"Comrade President, it would appear that we have launched a missile."

"A missile. What kind of missile?"

"I believe it is an inter-regional ballistic missile."

"And the target?" he asked.

Sun immediately recalled Zhao's last words, "None shall have her." "Comrade President, I believe the target is Taipei."

"Admiral, what can we do?"

Sun sighed as he ignored the blood-spatter on the chair next to him. He fell into it heavily, as if the weight of all China were upon him.

"Admiral, did you hear me? What can we do?"

Sun looked at the icon and blinked heavily. His mind turned back to General Yau's mobile command post and his previous moments of despair. Suddenly, that predicament paled in comparison.

CHAPTER FIFTEEN
ANVIL

With the destruction of the two Chinese patrol boats and a submarine, the Chinese amphibious troop ships reversed course for home. Still at General Quarters, *Princeton* turned her attention to damage control, helping the injured, and accounting for the dead. Lieutenant Commander Daniels, now wearing a bandage over the gash in his forehead, gave the order to continue for the rendezvous with USS *Ronald Reagan*. Ben watched as Daniels reported their status to Seventh Fleet via secure radio.

"Continue," a disembodied male voice said through a red-colored speaker in Combat.

"The President and National Security Advisor are safe and well. I regret to inform you that *John Paul Jones* took a missile strike during the initial attack. She was lost with all hands," said Daniels.

Pause.

"Roger. Copy all. Continue," the voice finally responded.

"*Princeton* then engaged a submerged contact. Hearing transients, we believe their torpedo doors were opening. We destroyed that target with two surface-launched torpedoes.

They never got a shot off at us." Daniels almost puffed his chest as he spoke.

Lieutenant Juarez sat across from him at her station while Chief of Staff Aldridge, an unidentified chief petty officer, and Ben all stood within earshot.

"Copy all. Continue."

"I have fifteen injuries. The most serious of them are electrical burns. We would like them flown off the ship as soon as we're in range. I have nineteen fatalities. Those fatalities include Congresswoman Nina Anders and Captain Elizabeth Nation."

The radio again fell silent for a long moment. Ben knew the news of Nation's death would hit home aboard USS BLUE RIDGE, the Seventh Fleet flagship. Her last duty-station before taking command of *Princeton* was that of the Seventh Fleet Chief of Staff. "Continue. Over," the voice finally said.

"Damage from the missile hit is considerable. We've lost the port-phased array and the bridge. We've got electrical casualties all over the ship. The most serious of them prevents the use of the forward missile magazine. Engineering is making that one a priority. The engineering plant is fully operational, and we are making 26 knots. That completes my report. How copy?"

"PRINCETON, this is SEVENTH FLEET-Actual. Copy all. Good work out there, Commander. Units are on the way to the vicinity to backfill you in case the Chinese change their mind."

Ben's eyebrow went up at the transmission. Rather than one of the staff officers, the actual three-star admiral commanding the Navy's largest operational fleet was talking to Daniels.

"SEVENTH FLEET, this is PRINCETON. Roger. Out," Daniels ended the transmission and placed the red handset set in its holder.

A second-class corpsman, still wearing a stethoscope around her neck, entered the space and approached Daniels and the gathering of officers standing near him. The enlisted woman's blonde hair was coming loose from its gathering at the top of her head. Her face, smudged with soot, framed sad eyes. She swallowed hard as her gaze came up to meet Daniels'.

"We lost another one?" the ship's acting captain asked.

"Senior Chief Guerette died a few minutes ago," she replied.

Ben noticed all work in CIC came to a sudden stop. The space, which moments before was full of youthful voices, was quiet again. One or two of the operations specialists lowered their heads while others openly wept.

Daniels sighed as he shook his head. "Tell Doc not to lose any more. That's an order."

The corpsman nodded her understanding. She exchanged uneasy glances with some of her shipmates before turning to leave CIC. Ben and the others watched until she was out of the space.

"What are your orders, Skipper?" a burly Master Chief Sonar Technician asked. His name tag read "Wright."

Daniels looked at him with surprise. The two men exchanged a long, silent stare. "Put *Princeton* back together, Master Chief. Let's get this mess cleaned up."

"Who's this guy?" Aldridge whispered to Ben.

"Command Master Chief. Highest ranking enlisted man on board," he whispered back.

"Aye. Aye, sir," Wright responded boisterously. "Okay, people. You heard the man. Back to work! Let's get this ship cleaned up!" The Command Chief left their immediate vicinity as he continued shouting. He eventually departed the space for other reaches of the ship, and other crew members in need of "motivation."

Daniels stood from his console. Lieutenant Juarez looked up at her captain as he got to his feet. "Miss Juarez?"

"Yes, Captain?"

"Combat is yours. I need to tour the ship."

"We've got it under control, sir."

The two exchanged a long stare before Daniels eventually nodded. He took a scan of the space and walked toward the door. "Captain's out of Combat," someone announced as he cleared the plane of the broken door.

***

National Reconnaissance Office Operations Center
Washington, DC
7:09 PM

"I need telemetry!" Chris Koch, the watch leader, shouted.

"I'm working on it! I'll have it in a few minutes!" Harvey Walters replied.

"We don't have a few minutes!!"

Harvey Walters had just briefed his director on the goings-on in China. As he finished the meeting, he planned to call his wife. On the way back to his office, he decided to cruise by the Operations Center. Even as he entered the secure room's foyer, he heard elevated voices. Entering the space, he saw the status screens. Now in its fifth full minute of flight from a silo in northwestern Manchuria, a Chinese ballistic missile hurtled its way toward apogee.

Harvey jumped in to help monitor the missile and track its probable impact. A launch like this provided a superb intelligence-gathering opportunity, provided they got the right assets monitoring it into place. Harvey Walters took over a workstation near Kochs' console.

"I've got the President of China on the phone!" a senior member of the watch team shouted.

Harvey turned to see the man holding the phone. The short bald man with thick dark-rimmed glasses' name escaped him. It didn't matter anyway. Everyone was trying to get as much information as possible. They would need it when it came time to reconstruct the attack.

"What? Are you shitting me? What the hell does he want?" the leader asked.

Chris Koch's thick dark hair was all over his head because he kept running his hands through it. All around him, forty other controllers either stood or sat watching the screens in front of them. A nuclear missile was on its way to Taiwan, and there was nothing they could do about it.

"He wants us to shoot it down!" the unnamed man with the phone shouted back.

"Tell him we'd love to. I'll run out and get some fucking spitballs! Hang up that phone!"

Harvey frowned at Koch's remark as something sparked in his mind. In the last week, he'd been all over Washington in one briefing or another. Something existed on the edge of his memory.

"Walters, are you gonna do something or just sit there like a bump on a mule's ass?" Koch asked.

He ignored Koch as he closed his eyes to concentrate. He was sure he had seen something about Theatre Ballistic Missile Defense (TBMD). Who? Where had he been?

"Damn it, Harvey! I need you to clear that station for one of my guys or…"

Harvey's eyes flashed open as it came to him.

"Walters! Did you hear me?!" Koch insisted.

Still ignoring his colleague he picked up the phone. He did not know the number to the Pentagon. But he did have the number to the space in which he'd spent most of the week—The White House Situation Room. He quickly dialed the number.

***

USS Princeton (CG-59)
0711 Hours

"SLEDGEHAMMER. This is BAD KARMA, over. ANVIL. I say again, ANVIL," the red secure voice radio speaker crackled.

Ben frowned as he heard the radio call. He looked to his right and at Juarez. The woman's face seemed to lose all color as she reached for the handset as if it might bite her.

"Are they calling us? What the hell does that mean?" Ben asked Juarez.

"Sir, can you get the XO back up here? Fast?" she asked as she pulled the red receiver to her ear.

Ben nodded and grabbed the microphone for the 1MC, shipboard PA system.

"This is SLEDGEHAMMER, over," she replied.

"Executive Officer lay to Combat." Ben had no idea what the radio call was about. However, he read Juarez's body language. She sat up in her chair as all emotion drained from her face.

"SLEDGEHAMMER. ANVIL. ANVIL. This is no drill. Are you ANVIL-Capable?"

"Standby," she replied.

Daniels tore into Combat as he was reaching for the 21MC intercom. "What the hell is going on?" he asked breathlessly.

"ANVIL, sir," she replied softly.

"Shit." His face went taught. He hurried over to the console.

"What the hell is ANVIL?" Ben asked.

"Sir. May I have that chair?" Daniels asked as he came to sit down.

Ben did not bother to answer him. It did not make any difference. The acting captain of *Princeton* was sitting in that chair whether Ben got out of the way or not.

As soon as he was down, he picked up the 21MC. "Engineering, Combat," he called.

"Engineering, aye?" the Chief Engineer replied.

"Have we got power to the forward magazine yet?"

"That's affirmative. We just..."

Daniels did not bother listening to the rest of the man's sentence. Rather he grabbed the radio microphone. "This is SLEDGEHAMMER. We are ANVIL-Capable."

"Roger, SLEDGEHAMMER. Sending you targeting data. How copy over?" the voice on the other end of the radio said.

Daniels grabbed the 1MC. "All hands. Stand clear of the forward missile magazine for missile launch. I say again. Stand clear of the forecastle and the forward missile magazine. All hands, man your TBMD stations."

"What's happening now?" Aldridge asked as she came over to Ben.

He knew *Princeton*'s capabilities. As the Naval Attaché, Ben had made knowing as much as he could about each of the ships that entered the Taiwan Area of Operations. *Princeton* possessed the newest of the Navy's capabilities: she was a Ballistic Missile Defense ship. "I think you're about to see why you supported our budget request for the last three years."

Daniels and Juarez turned their attention to the air contact display. Ben followed their example. A second later, the top half of a diamond appeared in red. A long line, also red, extended from it toward the south, toward Taiwan. The icon neared the edge of the main part of the Asian landmass. Ben quickly read the telemetry information to the right of the contact. "Holy shit. Is that what I think it is?"

"Yes, sir." Daniels' answer was as succinct as any he had ever heard.

"What is that?" Aldridge asked.

"It's a nuclear missile. I assume it's headed toward Taiwan."

This time both Daniels and Juarez nodded.

"The hits just keep on coming," Ben said to himself softly.

"BAD KARMA, this is SLEDGEHAMMER. Targeting data received. Developing a solution."

"SLEDGEHAMMER, roger. You have weapons release authority."

"BAD KARMA, this is SLEDGEHAMMER. Roger, out." Daniels ended the communication.

Ben took in a deep breath to calm himself. The horror of the moment was almost more than he thought he could bear.

"Got a solution?" Daniels asked Juarez.

Juarez checked her console. She pointed at a bank of green lights and nodded her response. "Good to go, sir."

"Tactical Action Officer. You have weapons release authority for two SM-4 missiles," Daniels said to Juarez. "Make 'em count."

She smiled at him as she spoke into her headset. "Air Weapons. TAO. Two SM-6 missiles. Weapons Free."

"Aye, ma'am," a young voice responded from behind them.

Ben turned to see Senior Chief Guerette's replacement, a young second-class petty officer reach for and press the firing button.

Ben turned his attention to the closed-circuit television screen above the main watch console. He pointed at it for Aldridge. *Princeton* vibrated like one of those old beds in a cheap hotel as a door on the forecastle deck opened. Fire belched from inside just before a white cylindrical object shot forward and out of view as it climbed skyward.

"Bird One, away," the young petty officer reported.

A second door opened; the action repeated itself. Ben continued watching the closed-circuit television as the breeze generated by *Princeton*'s motion carried away the smoke. The door to the empty and smoldering magazine closed in one rapid mechanical motion.

"Birds away. Both returning nominal telemetry," the new Air Weapons watch-stander reported confidently.

Both Daniels and Juarez nodded as they returned to gaze at their air plot. Two more icons joined the already busy screen. These were green half diamonds. Like the red icon they hunted, the green symbols, separated by a few inches, displayed a long lead-line reaching toward their target.

"I take it that the line coming from those is their speed and direction?" Aldridge asked.

Ben only nodded. He was holding his breath, only letting it out when his lungs demanded relief. He remembered reading an article in Surface Warfare Magazine months before--maybe even a year earlier--about the Navy's Theater Ballistic Missile Defense Program. He had no idea then, or even half an hour ago, that he would ever get to see it in action.

"Air Weapons," Juarez called.

"Yes, ma'am."

"Get ready for another shot," she ordered.

Still not breathing regularly, Ben glanced at her.

"Just in case, sir," she replied.

He nodded as he let out and took another breath.

"How far are we from Taiwan?" Aldridge asked.

"Not far enough," Daniels shot back without taking his eyes off the large screen display.

Ben felt the President's Chief of Staff looking at him, perhaps for reassurance. He did not turn toward her, as he had none to offer.

The first missile closed on the target. He overheard others around him, even Aldridge and Congressman Jones offering up prayers, "Come on," and "Go, baby." He joined them as his mind turned to his family. He checked his watch and did the time math. They should be safely in bed, slumbering sweetly with no idea that on the other side of the world he was dancing with the outcome of technology supplied to the Navy by the lowest bidder.

He and the others watched as the SM6 Nr 1 merged with the target. Half a cheer went up and immediately died. Ben's heart sank to its lowest depths as it re-emerged on the other side of the target's red icon.

"Miss." Daniels said to himself but aloud.

"Where is it?" Aldridge asked.

Ben quickly read the information next to the blinking red light that caused him to starve his body for oxygen. "Ten thousand feet, a hundred and fifty miles from impact."

"We won't get another shot," Juarez murmured.

The other missile, as it flew on, now carried all their hopes and prayers. Ben took in one last breath as he closed his eyes. He decided he would not watch as he started praying again.

"Come on, damn it!" the White House Chief of Staff shouted at the screen. "Come on! Kill that fucker!!"

Ben jerked his eyes open at the Government executive's breach of CIC protocol. His eyes went wide with surprise as Daniels hurled a similar expletive at the screen and the engagement it represented.

Soon everyone in CIC was standing, screaming at the screen. "Go! Go! Go!" It reminded Ben of the films he had seen of Houston's Mission Control during the early days of America's space program. He mentally shrugged his shoulders and joined them. "GO!"

SM6 Nr2 closed on its target. First, their speed vectors crossed, reminding Ben of an "X" somewhere over the Taiwan Straits. A second later the screen blinked as it received a computer update. The noise in Combat ceased in concert with the update.

Ben leaned forward as he waited for the computers to process the new information. His lungs cursed him for their airless plight, but he ignored the protestation. Veronica Aldridge placed her hand on his shoulder as the screen redrew the images. When the update was complete, two icons were missing.

"TARGET DESTROYED!!!" the radar operator screamed from his station in Air Alley.

Princeton's CIC erupted in ecstatic cheers. Crew members and their civilian visitors embraced, exchanged high-fives and handshakes with abandon. Even their acting captain joined in the celebration. He hugged McGuire, Aldridge, Jones, and finally, his TAO.

CHAPTER SIXTEEN
THE FINEST TRADITIONS

(Three Weeks Later)
Friday, September 4th
Residence of Lieutenant Commander Paul Daniels
Honolulu, HI
1:45 AM

"I'm coming!" Paul Daniels shouted at the person pounding on his door and ringing the doorbell. "I said…I'm coming!"

Paul Daniels' eyes quickly adjusted to the light pounding its way into his brain. Just moments before, he was in bed, staring at a darkened ceiling. He had not slept well since the Chinese naval engagement in the Taiwan Straits. Each time he closed his eyes, a remembrance from the event crept into his subconscious and emerged as a nightmare. Before bringing *Princeton* home, he had filled the sleepless times with his famous nocturnal strolls.

Now at home, the nights seemed longer, and he grew more and more restless. He wondered if he suffered from Post-Traumatic Stress Disorder. After almost three weeks, he found himself growing desperate for sleep and taking a drink before bed to relax.

While he had spent some nights contemplating and reliving the events of the firefight with the Chinese patrol boats, tonight he dwelled on the day's Article 32 Hearing and JJ's testimony.

He pulled on his bathrobe and made his way down the partially lit hallway toward the front door and the relentless asshole on the other side. For the last few minutes, someone had been pounding on it so hard that it almost rattled pictures off the wall. They intermittently leaned on the doorbell as if it were a Morse Code key. *Who the hell is this at this hour?*

When he reached the door, he took a moment to peer through the privacy peephole. A complicated mix of emotions stirred in him at seeing JJ.

After filing a written report to the Seventh Fleet Commander detailing the events leading up to the attack and *Princeton*'s response, the fleet commander recommended his boss, the Pacific Fleet Commander, convene an investigative board to sort out all of the details. When *Princeton* pulled back into Pearl Harbor, families and the media were not the only people waiting for them.

Earlier that day, investigators spent several hours grilling Lieutenant Juarez. They focused on her failure to recognize the Chinese patrol boat's missile targeting radar. By the end of the day, it was clear the Navy thought her failure led to the Chinese Navy's successful attack on their ship and the subsequent loss of life.

Paul felt both happy and anxious about seeing her.

Nearly a year and a half had passed since she last stood at his door. Urges, primal and raw, stirred as the memory of her body lying next to his seized his thoughts. An instant later, the image of Captain Nation flashed into his mind's eye, once again admonishing him for not disclosing a romantic relationship with a subordinate.

As he reached for the deadbolt, he knew it was too late. He had irrevocably crossed that line. He unlocked the door and opened it for her. JJ brushed by him without speaking and barely acknowledging his presence. She marched through the foyer into the darker reaches of his home. The odor of cigarette smoke and liquor lingered along with the aroma of her perfume. Paul closed the door and trailed after her.

By the time he walked into the living room, she was sitting in the dark on the center section of the sofa. He flipped a wall switch, and a floor lamp bathed the space in warm yellow light. As Paul sat next to her, he felt as if he were creeping toward a small and timid animal.

Still wearing her Summer White uniform, JJ sat on the edge of the couch with her knees together and her hands folded on top of them. "It's good to see you," he said softly after a long moment.

She sighed. "Yeah. You, too."

JJ eventually turned to face him. He nearly melted when her dark brown eyes met his. At their first meeting, and at every encounter since, those eyes always left him helpless. He felt the world shift beneath him as he looked at her for answers. Even after more than a year of separate personal but close professional contact, he still fell under her spell. She looked away, as if something else in the room yanked at her attention.

Paul frowned in confusion. The sat alone in a still and dark room. He cleared his throat. "What's going on?"

Rather than answer, JJ sighed as she fell back into the folds of the sofa.

Paul followed her example and reclined as well. He stared into the darkness beyond for a long while before turning back to JJ. He found her probing eyes peering at him intently.

They edged closer until their lips touched. The year since their last caress felt like a millennium. As the kiss lingered, he felt JJ slip something into his hand. Paul pulled away and looked down to find the engagement ring.

"I can't marry you, Paul."

Paul dragged his attention from the ring to JJ's beautiful face. "Why? We love each other. Don't we?"

"Of course we do. Yes, I do. But..."

Paul pulled back even further from her. He caught himself frowning at her.

"I'm resigning tomorrow," she declared.

He wasn't surprised. If he had been in her place, he would probably do the same. "JJ, this is a huge step. Are you sure-"

"That's what I want to do?" she cut him off, finishing the sentence for him. "Paul, I fucked up, and I got our captain killed. Even if I wanted to stay, I couldn't."

"But why end us?"

"I love you, Paul. But I'm not gonna be one of those wives you see waiting on the pier when we come in from being at sea," she said as she stood.

He followed her with his eyes as she paced the floor just in front of him. Stumbling a bit, JJ put her right hand on her hip and used her left to gesture as she spoke.

"I'm not saying there's anything wrong with those women. I just don't want to be one of them. Mostly because I'm supposed to be out there, too." She slurred her words as she spoke.

She stopped moving and once again brought her beautiful eyes to his. "I need you to call me a taxi, please. I'm in no condition to drive," she said.

"Please don't do this," he begged.

"Paul, don't make this any more difficult than it already is. Please."

Paul fought the urge to cry as the lump in his throat almost choked him. Shit.

***

People's Army-Navy Headquarters
Beijing China
1100 Hours

Restored to office, Vice Admiral Xueliang Sun sat at his desk preparing for the day's meetings. The agenda consisted of his normal intelligence briefing, evaluation sessions with several of his staff, and an introductory meeting with Admiral Chang's successor. Since the near coup, nearly every branch of China's government experienced some form of reorganization. Chairman Fei's reach proved long and deep. President Ho took great care in removing the cancer from his country's government.

The phone on Sun's desk rang pulling him his attention from the files.

"Yes?"

"Sir, I have President Ho on the line."

Sun removed his readers. "Yes, yes. Put him on."

The line made a clicking noise indicating the change in modes. "Mr. President?"

"Good afternoon, Admiral. Is this a good time to speak?"

"Of course, sir. Yes, sir."

"Admiral, I have just concluded a meeting with the CMCC that I think you will find interesting."

"Oh?"

"Admiral, I have forwarded your name as the next leader of China's armed forces. The CMCC has endorsed my recommendation."

Sun fell back in his office chair. He felt his body go limp at the news. Even holding the phone to his ear took energy.

"Admiral? Are you there?"

Sun forced himself to answer. "Yes, Mr. President."

"So, will you do it?"

Sun thought of his wife. They had plans for their retirement which he assumed was near. What would she say to staying in Government longer?

"Mr. President. It would be my honor."

***

Vladivostok Naval Base

Vladivostok, Russia
22:49 Hours

Jake Harrison peered out the cabin window at the military air terminal. As his Falcon 2000EX jet taxied toward the terminal, Russian aircraft and their personnel came into view. He shook his head at the irony. When he joined the Agency in the mid-eighties, the idea of a US aircraft landing here was beyond comprehension.

"Mr. G-Man," Alexi Pugachev called from his seat at the rear of the aircraft. "Welcome to Mother Russia."

Jake counted his blessings that his time with Pugachev was almost over. After almost three weeks of constant contact and nearly a day of traveling with him, he was more than ready to part ways.

Jake turned in his seat to face the shackled prisoner, wishing he had gagged him as well. Almost since leaving Guam, Pugachev had been something of a chatterbox, saying whatever he could think of to talk them out of handing him over to Russian authorities.

Jake didn't respond. He scrutinized his bonds and the two burly agents seated near him. A long metal chain connected cuffs on his wrists and ankles. Comfortable with Pugachev's security, he returned to looking out the window.

After ensuring the National Reconnaissance Office had Pugachev's freighter under drone coverage, Langley projected the ship would pass within a hundred miles of Guam. Shortly after seeing Ciara off, Jake boarded an aircraft for the US Territory.

With a transit time of almost two and a half days, Jake had plenty of time to coordinate an operation with the Navy. The Special Operations Command placed a SEAL Team on the ship in the night. After extracting Pugachev without firing a shot, they turned him over to the CIA.

GENERAL QUARTERS

The pilots brought the aircraft to a stop in front of a large white building. Jake made out several men in Russian Army uniforms standing beside a green van. The sound of the jet engines winding down accompanied the action of his men opening the aircraft cabin door.

Crisp fresh air rushed into the cabin as airfield personnel pushed a small gantry to the Falcon's open door. Jake stood and adjusted his necktie before walking over to Pugachev. Still seated, the man looked up at him and gave a sardonic smile.

Jake, sensing he was looking for a reaction, gave none. "Let's go," he said to the other agents. The men pulled Pugachev to his feet, the chains jingling with the prisoner's every move.

Jake led the two other agents and their prisoner out the aircraft door. As he took his first steps down the gantry, he looked over his shoulder to see Pugachev struggling against his shackles to follow him. The two other agents each took Pugachev's arms to support him.

"American!" Pugachev called above the noise of the wind and other aircraft.

Jake ignored the prisoner yet again as he greeted his Russian counterpart at the bottom of the stairs.

"Mr. Harrison," a short but very fit-looking man in Army uniform greeted him with a salute.

"Colonel Nerinov, I presume?"

"You presume correctly," the man replied in near-perfect English but with a strong Slavic accent.

Jake reached into his coat pocket and withdrew several folded papers. He handed them over to Nerinov, with a slight smile. "He's all yours."

The prisoner and his two escorts finally arrived at the bottom of the stairs. The sound of the jingling chains punctuated his final, difficult step. The Russian officer examined the transfer documents before examining Pugachev with a long evaluative gaze.

"He looks in good health," Nerinov commented.

"You can't believe everything you hear from our news media. We haven't laid a hand on him," Jake cracked with a smile.

Nerinov signaled for two of his soldiers to join him with a nod of his head. Two guards, just as burly as Jake's comrades, marched forward and took their places on each side of the prisoner.

"American!" he called out to Jake once more as they were ready to lead him away.

"What?" Jake replied in a put-upon tone. "You're worse than a wife," he added.

The other men laughed at his humor.

"I'll give you one last chance to let me go," Pugachev threatened.

This was the fourth or fifth time the man made the veiled threat. Jake was ready to dismiss it as he had before, but something kept him from ignoring the man as he has done previously. "Tell you what: If you still feel this way in a few months, I'll see what I can do. But from what these guys have told me," Jake said as he nodded at the Russian Army officer, "you won't be feeling much below the waist in a couple of days. I hear your new husband is waiting for you."

Pugachev's face grew even sterner. He grimaced as if he had terrible taste in his mouth. "Until we meet again," was all he said as the soldiers pulled him away.

Jake followed him with his eyes for a long while before he turned back to Colonel Nerinov. "I guess we're out of here." He took one last look as the soldier's hoisted Pugachev into the back of a green van.

Nerinov came to attention and saluted. "On behalf of the Russian people, thank you for returning this criminal to us."

Jake nodded. "Any time. Just make sure you hold on to him this time."

"We will."

Jake nodded as he and his agents turned and climbed the stairs to their waiting aircraft. Once inside, one agent pulled the door shut as Jake watched ground personnel pull away the gantry.

"Comrade Major," the soldier who helped him into the vehicle began. "You look well."

Pugachev smiled. "Get these chains off me," he ordered.

The man pulled a key from his jacket and inserted it into the upper lock. Pugachev's wrist bonds fell free with a loud clank.

The vehicle was just big enough for the passengers. Another Army soldier sat in the front seat at the controls. He turned, glanced over his right shoulder, and shot Pugachev a wide smile.

"What are we waiting for?" Pugachev snapped.

Suddenly the rear door to the van flew open. "What the hell is going on?!! Why is that man unshackled?!!" Colonel Nerinov shouted as he placed his hand on his pistol.

Rather than answer, the guard brought up his Makarov 9mm and fired a single round into the Army officer's head. Nerinov fell into a bloody heap, and the guard closed the door.

"Drive," he said to the man behind the wheel.

"When can we get me to the United States? I have unfinished business," Alexi Pugachev asked as he used the key to free his leg bonds.

"All in due time, Comrade. Our superiors have many questions for you."

Pugachev sat up as the chains around his feet came loose. "Good. I have questions for them, too."

***

Over the Bering Sea

25,000 Feet

Jake Harrison, now free of his responsibilities, slumped in his seat for the first time in nearly a day. When the whine from the jet engines pushing the aircraft into flight got to be too much, he reached for his MP3 player and the relative comfort it offered.

As the sound of Chris Botti's trumpet filled his ears, his mind finally started to unclench and relax. A second later, his eyes ratcheted open as he sat up in his chair. "Shit!"

The other two agents, one of whom was already asleep, jumped with a start. "What?" they both asked.

His mind had just played back the last few moments he had spent on the tarmac in Vladivostok. Why hadn't his conscious mind registered it? Why hadn't he reacted? Was he dreaming? Without a doubt, Pugachev and the guard helping him into the Army vehicle exchanged a knowing and friendly glance. Further, the guard patted Pugachev on the back just before climbing in behind the prisoner.

Jake rushed to the cockpit and opened the door. The pilots turned with a jerk to face him. "Sir?"

"Call Vlad," he said, referring to Vladivostok. "I think the prisoner has escaped."

Jake slowly made his way back to his seat as he eavesdropped on the pilot's radio call. He took his seat as his mind conjured Pugachev's last words to him: "Until we meet again."

Jake smiled to himself. Ending it this way had not been his choice. Rather, he followed Washington's orders. Now, just maybe, they would let him take care of this his way.

Jake reclined in his chair when he heard the pilots getting the news that Pugachev had indeed escaped. He placed the earbuds back in place and hit the play button yet again. He closed his eyes and drifted off to one of the most restful slumbers he had hosted in weeks.

****

The Pentagon
Washington, D.C.
1040 Hours

"There is little doubt that the events of 16th August will be the subject of historical discussion for many years to come," Secretary of Defense Andrew Lancaster said from behind the large wooden lectern in the stage's center.

In Ben McGuire's many visits to the Pentagon, he had never seen the impressive auditorium. He took note of some of the room's more alluring features. A tall set of blue curtains served as the backdrop. A large Department of Defense crest rested in the center of the blue curtains above Ben and the rest of the official party. Five flags representing America's Armed Forces branches, Army, Navy, Marine Corps, Air Force, and Space Force stood beneath the crest.

The event began promptly at ten o'clock with another Navy captain calling the room to attention. The Secretaries of State and Defense entered the room first. Ben followed closely behind his mentor, the Chairman of the Joint Chiefs of Staff, Vice-Admiral Frederick Kiatkowski. The Admiral and Ben, dressed in Service Dress Blues, stood to the right of the two cabinet members as they each made speeches.

The Secretary of State's address covered the same ground as his Defense Department peer, but from a diplomatic context. Ben did his best to look attentive as the officials gave their addresses, but time and again, he found himself scanning the room and the sea of people in the audience.

Almost half of the estimated two hundred onlookers consisted of uniformed military personnel. Most of the rest appeared to be DoD civilians and news media. ABC, CNN, CBS, Fox, to name but a few. The PRC even sent a news crew from their State Television network.

Ben mentally pinched himself each time he looked at them. Holy shit!

"The military forces of the People's Republic of China are once again under the positive control of their government," the Secretary of Defense continued.

Ben's wife, Claire, and his two kids, Adam and Vanessa, sat in the audience just a few feet from him. Claire kept shooting him the same glance she used to prod Adam into paying attention. Whenever their eyes met, Ben smirked.

Just a week after the sea battle with the Chinese, Ben turned over the job of Naval Attaché to his designated relief. Corrigan, though he had been chomping at the bit to take over, was a little disappointed, "that all of the excitement had occurred on Ben's watch." Ben smiled at Corrigan's complaint and reminded him, "The very nature of our work is that we spend years of boredom separated by moments of sheer terror. Enjoy the quiet time."

"As I mentioned a few moments ago," Secretary Lancaster said as Ben tuned back into the address. "The lead up to the events of that day will be debated for years. However, there is one aspect of that day that will remain unchallenged. And that is the fact that Captain Benjamin McGuire quite literally saved the day when he saved the life of the Chinese President."

The audience stood in applause as the two cabinet members and the JCS Chairman all turned toward Ben and clapped as well. Surprised by the sudden spotlight, Ben momentarily felt like taking a step or two back. He glanced at his wife, smiling widely and shook her head before she started applauding.

Not knowing what to do, Ben just stood there at first.

"Smile," VADM Kiatkowski leaned over and whispered to him.

Ben followed his order. He eventually raised his hand and waved at the crowd. As he examined the faces of the people applauding his actions, he recalled White House Chief of Staff Veronica Aldridge's words to him, "Your life just changed."

"Admiral, if you and Captain McGuire would join us at the podium," Secretary Lancaster invited as the ovation died and the gathering retook their seats.

Vice Admiral Kiatkowski led the way to the podium as Ben followed. Once there, the two men came to a stop, and the admiral turned and faced Ben.

"Citation to accompany the award," the same Navy Captain who had initiated the proceedings announced.

The military personnel in the gathering came to attention. The civilians, albeit at a more leisurely pace, climbed to their feet as well.

"The Secretary of Defense takes pleasure in presenting the Defense Distinguished Service Medal to Captain Benjamin McGuire, United States Navy, as set forth in the following citation: 'For heroic achievement while serving as Naval Attaché, US Embassy, Taipei, Taiwan. On 16 August, a Chinese National attempted to murder the President of the People's Republic of China during a State Dinner. Captain McGuire noted the abnormal demeanor of his fellow dinner guest as one of the members of the head table fell with a seizure.

When the would-be assailant was about to strike, Captain McGuire placed himself in mortal danger by hurtling himself through the air, knocking the assailant temporarily off-balance, and thereby giving security personnel time to react. The assailant was subsequently killed before he could complete his attack.'"

Ben stood at attention as the announcer read the citation and as Admiral Kiatkowski pinned the Navy Distinguished Service medal to his left chest.

"'Thanks to Captain McGuire's alertness, intrepidity, and heroism, the life of the President of the People's Republic of China was saved, thereby allowing him to put down a coup d'état which would have undoubtedly led to dangerous instability in the region. His heroic action and outstanding leadership inspired all who observed him and contributed significantly to the National Security of the United States. By his courage and selfless devotion to duty, Captain McGuire upheld the finest traditions of the United States Naval Service. Signed, Andrew K. Lancaster, Secretary of Defense.'"

Admiral Kiatkowski, wearing a wide smile, shook his hand when he finished the pinning. "Nice work. I knew I could count on you," he said with a smile as he placed his hand on Ben's shoulder before shaking his hand.

"Thank you, sir."

THE END

KEN CARODINE ADMIRAL (RET)

C. Kenneth "Ken" Carodine is a 1982 graduate of the US Naval Academy, a combat-veteran of the 1991 Gulf War, and a retired US Navy Rear Admiral.

A native of Huntsville, Alabama, he is the 25th African American Flag Officer in US Navy history and the third from the State of Alabama. As a Navy Flag Officer, he commanded the US Navy Warfare Development Command leading the research and documentation of new uses of currently deployed sensors and weapons. Following his tour of duty at NWDC, Carodine joined the US Navy's Headquarters Staff in the Pentagon where he formulated and executed policy in the areas of information technology implementation, personnel management, and National Security. Carodine retired from the US Navy in October 2013.

Ken won the 1991 Rose Trilogy Award for Best New Fiction. His first book, NUCLEAR DRAGON, was originally published as ALL THE TEA in 2000. ALL THE TEA was republished as NUCLEAR DRAGON in 2024. Carodine has also authored several non-fiction articles addressing current events and politics for the New York Center for Foreign Policy Affairs and TC Palm News.

Carodine's civilian career includes Information Technology executive leadership for several large firms in Banking, Healthcare, Transportation, and Energy. His IT background spans application development, analytics, data management, and data governance.

Ken is currently working on another chapter of the Ben McGuire Series, FLAG COUNTRY.

IF YOU ENJOYED THIS BOOK VISIT

PENMORE PRESS

www.penmorepress.com

All Penmore Press books are available directly through our website,

NUCLEAR DRAGON

BY

KEN CARODINE

Japan and the US have been working in secret at a disused nuclear research center on Senkaku, a remote island in the South China Sea, to perfect a viable nuclear fusion reactor, the Holy Grail of the utility industry promising unlimited energy. Suddenly the black veil of secrecy is shredded, the long shot project is on the verge of a breakthrough, and the Chinese want the prize located in their backyard. Navy Reserve Commander Ben McGuire and a Navy SEAL team leap into their mission to get the radical new reactor off the island before the rapidly approaching Chinese fleet can get boots on the ground, struggling with sabotage, a typhoon, and the isolated group of scientists, some of whom are terrified of shutting down the Nuclear Dragon. This fast-paced, frightening and very realistic book by a retired Rear Admiral and Surface Warfare Officer keeps the reader turning pages. The author knows his stuff.

PENMORE PRESS
www.penmorepress.com

The Simushir Island Incident
BY

Marc Liebman

Manufacturing and selling illicit drugs is a lucrative business. But what good is being rich if you can't enjoy your wealth?

North Korean officers Admiral Pak and General Jang are in charge of an operation that produces high-grade heroin to be sold in the United States as Asian Pure. But an alarming number of high-ranking officers in the Democratic People's Republic of Korea are being accused of treason -- and not surviving their arrests. Admiral Pak and General Jang suspect it is only a matter of time before their own heads will be on the execution block, unless they can make themselves to valuable to kill off. They figure out a way to dramatically reduce costs and increase the profit margin: rent Simushir Island from Russia and manufacture the drugs closer to their market destination. They even concoct a plausible cover story of establishing a maritime base for merchant shipping. It's a great plan -- until other heads of state decide to militarize the operation with a ballistic missile launch facility.

PENMORE PRESS
www.penmorepress.com

NORTH SEA WIND STORM

BY

JAMES BOSCHERT

A major drug deal is underway and loose ends are being taken care of when two things go wrong: two murders that were supposed to look like a suicide and an accident get noticed – one on an English railroad, and one on board an ocean-going barge.

As police are sent to investigate both seemingly unrelated incidents, the men at sea find themselves in dangerous waters. Who among them is on the take, and who is on the level? Who can be trusted when all of them are enduring the special man-made hell of life on an oil barge? As if deadly drug runners weren't enough to contend with, a convergence of storm winds and tides is creating the kind of waves that can make even the largest ships disappear without a trace...

PENMORE PRESS
www.penmorepress.com

Brewer and the Portuguese Gold
By

James Keffer

The year is 1840. Twenty-three years ago, Horatio Lord Hornblower was governor of the island of St. Helena and hailer to its only prisoner, Napoleon Bonaparte. First mutual respect and later shared tragedy forged a clandestine friendship between the two men. Now King Louis Philippe of France has requested that the remains of the late emperor be returned, and Queen Victoria has granted that request. The French have also requested that the former-Governor Lord Hornblower attend the exhumation as the official British representative! Hornblower knows the situation is a veritable powder keg; the Ultra-Royalists, led by the ruthless Duke of Angouleme, will stop at nothing to prevent Bonaparte's remains from returning to France, while the Bonapartists, led by the late-emperor's nephew Louis-Napoleon, hope to use the return to stage a coup and establish a renewed French Empire. Hornblower must do his utmost to ensure the mortal remains reach French shores safely to pay a debt he has owed for over twenty years.

Penmore Press

Challenging, Intriguing, Adventurous, Historical and Imaginative

www.penmorepress.com